Tarzan struggled vainly against the net of rawhide strips as the old sorcerer gloated.

"In the meantime, I shall show you that Woora can be kind, even to an enemy. I would save you from unnecessary suffering. The sight of the preparations I must make for your torture and death would depress you—therefore I am going to burn out your eyes so you do not see them!"

Woora came close and raised the red-hot iron to the level of Tarzan's eyes, then jabbed at them. The victim warded off the searing point from its intended target, only his hand was burned. Again and again he diverted the iron.

Enraged, Woora wound coils of rope around the net, pinioning Tarzan's arms tightly, and heated the iron to a brighter glow. Tarzan faced his approach stoically.

"You pretend you are not afraid!" Woora screamed. "But I'll make you shriek for mercy yet!" And he came forward, holding the red point on a level with the ape-man's eyes.

Edgar Rice Burroughs

TARZAN NOVELS

now available from Ballantine Books:

COMPLETE AND UNABRIDGED!

TARZAN
the
Magnificent

Edgar Rice Burroughs

BALLANTINE BOOKS • NEW YORK

To Cyril Ralph Rothmund

Tarzan the Magnificent was first published in two parts as follows:

Part 1: "Tarzan and the Magic Men"
      Copyright © 1936 Edgar Rice Burroughs, Inc.

Part 2: "Tarzan and the Elephant Men"
      Copyright © 1937 Edgar Rice Burroughs, Inc.

Cover illustration copyright © 1977 by Edgar Rice Burroughs, Inc.

ISBN 0-345-28980-3

This authorized edition published by arrangement with Edgar Rice Burroughs, Inc.

Manufactured in the United States of America

First U.S. Printing: March 1964
Eighth U.S. Printing: March 1984

First Canadian Printing: August 1964

Cover illustration by Boris Vallejo

CONTENTS

CHARACTERS AND PLACES

NEUBARI RIVER
MAFA—an affluent of the Neubari
THE KAJI—a tribe of warrior women
LORD AND LADY MOUNTFORD—lost in Africa twenty years
ago
STANLEY WOOD—An American travel writer
ROBERT VAN EYK—Wood's friend and companion
SPIKE AND TROLL—white hunters attached to Wood—van
Eyk safari
MAFKA—magician of the Kaji
GONFALA—Queen of the Kaji
GONFAL—the great diamond of the Kaji
ZULI—a tribe of warrior women; enemies of the Kaji
LORD—an Englishman; captive of the Zuli
WOORA—magician of the Zuli
LORRO—A Zuli warrior-woman
THE GREAT EMERALD OF THE ZULI
KAMUDI—a black man
MUVIRO—Chief of the Waziri
BANTANGO—a cannibal tribe
WARANJI—A Waziri warrior
TOMOS—Prime Minister of Cathne, City of Gold
ALEXTAR—King of Cathne
VALTHOR—Athnean noble
PHOROS—Dictator of Athne, City of Ivory
ZYGO—King of Athne
MENOFRA—Wife of Phoros
DYAUS—Athnean elephant-god
DAIMON—a demon
KANDOS—righthand man of Phoros
GEMBA—a black slave
HYARK—warrior killed in arena by Tarzan

TRUTH IS STRANGER than fiction.

If this tale should seem in part incredible, please bear this axiom in mind. It had its beginning more than twenty years ago, unless one wishes to go further back to the first amoeba or even beyond that to the cosmos shattering clash of two forgotten suns; but we shall confine our story, other than by occasional reference, to the stage, the actors, and the business of the present time.

The searing sun rays scorch down upon a shriveled plain a scant five degrees north of the equator. A man, clothed in torn shirt and trousers upon which dried blood has caked and turned a rusty brown, staggers and falls to lie inert.

A great lion looks down upon the scene from the summit of a distant rocky ledge where a few tenacious bushes cling to give shade to the lair of the king; for this is Africa.

Ska, the vulture, wheels and circles in the blue, sky-writing anticipation far above the body of the fallen man.

Not far to the south, at the edge of the dry plain, another man swings easily toward the north. No sign of fatigue or exhaustion here. The bronze skin glows with health, full muscles glide beneath it. The free gait, the noiseless tread might be those of Sheeta, the panther; but there is no slinking here. It is the carriage of one who knows neither doubt nor fear, of a lord in his own domain.

He is encumbered by but a single garment, a loincloth of doe-skin. A coil of grass rope is looped over one shoulder, behind the other hangs a quiver of arrows; a scabbarded knife swings at his hip; a bow and a short spear complete his equipment. A shock of black hair falls in disorder above serene, grey eyes, eyes that can reflect the light of a summer sea or the flashing steel of a rapier.

7

The Lord of the Jungle is abroad.

He is far to the north of his ancient haunts, yet this is no unfamiliar terrain. He has been here many times before. He knows where water may be had for the digging. He knows where the nearest water hole lies where he can make a kill and fill his belly.

He has come north at the behest of an emperor to investigate a rumor that a European power is attempting to cause the defection of a native chief by means of bribery. War and rumors of war are in the air, but of this tale such things are not a part—we hope. However, we are no prophet. We are merely a chronicler of events as they transpire. We follow the activities of our characters to the bitter end, even to war; but we hope for the best. However, only time can tell.

As Tarzan swung with easy strides out across the plain, no sound escaped his keen ears; no moving thing, his eyes; no scent, borne upon the soft bosom of Usha the wind, went unidentified. Far in the distance he saw Numa the lion standing upon his rocky ledge; he saw Ska the vulture circling above something that Tarzan could not see. In all that he saw or heard or smelled he read a story; for to him this savage world was an open book, sometimes a thrilling, always an interesting narrative of love, of hate, of life, of death.

Where you or I might occasionally pick out a letter or a word, Tarzan of the Apes grasped the entire text and countless implications that we might never guess.

Presently, ahead of him, he saw something white shining in the sunlight—a human skull; and as he came closer his eyes picked out the skeleton of a man, the bones only slightly disarranged. From among them grew a low desert shrub proclaiming that the skeleton had lain there for a long time.

Tarzan paused to investigate, for to him in his world nothing is too trivial to pass by without question. He saw that the skeleton was that of a Negro and that it had lain there for a long time, years probably; which was entirely possible in this hot, dry plain. He could not tell how the man had come to his death, but he guessed that it might have been from thirst.

Then he saw something lying by the bones of a hand, something half buried by shifting soil; and he stopped and picked it up, drawing it carefully out of the earth. It was a

split stick of hardwood in the split end of which was
wedged a thin parcel of oiled silk.

The silk was stained and brittle and dry. It seemed that
it might crumble to his touch, but that was only the outer
layer. As he carefully unwrapped it, he found the inner
layers better preserved. Inside the silk wrapper he found
what he had expected—a letter.

It was written in English in a small, extremely legible
hand. Tarzan read it with interest, interest that was perhaps
stimulated by the date at the top of the sheet. Twenty years
had elapsed since that letter had been written. For twenty
years it had lain here beside the skeleton of its bearer in
mute testimony to the loneliness of this barren plain.

Tarzan read it:

*To Whom This May Come: I am dispatching this
without much hope that it will even get out of this
damnable country, still less that it will reach any white
man; but if it does, please contact the nearest Resi-
dent Commissioner or any other authority that can get
help to us quickly.*

*My wife and I were exploring north of Lake Rudolph.
We came too far. It was the old story. Our boys became
frightened by rumors of a fierce tribe inhabiting the
country in which we were. They deserted us.*

*Where the Mafa River empties into the Neubari we
turned up the gorge of the former as though drawn by
some supernatural power, and were captured by the wild
women of Kaji, when we reached the plateau. A year
later our daughter was born and my wife died—the
she-devils of Kaji killed her because she did not bear
a son. They want white men. That is why they have not
killed me and a dozen other white men captives.*

*The Kaji country lies on a high plateau above the falls
of the Mafa. It is almost inaccessible, but can be reached
by following the gorge of the Mafa from the Neubari.*

*It will require a strong expedition of white men to
rescue me and my little daughter, as I doubt that blacks
can be induced to enter the country. These Kaji women
fight like devils, and they have strange, occult powers of
some nature. I have seen things here that—well, things
that just can't be but are.*

*No native tribes will live near this mysterious, ill-
omened country; so, little is known of the Kaji; but*

*rumors of their terrifying practices have become part
of the folklore of their nearest neighbors, and it is the
hushed recital of these that frightens the bearers of any
safari that comes within the sphere of their baneful influence.*

*The white men may never know the cause of it, for
the blacks fear to tell them, thinking that the black
magic of the Kaji will reach out and destroy them; but
the result is always the same—if the safari approaches
too close to Kaji, the blacks all desert.*

*Then that happens which happened to my wife and
me—the whites are lured by some mysterious means to
the plateau and made prisoners.*

*Perhaps even a large force might be overcome, for
the whites would not be contending against natural
forces; but if they succeeded, the reward might be very
great. It is the hope of this reward that I hold out
against the dangers involved.*

*The Kaji own an enormous diamond. Where it came
from, where it was mined, I have been unable to ascertain; but I suspect that it came from the soil of their
own country.*

*I have seen and handled the Cullinan diamond,
which weighed over three thousand carats; and I am
certain that the diamond of Kaji weighs fully six thousand. Just what its value may be I do not know, but
using the value of the Brazilian stone, Star of the South,
as a measure, it must be worth close to £2,000,000—
a reward well worth some risk.*

*It is impossible for me to know whether I shall ever
get this letter out of Kaji, but I have hopes of doing
so by bribing one of their black slaves who occasionally leave the plateau to spy in the lowlands.*

God grant this be delivered in time.

                                              Mountford.

Tarzan of the Apes read the letter through twice. Mountford! Almost ever since he could remember, it seemed, the
mysterious disappearance of Lord and Lady Mountford had
been recalled to the minds of men by rumors that they still
lived, until they had become a legend of the wilderness.

No one really believed that they lived, yet at intervals
some wanderer from the interior would revive the rumor
with more or less circumstantial evidence. He had had the

story from the chieftain of a remote tribe, or perhaps from
the lips of a dying white man; but there never came any
definite clew as to the exact whereabouts of the Mount-
fords—they had been reported from a score of places all
the way from the Soudan to Rhodesia.

And now at last the truth had come, but too late. Lady
Mountford had been dead for twenty years, and it was quite
improbable that her husband still lived. The child must, of
course, have died or been killed by the Kaji. It could
scarcely have survived among those savage people through
infancy.

To the jungle bred ape-man death was a commonplace
phenomenon of existence and far less remarkable than many
other manifestations of nature, for it came eventually to all
living things; so the possibility of the death of the man and
the child induced no reaction of sorrow or regret. It simply
meant nothing to him whatsoever. He would deliver the
letter to the English authorities at the first opportunity, and
that would be all that there would be to it. Or so Tarzan
thought. He continued his way, putting the matter from
his mind. He was more interested in the maneuvers of Ska
the vulture, for they indicated that Ska was circling about
some creature not yet dead and which, because of its size
or nature, he hesitated to attack.

As Tarzan approached the spot above which Ska wheeled
on static wings he saw Numa the lion drop from the ledge
upon which he had been standing and move cautiously
toward the thing that had aroused the man's curiosity.
Though the latter was in plain sight, Numa seemingly ignored
his presence; nor did Tarzan alter his course because of the
lion. If neither changed his pace or his direction they would
meet close to the thing above which Ska hovered.

As the ape-man came nearer the object of his interest
he saw the body of a man lying in a little natural depres-
sion of the ground—the body of a white man.

To the right of it, a hundred yards away, was Numa.
Presently the man stirred. He was not dead. He raised his
head and saw the lion; then he struggled to rise, but he was
very weak and could only manage to raise himself to one
knee. Behind him was Tarzan, whom he did not see.

As the man half rose, the lion growled. It was only a
warning in which there was no immediate menace. Tarzan
recognized it as such. He knew that Numa had been attracted by curiosity and not by hunger. His belly was full.

But the man did not know these things. He thought it was the end, for he was unarmed and helpless; and the great carnivore, the king of beasts, was almost upon him.

Then he heard another low growl behind him and, turning his eyes quickly in that direction, saw an almost naked man coming toward him. For an instant he did not understand, for he saw no other beast; then he heard the growl again and saw that it came from the throat of the bronzed giant approaching him.

Numa heard the growl too and paused. He shook his head and snarled. Tarzan did not pause; he continued on toward the man. There was no sanctuary should the lion attack, no tree to offer the safety of its branches; there were only Tarzan's weapons and his great strength and his skill; but greatest of all was his conviction that Numa would not attack.

The Lord of the Jungle well knew the art of bluff and its value. Suddenly he raised his head and voiced the hideous warning-cry of the bull ape. The man shuddered as he heard the bestial cry issue from the lips of a human being. Numa, with a parting growl, turned and stalked away.

Tarzan came and stood over the man. "Are you hurt?" he demanded, "or weak from hunger and thirst?"

The voice of a beast coming from the lips of this strange white giant had been no more disconcerting to the man than now to hear him speak in English. He did not know whether to be afraid or not. He glanced hurriedly in the direction of the lion and saw it moving off in the direction from which it had come, and he was filled with a new awe of this creature who could frighten the king of beasts from its prey.

"Well," demanded the ape-man, "do you understand English?"

"Yes," replied the other; "I am an American. I am not hurt. I have been without food for several days. I have had no water today."

Tarzan stooped and lifted the man to a shoulder. "We will find water and food," he said, "and then you may tell me what you are doing alone in this country."

2

A Strange Tale

A S TARZAN CARRIED the man toward safety, the limp, dead
weight of his burden told him that his charge had lost
consciousness. Occasionally he mumbled incoherently,
but for the greater part of the journey he was as one dead.

When they came at last to water, Tarzan laid the man in the
shade of a small tree; and, raising his head and shoulders,
forced a few drops of the liquid between his lips. Presently
he could take more, and with its revivifying effects he commenced to speak—broken, disjointed, sometimes incoherent
snatches of sentences; as one speaks in delirium or when
emerging from an anesthetic.

"She-devil," he mumbled. ". . . beautiful . . . God! how
beautiful." Then he was silent for a while as Tarzan bathed
his face and wrists with the cool water.

Presently he opened his eyes and looked at the ape-man,
his brows wrinkled in questioning and puzzlement. "The
diamond!" he demanded. "Did you get the diamond? Huge
. . . she must have been sired by Satan . . . beautiful—
enormous—big as . . . what? It can't be . . . but I saw it—
with my own eyes—eyes! eyes! . . . what eyes! . . . but a
fiend . . . ten million dollars . . . all of that . . . big . . .
big as a woman's head."

"Be quiet," said the ape-man, "and rest. I will get food."

When he returned, the man was sleeping peacefully and
night was falling. Tarzan built a fire and prepared a brace
of quail and a hare that he had brought down with arrows
from his bow. The quail he wrapped in wet clay and laid
in the embers; the hare he jointed and grilled on sharpened
sticks.

When he had done, he glanced at the man and saw that
his eyes were open and upon him. The gaze was quite
normal, but the expression was one of puzzlement.

"Who are you?" asked the man. "What happened? I do
not seem to be able to recall."

"I found you out on the plain—exhausted," explained Tarzan.

"O-oh!" exclaimed the other. "You are the—the man the lion ran away from. Now I remember. And you brought me here and got food?—and there is water, too?"

"Yes; you have had some. You can have more now. There is a spring behind you. Are you strong enough to reach it?"

The man turned and saw the water; then he crawled to it. Some of his strength had returned.

"Don't drink too much at once," cautioned the ape-man.

After the man had drunk he turned again toward Tarzan. "Who are you?" he asked. "Why did you save me?"

"You will answer the questions," said the Lord of the Jungle. "Who are you? And what are you doing in this country alone? What are you doing here at all?"

The voice was low and deep. It questioned, but it also commanded. The stranger felt that. It was the well modulated, assured voice of a man who was always obeyed. He wondered who this almost naked white giant could be. A regular Tarzan, he thought. When he looked at the man he could almost believe that such a creature existed outside of story and legend and that this was, indeed, he.

"Perhaps you had better eat first," said the ape-man; "then you may answer my questions." He took a ball of hard baked clay from the fire, scraping it out with a stick; then with the hilt of his knife he broke it open, and the baked clay fell away from the body of the quail, taking the feathers with it. He impaled the bird on the stick and handed it to the man. "It is hot," he said.

It was, but the half-famished stranger risked burning for an initial morsel. Without seasoning, as it was, no food had ever tasted better. Only its high temperature restrained him from wolfing it. He ate one quail and half the rabbit before he lay back, at least partially satisfied.

"To answer your questions," he said, "my name is Wood. I am a writer—travel stuff. Thus I capitalize my natural worthlessness, which often finds its expression and its excuse in wanderlust. It has afforded me more than a competence; so that I am now able to undertake expeditions requiring more financing than a steamer ticket and a pair of stout boots.

"Because of this relative affluence you found me alone and on the point of death in an untracked wilderness; but though you found me deserted and destitute without even a crust of bread, I have here in my head material for such a travel book as has never been written by modern man. I have seen things of which civilization does not dream and will not believe; and I have seen, too, the largest diamond in the world. I have held it in my hands. I even had the temerity to believe that I could bring it away with me.

"I have seen the most beautiful woman in the world—and the cruelest; and I even had the temerity to believe that I could bring her away with me, too; for I loved her. I still love her, though I curse her in my sleep, so nearly one are love and hate, the two most powerful and devastating emotions that control man, nations, life—so nearly one that they are separated only by a glance, a gesture, a syllable. I hate her with my mind; I love her with my body and my soul.

"Bear with me if I anticipate. For me she is the beginning and the end—the beginning and the end of everything; but I'll try to be more coherent and more chronological.

"To begin with: have you ever heard of the mysterious disappearance of Lord and Lady Mountford?"

Tarzan nodded. "Who has not?"

"And the persistent rumors of their survival even now, twenty years after they dropped from the sight and knowledge of civilized man?

"Well, their story held for me such a glamour of romance and mystery that for years I toyed with the idea of organizing an expedition that would track down every rumor until it had been proved false or true. I would find Lord and Lady Mountford or I would learn their fate.

"I had a very good friend, a young man of considerable inherited means, who had backed some of my earlier adventures—Robert van Eyk, of the old New York van Eyks. But of course that means nothing to you."

Tarzan did not comment. He merely listened—no shadow of interest or emotion crossed his face. He was not an easy man in whom to confide, but Stanley Wood was so full of pent emotion that he would have welcomed the insensate ears of a stone Buddah had there been no other ear to listen.

"Well, I gabbled so much about my plans to Bob van Eyk that he got all hepped up himself; and insisted on going along and sharing the expenses; which meant, of course, that we could equip much more elaborately than I had planned to and therefore more certainly ensure the success of our undertaking.

"We spent a whole year in research, both in England and Africa, with the result that we were pretty thoroughly convinced that Lord and Lady Mountford had disappeared from a point on the Neubari River somewhere northwest of Lake Rudolph. Everything seemed to point to that, although practically everything was based on rumor.

"We got together a peach of a safari and picked up a couple of white hunters who were pretty well familiar with everything African, although they had never been to this particular part of the country.

"Everything went well until we got a little way up the Neubari. The country was sparsely inhabited, and the farther we pushed in the fewer natives we saw. These were wild and fearful. We couldn't get a thing out of them about what lay ahead, but they talked to our boys. They put the fear o' God into 'em.

"Pretty soon we commenced to have desertions. We tried to get a line on the trouble from those who remained, but they wouldn't tell us a thing. They just froze up—scared stiff—didn't even admit that they were scared at first; but they kept on deserting.

"It got mighty serious. There we were in a country we didn't know the first thing about—a potentially hostile country—with a lot of equipment and provisions and scarcely enough men to carry on with.

"Finally one of the headmen told me what they were scared of. The natives they had talked with had told them that there was a tribe farther up the Neubari that killed or enslaved every black that came into their territory, a tribe with some mysterious kind of magic that held you—wouldn't let you escape, or, if you did escape, the magic followed you and killed you before you got back to your own country— maybe many marches away. They said you couldn't kill these people because they were not human—they were demons that had taken the form of women.

"Well, when I told Spike and Troll, the white hunters, what the trouble was, they pooh-poohed the whole business, of course. Said it was just an excuse to make us turn back because our carriers didn't like the idea of being so far from their own country and were getting homesick.

"So they got tough with the boys. Whaled hell out of 'em, and drove 'em on like slaves. As Spike said, 'Put the fear o' God into 'em', and the next night all the rest of 'em deserted—every last mother's son of 'em.

"When we woke up in the morning there were the four of us, Bob van Eyk, Spike, Troll, and myself, four white men all alone with loads for fifty porters; our personal boys, our gun bearers, our askaris all gone.

"Spike and Troll back-tracked to try to pick up some of the boys to take us out, for we knew we were licked; but they never found a one of them, though they were gone for two days.

"Bob and I were just about to pull out on our own when they got back; for, believe me, if we'd had plenty of it before they left we'd had a double dose while they were away.

"I can't tell you what it was, for we never saw anyone. Maybe we were just plain scared, but I don't think that could have been it. Van Eyk has plenty of nerve, and I have been in lots of tough places—lost and alone among the head-hunters of Equador, captured in the interior of New Guinea by cannibals, stood up in front of a firing squad during a Central American revolution—the kind of things, you know, that a travel writer gets mixed up in if he's really looking for thrills to write about and hasn't very good sense.

"No, this was different. It was just a *feeling*—a haunting sense of being watched by invisible eyes, day and night. And there were noises, too. I can't describe them—they weren't human noises, nor animal either. They were just noises that made your flesh creep and your scalp tingle.

"We had a council of war the night Spike and Troll got back. At first they laughed at us, but pretty soon they commenced to feel and hear things. After that they agreed with us that the best thing to do would be to beat it back.

"We decided to carry nothing but a revolver and rifle apiece, ammunition, and food, abandoning everything else. We were going to start early the following morning.

"When morning came we ate our breakfasts in silence, shouldered our packs, and without a word started out *up* the Neubari. We didn't even look at one another. I don't know about the rest of them, but I was ashamed to.

"There we were, doing just the opposite of the thing we had decided on—going deeper and deeper into trouble—and not knowing why we were doing it. I tried to exercise my will and force my feet in the opposite direction, but it was no go. A power far greater than my own will directed me. It was terrifying.

"We hadn't gone more than five miles before we came

across a man lying in the trail—a white man. His hair and
beard were white, but he didn't look so very old—well under
fifty, I should have said. He seemed pretty well done in,
notwithstanding the fact that he appeared in good physical
condition—no indication of starvation; and he couldn't very
well have been suffering from thirst, for the Neubari river
was less than fifty yards from where he lay.

"When we stopped beside him, he opened his eyes and
looked up at us.

" 'Go back!' he whispered. He seemed very weak, and it
was obviously an effort for him to speak.

"I had a little flask of brandy that I carried for emer-
gencies, and I made him drink a little. It seemed to revive
him some.

" 'For God's sake turn back,' he said. 'There are not
enough of you. They'll get you as they got me more
than twenty years ago, and you can't get away—you can't
escape. After all these years I thought I saw my chance;
and I tried it. But you see! They've got me. I'm dying. His
power! He sends it after you, and it gets you. Go back and
get a big force of white men—blacks won't come into this
country. Get a big force and get into the country of the
Kaji. If you can kill him you'll be all right. He is the power,
he alone.'

" 'Whom do you mean by "he"?' I asked.

" 'Mafka,' he replied.

" 'He's the chief?' I asked.

" 'No; I wouldn't know what to call him. He's not a chief,
and yet he's all-powerful. He's more like a witch-doctor. In
the dark ages he'd have been a magician. He does things
that no ordinary witch-doctor ever dreamed of doing. He's
a devil. Sometimes I have thought that he is *the* Devil. And
he is training her—teaching her his hellish powers.'

" 'Who are you?'

" 'I'm Mountford,' he replied.

" 'Lord Mountford?' I exclaimed.

"He nodded."

"Did he tell you about the diamond?" asked Tarzan.

Wood looked at the ape-man in surprise. "How did you
know about that?"

"You rambled a little while you were delirious, but I knew
about it before. Is it really twice the size of the Cullinan?"

"I never saw the Cullinan, but the Kaji diamond is
enormous. It must be worth ten million dollars at least, pos-

sibly more. Troll used to work at Kimerly. He said somewhere between ten and fifteen million. Yes, Mountford told us about it; and after that Troll and Spike were keen on getting into this Kaji country, hoping to steal the diamond. Nothing Mountford said could deter them. But after all it made no difference. We couldn't have turned back if we'd wanted to."

"And Mountford?" asked Tarzan. "What became of him?"

"He was trying to tell us something about a girl. He rambled a little, and we couldn't quite make out what he was driving at. His last words were, 'Save her . . . kill Mafka.' Then he died.

"We never did find out whom he meant even after we got into the Kaji country. We never saw any woman captive. If they had one they kept her hidden. But then, we never saw Mafka either. He lives in a regular castle that must have been built centuries ago, possibly by the Portuguese, though it may have antedated their excursion into Abyssinia. Van Eyk thought it may have been built during the Crusades, though what the Crusaders were doing in this neck of the woods he couldn't explain. At any rate, the Kaji never built it; though they had done considerable toward restoring and preserving it.

"The diamond is kept in this castle and is guarded along with Mafka and the queen by Kaji warriors who are constantly on guard at the only entrance.

"The Kaji attribute all their powers and the power of Mafka to the diamond; so naturally they guard it very carefully. For the stone itself they show no particular reverence. They handle it and allow others to handle it as though it were quite an ordinary stone. It is for the queen that they reserve their reverence.

"I am not certain that I correctly fathomed the connection between the queen and the diamond; but I think that they consider her the personification of the stone, into whose body has entered the spirit and the flame of the brilliant.

"She is a gorgeous creature, quite the most beautiful woman I have ever seen. I do not hesitate to say that she is the most beautiful woman in the world; but a creature of such radical contradictions as to cast a doubt upon her sanity. One moment she is all womanly compassion and sweetness, the next she is a she-devil. They call her Gonfala, and the diamond Gonfal.

"It was during a moment of her femininity that she

helped me to escape; but she must have repented it, for it could have been only Mafka's power that reached out and dragged me down. Only she knew that I had gone; so she must have told him."

"What became of the other three men?" asked Tarzan.

"They are still prisoners of the Kaji. When Gonfala helped me to escape, I planned to come back with a force of whites large enough to rescue them," Wood explained.

"Will they be alive?"

"Yes; the Kaji will protect them and marry them. The Kaji are all women. Originally they were blacks who wished to turn white; so they married only white men. It became a part of their religion. That is why they lure white men to Kaji—and frighten away the blacks.

"This must have been going on for generations, as there is not an unmixed black among them. They range in color all the way from brown to white. Gonfala is a blond. Apparently there is not a trace of Negro blood in her veins.

"If a baby is born black it is destroyed, and all male babies are destroyed. They believe that the color of the skin is inherited from the father."

"If they kill all the males, where do they get their warriors?"

"The women are the warriors. I have never seen them fight; but from what I heard I imagine they are mighty ferocious. You see, we walked right into their country like long-lost friends, for we didn't want to fight 'em. All two of us wanted was their diamond, Bob van Eyk wanted adventure, and I wanted material for another book. If we could make friends, so much the better.

"That was six months ago. Bob has had adventure and I have material for a book, though much good it will ever do me. Spike and Troll haven't the diamond, but they each have seven Kaji wives—all properly married, too, by Gonfala in the presence of the great diamond.

"You see, Gonfala, as queen, selects the wives for all captured whites; but she herself is not allowed to marry.

"This allotting of the whites is more or less of a racket. The women make offerings to Gonfala, and the ones who make the most valuable offerings get the husbands.

"Well, we saw a lot of Gonfala. She seemed to take a liking to Bob and me, and I sure took a liking to her. In fact, I fell in love with her, and even after I guessed the truth I didn't care.

"She liked to hear about the outside world, and she'd listen to us by the hour. You know how people are. Seeing so much of her and being near her broke down my revulsion for her cruelties; so that I was always mentally making excuses for her. And all the time I kept on loving her more and more, until finally I told her.

"She looked at me for a long time without saying a word. I didn't know whether she was sore or not. If you knew what a big shot the queen of the Kaji is, you'd realize how presumptuous I was in declaring my love. She's more than a queen; she's a sort of deity that they worship—all mixed up with their worship of the diamond.

" 'Love,' she said in a little, low voice. 'Love! So that is what it is!'

"Then she straightened up and became suddenly very regal. 'Do you know what you have done?' she demanded.

" 'I have fallen in love with you,' I said. 'That is about all I know or care.'

"She stamped her foot. 'Don't say it,' she commanded. 'Don't ever say it again. I should have you killed; that is the penalty for daring to aspire to the love of Gonfala. She may not love; she may never marry. Do you not understand that I am a goddess as well as a queen?'

" 'I can't help that,' I replied. 'And I can't help loving you any more than *you can help loving me!*'

"She gave a little gasp of astonishment and horror. There was a new expression in her eyes; it was not anger; it was fear. I had voiced a suspicion that I had had for some time, and I had hit the nail on the head—Gonfala was in love with me. She hadn't realized it herself until that very moment—she hadn't known what was the matter with her. But, now she did, and she was afraid.

"She didn't deny it; but she told me that we would both be killed, and killed horribly, if Mafka suspected the truth. And what she was afraid of was that Mafka would know because of his uncanny powers of magic.

"It was then that she decided to help me escape. To her it seemed the only way to insure our safety; to me it presented an opportunity to effect the rescue of my friends with the possibility of persuading Gonfala to come away with me if I were successful.

"With her help, I got away. The rest you know."

3

The Power of Mafka

THE APE-MAN HAD listened patiently to Stanley Wood's recital. How much he could believe of it, he did not know; for he did not know the man, and he had learned to suspect that every civilized man was a liar and a cheat until he had proved himself otherwise.

Yet he was favorably impressed by the man's personality, and he had something of the wild beast's instinctive knowledge of basic character—if it may be called that. Perhaps it is more an intuitive feeling of trust for some and distrust of others. That it is not infallible, Tarzan well knew; so he was cautious, always. And in that again the beast showed in him.

"And what do you propose doing now?" he asked.

Wood scratched his head in perplexity. "To be perfectly frank, I don't know. I am confident that Mafka found out that I had escaped and that it was his magic that followed and brought me down. Perhaps Gonfala told him. She is a Jekyll and Hyde sort of person. In one personality she is all sweetness and tenderness, in another she is a fiend.

"As far as my future actions are concerned, I have a very definite premonition that I am not a free agent."

"What do you mean?" demanded the ape-man.

"Since it commenced to get dark haven't you felt an invisible presence near us, haven't you sensed unseen eyes upon us, and heard things, and almost seen things? These are the manifestations of Mafka. We are in his power. Where he wills us to go, we'll go; and you can lay to that."

A shadow of a smile moved the lips of the Lord of the Jungle. "I have seen and heard and sensed many things since we stopped here, but none of them was Mafka. I have identified them all either through my ears or my nose. There is nothing to fear."

"You do not know Mafka," said Wood.

"I know Africa, and I know myself," replied the ape-man,

simply. There was no bravado in his tone, but absolute assurance. It impressed the American.

"You are a regular Tarzan," he said.

The other shot a quick glance at him, appraising. He saw
that the man spoke without knowledge of his identity, and
he was satisfied. His mission required that he remain unknown, if possible. Otherwise, he might never gain the information he sought. He had felt safe from recognition, for
he was unknown in this district.

"By the way," continued Wood. "You have not told me
your name. I have seen so many unbelievable things since I
came into this country that not even the sight of an evidently
highly civilized man wandering almost naked and alone in a
wilderness surprised me as much as it otherwise might have.
Of course, I don't want to pry into your affairs, but naturally
my curiosity is aroused. I wonder who you are and what you
are doing here." He stopped suddenly and looked intently at
Tarzan. His eyes registered suspicion and a shadow of
fear. "Say!" he exclaimed. "Did Mafka send you? Are you
one of his—his creatures?"

The ape-man shook his head. "You are in a most un-
fortunate situation," he said. "If I were not one of Mafka's
creatures, or if I were, my answer, quite conceivably, might
be the same—I should deny it; so why answer you? You
will have to find out for yourself, and in the meantime
you will have to trust me or distrust me as seems wisest
to you."

Wood grinned. "I *am* up against it, ain't I?" He shrugged.
"Well, we're both in the same boat. At least you don't
know any more about me than I do about you. I may have
been giving you a cock-and-bull story. I admit it must sound
fishy. But at least I told you my name. You haven't told
me that much about yourself yet. I don't know what to call
you."

"My name is Clayton," said the ape-man. He might also
have said, John Clayton Lord Greystoke—Tarzan of the
Apes; but he didn't.

"I suppose you want to get out of this country," said
Tarzan, "and get help for your friends."

"Yes, of course, but there isn't a chance now."

"Why not?"

"Mafka—Mafka and Gonfala."

"I can't take you out at present," said the ape-man,
ignoring the implied obstacle. "You may come along to the

Lake Tana country with me if you wish to. You'll get a
story there—a story that you must never write. You'll have
to give me your word as to that. My only alternative is to
leave you here. You will have to decide."

"I'll come with you," said Wood, "but neither of us will
ever reach Lake Tana." He paused and strained his eyes into
the lowering dusk of the brief twilight. "There!" he said in a
whisper. "It's back; it's watching us. Don't you hear it?
Can't you feel it?" His voice was tense, his eyes slightly
dilated.

"There is nothing," said Tarzan. "Your nerves are upset."

"You mean to tell me you don't hear it—the moaning, the
sighing?"

"I hear the wind, and I hear Sheeta the panther a long
way off," replied the ape-man.

"Yes, I hear those, too; but I hear something else. You
must be deaf."

Tarzan smiled. "Perhaps," he said. "But go to sleep; you
need rest. Tomorrow you will not hear things."

"I tell you I hear it. I almost see it. Look! There, among
those trees—just a shadow of something that has no sub-
stance."

Tarzan shook his head. "Try to sleep," he said. "I will
watch."

Wood closed his eyes. The presence of this quiet stranger
gave him a feeling of security despite his conviction that
something weird and horrible hovered there in the darkness
—watching, always watching. With the dismal keening still
ringing in his ears, he fell asleep.

For a long time Tarzan sat in thought. He heard nothing
other than the usual night noises of the wilderness, yet he
was sufficiently conversant with the mystery and the magic
of black Africa to realize that Wood *had* heard something
that he could not hear. The American was intelligent, sane,
experienced. He did not seem the type to be carried away
by imaginings or hysteria. It was just possible that he was
under the spell of hypnotic suggestion—that Mafka could
project his powers to great distances. This was rather borne
out by the evidence that Tarzan had had presented to him
within the past few hours: the death of Mountford's mes-
senger twenty years before, the striking down of Wood
within a short distance of the same spot, the death of Mountford for no apparent good reason upon the very threshold
of escape.

Mafka's was indeed a sinister power, but it was a power that the ape-man did not fear. All too often had he been the object of the malign necromancy of potent witch-doctors to fear their magic. Like the beasts of the jungle, he was immune. For what reason he did not know. Perhaps it was because he was without fear; perhaps his psychology was more that of the beast than of man.

Dismissing the matter from his mind, he stretched and fell asleep.

The sun was half a hand-breadth above the horizon when Wood awoke. He was alone. The strange white man had disappeared.

Wood was not greatly surprised. There was no reason why this stranger should wait and be burdened by a man he did not know, but he felt that he might at least have waited until he was awake before deserting him and leaving him prey for the first lion or leopard that might chance to pick up his scent.

And then there was Mafka. The thought aroused questions in the mind of the American. Might not this fellow who called himself Clayton be a tool of the magician of the Kaji? The very fact that he denied that he had heard any strange sounds or sensed any unusual presence lent color to this suspicion. He must have heard; he must have sensed. Then why did he deny it?

But perhaps he was not Mafka's spy. Perhaps he had fallen a victim to the sorcery of the old Devil. How easy it would have been for Mafka to lure him away. Everything seemed easy for Mafka. He could have lured him away to captivity or destruction, leaving Wood to die as Mafka intended—alone by starvation.

Wood had never seen Mafka. To him he should have been no more than a name; yet he was very real. The man even conjured an image of him that was as real and tangible as flesh and blood. He saw him as a very old and hideous black man, bent and wrinkled. He had filed, yellow teeth, and his eyes were close-set and blood-shot.

There! What was that? A noise in the trees! The thing was coming again!

Wood was a brave man, but things like these can get on the nerves of the bravest. It is one thing to face a known danger, another to be constantly haunted by an unseen thing —a horrible, invisible menace that one can't grapple with.

The American leaped to his feet, facing the direction of

the rustling among the foliage. "Come down!" he cried, "Come down, damn you, and fight like a man!"

From the concealing foliage a figure swung lightly to the ground. It was Tarzan. Across one shoulder he carried the carcass of a small buck.

He looked quickly about. "What's the matter?" he demanded. "I don't see anyone"; then a faint smile touched his lips. "Hearing things again?" he asked.

Wood grinned foolishly. "I guess it's sort of got me," he said.

"Well, forget it for a while," counseled the ape-man. "We'll eat presently; then you'll feel better."

"You killed that buck?" demanded Wood.

Tarzan looked surprised. "Why, yes."

"You must have killed it with an arrow. That would take an ordinary man hours—stalk an antelope and get close enough to kill it with an arrow."

"I didn't use an arrow," replied the ape-man.

"Then how did you kill him?"

"I killed him with my knife—less danger of losing an arrow."

"And you brought him back through the trees on your shoulder! Say, that bird Tarzan has nothing on you. How did you ever come to live this way, Clayton? How did you learn to do these things?"

"That is a long story," said Tarzan. "Our business now is to grill some of this meat and get on our way."

After they had eaten, Tarzan told the other to carry some of the meat in his pockets. "You may need food before I can make another kill," he said. "We'll leave the rest for Dango and Ungo."

"Dango and Ungo? Who are they?"

"The hyena and the jackal."

"What language is that? I never heard them called that before, and I am a little bit familiar with a number of native dialects."

"No natives speak that language," replied the ape-man. "It is not spoken by men."

"Who does speak it, then?" demanded Wood; but he got no reply, and he did not insist. There was something mysterious about him, and that in his mien and his manner of speech that discouraged inquisitiveness. Wood wondered if the man were not a little mad. He had heard of white men going primitive, living solitary lives like wild animals; and they were always a little bit demented. Yet his companion seemed sane enough. No, it was not that; yet undeniably the man was different from other men. He reminded Wood of a lion. Yes, that was it—he was the personification of the strength and majesty and the ferocity of the lion. It was controlled ferocity; but it was there—Wood felt it. And that, perhaps, was why he was a little afraid of him.

He followed in silence behind the bronzed white savage back up the valley of the Neubari, and as they drew closer to the country of the Kaji he felt the power of Mafka increasing, drawing him back into the coils of intrigue and sorcery that made life hideous in the land of the women who would be white. He wondered if Clayton felt it too.

They came at length to the junction of the Mafa and the Neubari. It was here, where the smaller stream emptied into the larger, that the trail to the Kaji country followed up the gorge of the Mafa. It was here that they would *have* to turn up the Mafa.

Tarzan was a few yards in advance of Wood. The latter watched him intently as he came to the well-marked forking of the trail to the right leading to the crossing of the Neubari and up the Mafa. Here, regardless of his previous intentions, he would have to turn toward Kaji. The power of Mafka would bend his will to that of the malign magician; but Tarzan did not turn—he continued upon his way, unperturbed, up the Neubari.

Could it be that Mafka was ignorant of their coming? Wood felt a sudden sense of elation. If one of them could pass, they could both pass. There was an excellent chance that they might elude Mafka entirely. If he could only get by—if he could get away somewhere and organize a large expedition, he might return and rescue Van Eyk, Spike, and Troll.

But could he get by? He thought of the invisible presence that seemed to have him under constant surveillance. Had that been only the fruit of an overwrought imagination, as Clayton had suggested?

He came then to the forking of the trails. He focused all his power of will upon his determination to follow Clayton up the Neubari—and his feet turned to the right toward the crossing that led up the Mafa.

He called to Clayton, a note of hopelessness in his voice. "It's no go, old man," he said. "I've got to go up the Mafa—Mafka's got me. You go on—if you can."

Tarzan turned back. "You really want to go with me?" he asked.

"Of course, but I can't. I tried to pass this damnable trail, but I couldn't. My feet just followed it."

"Mafka makes strong medicine," said the ape-man, "but I think we can beat him."

"No," said Wood, "you can't beat him. No one can."

"We'll see," said Tarzan, and lifting Wood from the ground he threw him across a broad shoulder and turned back to the Neubari trail.

"You don't feel it?" demanded Wood. "You don't feel any urge to go up the Mafa?"

"Only a strong curiosity to see these people—especially Mafka," replied the ape-man.

"You'd never see him—no one does. They're afraid someone will kill him, and so is he. He's pretty well guarded all the time. If one of us could have killed him, most of the Kaji's power would be gone. We'd all have had a chance to escape. There are about fifty white prisoners there. Some of them have been there a long time. We could have fought our way out, if it hadn't been for Mafka; and some of us would have come through alive."

But Tarzan did not yield to his curiosity. He moved on toward the North with an easy grace that belied the weight of the burden across his shoulder. He went in silence, his mind occupied by the strange story that the American had told him. How much of it he might believe, he did not know; but he was inclined to credit the American with believing it, thus admitting his own belief in the mysterious force that enslaved the other mentally as well as physically; for the man seemed straightforward and honest, impressing Tarzan with his dependability.

There was one phase of the story that seemed to lack any confirmation—the vaunted fighting ability of the Amazonian Kaji. Wood admitted that he had never seen them fight and that they captured their prisoners by the wiles of Mafka's malign power. How, then, did he know that they were such redoubtable warriors? He put the question to the American. Whom did they fight?

"There is another tribe farther to the East," explained Wood, "across the divide beyond the headwaters of the Mafa. They are called Zuli. Once the Kaji and the Zuli were one tribe with two medicine-men, or witch-doctors, or whatever you might call them. One was Mafka, the other was a chap called Woora.

"Jealousy arose between the two, causing a schism. Members of the tribe took sides, and there was a battle. During the fracas, Woora swiped one of the holy fetishes and beat it, telling some of his followers where he was going and to join him when the fight was over. You see, like the people who cause civilized wars, he was not taking part in it personally.

"Well, it seems that this other fetish that he lifts is the complement of the great diamond, the Gonfal, of the Kaji. United, their power is supreme; but separated, that of each is greatly reduced. So the Kaji and the Zuli are often battling, each seeking to obtain possession of the fetish of the other.

"It was the stories of the raids and skirmishes and battles for these prizes, as told me by Gonfala and others of the Kaji, that gave me the hunch that these ladies are pretty mean warriors. Some of the yarns I've heard were sure tall; but the scars of old wounds on most of them sort of bear them out, as do the grisly trophies that hang from the outer walls of Gonfala's palace—the shriveled heads of women, suspended by their long hair.

"An interesting feature of the story is the description of the fetish of the Zuli—a green stone as large as the Gonfal and as brilliant. It glistens like an emerald; but, holy cats! Think of an emerald weighing six thousand carats! That would be something worth battling for, and they don't know the value of it."

"Do you?" asked Tarzan.

"Well, no, not exactly—perhaps twenty million dollars at a rough guess."

"What would that mean to you—luxuries and power? The Kaji probably know little of luxuries; but, from what you have told me, power is everything to them; and they believe that this other fetish would give them unlimited power, just as you think that twenty million dollars would give you happiness.

"Probably you are both wrong; but the fact remains that they know quite as well the value of it as you, and at least it does less harm here than it would out in the world among men who would steal the pennies from the eyes of the dead!"

Wood smiled. This was the longest speech that his strange

companion had vouchsafed. It suggested a philosophy of life that might make an uninhabited wilderness preferable to contacts of civilization in the eyes of this man.

For an hour Tarzan carried the American; then he lowered him to his feet. "Perhaps you can go it on your own now," he said.

"I'll try. Come on!"

Tarzan started again along the trail toward the North. Wood hesitated. In his eyes and the strained expression of his face was reflected the stupendous effort of his will. With a groan of anguish he turned and started briskly toward the South.

The ape-man wheeled and hastened after him. Wood glanced back and broke into a run. For an instant Tarzan hesitated. The fellow meant nothing to him; he was a burden. Why not let him go and be relieved of him? Then he recalled the terror in the man's face and realized, also, the challenge that Mafka was hurling at the Lord of the Jungle.

Perhaps it was the latter that motivated him more strongly than aught else when he started in pursuit of the fleeing American.

Mafka's power might be unquestionably great, but it could not lend sufficient speed to the feet of Stanley Wood to permit him to outdistance the ape-man. In a few moments Tarzan overhauled and seized him. Wood struggled weakly to escape at the same time that he was thanking Tarzan for saving him.

"It's awful," he groaned. "Don't you suppose I can ever escape from the will of that old devil?"

Tarzan shrugged. "Perhaps not," he said. "I have known ordinary witch-doctors to kill men after a period of many years at distances of hundreds of miles, and this Mafka is evidently no ordinary witch-doctor."

That night they camped beside the Neubari, and in the morning when the ape-man awoke Stanley Wood had disappeared.

4

Sentenced to Death

WITH THE REALIZATION that the American had gone
there came to Tarzan a fuller realization of the po-
tency of Mafka's necromancy; for he did not for a
moment doubt that it was the influence of the Kaji magician
that had forced the desertion of the unwilling Wood.

The ape-man conceded admiration to the cunning and the
power that had stolen the man from him, for he had taken
particular pains to circumvent just such a possibility. When
they had lain down to sleep, Tarzan had fastened one end of
his grass rope securely to an ankle of the man he had taken
under his protection and the other end to one of his own
wrists; but that upon which he had depended most was
his own preternatural keenness of sense which ordinarily
functioned only a little less actively when he slept than
when he was awake.

That Wood had been able to free himself and escape could
have been due to no powers of his own; but must have been
attributable solely to the supernatural machinations of Mafka, constituting in the eyes of the ape-man a direct challenge
to his own prowess.

Perhaps this motivated him in part, but it was also a desire
to save the young American from an unknown fate that
prompted him to turn back in pursuit.

He did not follow the back trail to the Mafa River, but
struck out in a south-easterly direction into the mountainous
country that forms an almost impregnable protection for the
stronghold of the Kaji.

Deep gorges and precipitous cliffs retarded the progress of
the ape-man; so that it was over three days before he reached
his objective: a point near the headwaters of the Mafa a full
day's march to the east of the City of Kaji.

He had foreseen that Mafka might expect him to follow
Wood, which would offer the magician an opportunity to
have Tarzan waylaid and destroyed at some point upon the

trail where he would be helpless against the onslaught of a
well-placed detachment of Kaji warrior-women; and so he
had elected to come upon Kaji from an unexpected direction
and depend upon his animal cunning and his great strength
and agility to carry him into the very presence of the
malign power the destruction of which appeared to be the
only means whereby Wood and his companions might be set
at liberty permanently.

But above all, his success depended upon the verity of his
conviction that he was immune to the supernatural powers of Mafka; though upon this point there was one thing that
troubled him; it seemed to him that Mafka must have known
of his befriending of Wood. The very fact that he had taken
Wood from him suggested that. Yet this might have been
accomplished by means of spies, which the American had
specifically stated were employed by the Kaji. There was also
the possibility that Mafka's power over his victims was so
great that he could read their minds even at great distances
and thus see through their eyes the things that they saw; so
that while Tarzan had been in the company of the American,
Mafka had been as well aware of him and his activities as
though he had been present in person; but when Wood was
no longer with him, the magician could not exercise his
telepathic surveillance over him. This was the premise upon
which the ape-man based his strategy.

It was late in the afternoon of the third day after Wood's
disappearance that Tarzan paused upon a lofty mountain ridge
and surveyed the country about him. In a canyon below and
to the south of him raced a turbulent mountain stream. With
his eyes he followed its meanderings toward the west where,
in the dim and hazy distance, he saw a cleft in the serried
range that he knew must be the gorge of the Mafa leading
down to its confluence with the Neubari.

He stood, then, near the headwaters of the former stream
between the countries of the Kaji and the Zuli.

A west wind blew gently from the lower country toward
the summit of the range, carrying to the nostrils of the ape-
man evidence of things unseen—of Tongani the baboon,
Sheeta the leopard, of the red wolf, and the buffalo; but of
the east he had no knowledge except that which his eyes
and his ears furnished; and so, facing the west, he was unaware of the eyes that watched him from behind the summit of the ridge above him, eyes that disappeared when the
ape-man turned in their direction.

There were a dozen pairs of them, and their owners formed a motley crew of unkempt, savage warriors. Of them, seven were bearded white men and five were blacks. All were similarly garbed in well worn loin-cloths of the skins of wild beasts. They carried bows and arrows and short, heavy spears; and all the blacks and some of the whites wore barbaric ornaments—necklaces of the teeth of animals and armlets and anklets. Upon their backs were small shields of the hide of the buffalo.

They watched Tarzan as he descended into the gorge of the Mafa and slaked his thirst. They saw him take a piece of meat from his quiver and eat, and every move that he made they watched. Sometimes they spoke together in low whispers that could not carry against the wind to the ears of the apeman.

One, who seemed to be the leader, spoke most often. He was a white man whose brown hair had greyed at the temples and whose beard was streaked with grey. He was well built, with the hard leanness of the athlete. His forehead and his eyes denoted intelligence. His companions called him Lord.

Tarzan was tired. For three days he had scaled cliffs and crags, descended into abysses, and clambered to lofty summits; and the previous night his rest had been broken by hunting leopards that had caught his scent and stalked him. He had killed one that had attacked him; but others had kept him constantly on the alert, precluding the possibility of continued rest.

The sun was still an hour high when he lay down to sleep behind a bush on the slope above the Mafa. That he was dogtired must account for that which followed, for ordinarily nothing could have approached without arousing him.

When he did awaken, it was still daylight; and a dozen warriors formed a close circle about him, the points of their spears directed at his unprotected body. He looked up into the savage, unfriendly eyes of a black man; then he glanced quickly around the circle and noted the composition of the group. He did not speak. He saw that he was outnumbered and a captive. Under the circumstances there was nothing that he could say that would serve him any purpose.

His silence and his composure set his captors aback. They had expected him to show fear and excitement. He did neither. He just lay there and appraised them through steady, grey eyes.

"Well, Kaji," said Lord at last, "we've got you."

The truth of the statement was too obvious to require comment; so Tarzan remained silent. He was interested less in what the man said than in the language in which he said it. The fellow appeared definitely Anglo-Saxon, yet he spoke a bastard tongue the base of which was Galla but so intermixed with other tongues that it would have been unintelligible to one less versed in African dialect and European languages than Tarzan. In his brief speech, that could be translated into six English words, he had used as many tongues.

Lord shifted his weight from one foot to the other. "Well, Kaji," he said after a brief silence, "what have you got to say?"

"Nothing," replied the ape-man.

"Get up!" directed Lord.

Tarzan arose and stretched with the easy indifference of a lion in its own lair.

"Take his weapons," snapped Lord; and then, half to himself and in English: "By Jove, but he's a rum 'un."

Then, indeed, was Tarzan interested. Here was an Englishman. There might be some reason to speak now—to ask questions.

"Who are you?" he demanded. "What makes you think that I'm a Kaji?"

"For the same reason that you know that we are Zuli," replied Lord. "Because there are no other people in these mountains." Then he turned to one of his fellows. "Tie his hands behind his back."

They led him then across the ridge and down the other side of the divide; but it was dark now, and Tarzan saw nothing of the country through which they passed. He knew that they followed a well worn trail that often dropped precipitously down the side of a rocky gorge until it reached a gentler descent and wound tortuously as though following the meanderings of the stream that splashed or purled or gurgled at their right.

It was very dark in the gorge; but at length they came out into open, level country; and there it was lighter; though still no landmarks were visible to give the ape-man a suggestion of the terrain of this unfamiliar land.

A dim, flickering light showed far ahead. For half an hour they approached it before its closer aspect explained it. Then Tarzan saw that it was from an open fire burning behind the stockade of a village.

As they approached the gates, Lord hallooed; and when he

had identified himself they were admitted, and Tarzan found himself in a village of stone huts thatched with grass. The light from the fire burning in the center of the main street revealed only a portion of the village, which evidently was of considerable size; the rest was lost in the shadows beyond the limit of the firelight.

Before him, built directly across the principal avenue, loomed a large two-storied stone building. At the village gate were several women garbed and armed similarly to his captors. In the none-too-brilliant light of the fire they appeared to be white women; and there were others, like them, lounging in the doorways of huts or about the fire. Among them were a number of white men; and all of them, but especially the women, evinced considerable interest in Tarzan as Lord led him through the village.

"Ai, Kaji!" they yelled at him. "You will soon be dead, Kaji."

"It is too bad he is a Kaji," shouted one woman. "He would make a fine husband."

"Perhaps Woora will give him to you," bantered another, "when he gets through with him."

"He will be no good for a husband then. I do not want lion meat for a husband."

"I hope Woora feeds him to the lions alive. We have had no good sport since before the last rains."

"He will not turn this one to the lions. The fellow has too good a head. He looks as though he might have brains, and Woora never wastes good brains on the lions."

Through this barrage of comment, Lord led his captive to the entrance to the big building that dominated the village. At its portals were a dozen warrior-women, barring entrance. One of them advanced to meet Lord, the point of her spear dropped to the level of the man's abdomen.

Lord halted. "Tell Woora that we bring a Kaji prisoner," he said.

The woman turned to one of her warriors. "Tell Woora that Lord brings a Kaji prisoner," she directed; then her eyes travelled over the ape-man appraisingly.

"A good specimen, eh?" said Lord. "What a fine mate he'd make for you, Lorro."

The woman spat reflectively. "M-m-m, yes," she agreed; "he has good conformation, but he is a little too dark. Now, if one were sure he had nothing but white blood, he'd be well worth fighting for. Do you suppose he's all white? But what's the difference? He's a Kaji, and that's the end of him."

Since his capture Tarzan had spoken only a few words, and
these in the Gallic dialect. He had not denied that he was a
Kaji for the same reason that he had made no effort to escape: curiosity prompted him to learn more of the Zuli—curiosity and the hope that he might learn something of advantage from these enemies of the Kaji that would aid him in
freeing the two Americans and their companions from captivity and releasing them permanently from the malign power of Mafka.

As he waited before the entrance to the palace of Woora
he decided that he was rather enjoying the adventure. The
frank appraisal of Lorro amused him. The idea of a woman
fighting for possession of him appealed to his sense of humor.
At the time he did not know exactly what the woman's words
connoted, but he made a shrewd guess based on what Wood
had told him of the customs of the Kaji.

Indifferently he appraised the woman. She might have
been an octoroon, or she might have been a white woman
with a coat of tan. Her features were not Negroid. Except
for her dark hair she might have passed easily for a Scandi-
navian. She was a well-formed woman of about thirty, clean
limbed and with the muscular contours of an athlete rendered
graceful by femininity. Her features were good, and by
any civilized standards she would have been accounted a
handsome woman.

The ape-man's reflections upon the subject were interrupted
by the return of the warrior Lorro had sent to advise
Woora of Lord's return with a prisoner.

"Lord is to take the Kaji to Woora," she announced. "See
that the prisoner bears no weapons, that his hands are tied behind him, and that a strong guard accompanies him and
Lord—a guard of women."

With six of her warriors, Lorro escorted Lord and his
prisoner into the palace, a palace only by virtue of its being
occupied by a ruler—a palace by courtesy, one might say.

They entered a gloomy hall lighted dimly by a burning
wick in a shallow pottery dish, a primitive cresset that gave
forth more soot than light. Upon either side of the corridor
were doorways, across most of which were drawn hangings
fashioned from the pelts of animals, mostly buffaloes.

One uncovered doorway revealed a chamber in which a
number of warrior-women were congregated. Some lay on
low, skin-covered cots; others squatted in a circle upon the

floor intent upon some game they were playing. The walls of
the room were hung with spears and shields and bows and
arrows. It was evidently a guard-room. Just beyond it, the
corridor ended before a massive door guarded by two warriors.

It was evident that the guards were expecting the party
and had received their instructions, for as they approached
the doors were swung open for them to enter.

Tarzan saw before him a large room at the far end of
which a figure was seated upon a dais. Two score or more of
smoking cressets lighted the interior, revealing walls hung
with a strange array of skins, weapons, rugs, silks, calicoes
—a veritable museum, Tarzan conjectured, of the loot of
many a safari; but by far the most outstanding and impressive feature of the decorations was the frieze of human
heads that encircled the chamber—the mummified heads of
women, hanging by their long hair, while from the smoke-
darkened beams of the ceiling depended a hundred more.

These things the eyes of the ape-man took in in a sweeping
glance; then they returned to the dais and the figure upon it.
A score of women warriors flanked the dais where the lone
figure sat upon a huge throne chair.

At first glance Tarzan saw only an enormous head thatched
with scraggly grey hair; and then, below the head, a
shrivelled body that was mostly abdomen—a hideously repulsive figure, naked but for a loin cloth. The skin of the
face and head were drawn like yellow parchment over the
bones of the skull—a living death's head in which were
set two deep, glowing eyes that smouldered and burned as
twin pits of Hell. And Tarzan knew that he was in the presence of Woora.

On a table directly in front of the magician rested an
enormous emerald that reflected the lights from the nearer
cressets and shot them back in scintillant rays that filled the
apartment with their uncanny light.

But it was the man rather than the emerald that interested
Tarzan. Woora was no black man, yet it was difficult to de-
termine to what race he might belong. His skin was yellow,
yet his features were not those of a Chinese. He might have
been almost anything.

For several minutes he sat staring at Tarzan after the latter
was halted before the dais. Gradually an expression of
puzzlement and frustration overspread his face; then he
spoke.

"How is my brother?" he demanded, the words squeaking like a rusty hinge.

The expression on Tarzan's face revealed no emotion, though inwardly he was greatly puzzled by the question.

"I do not know your brother," he replied.

"What?" demanded Woora. "You mean to tell me, Kaji, that you do not know that prince of liars, that thief, that murderer, that ingrate, my brother?"

The ape-man shook his head. "I do not know him," he repeated, "and I am no Kaji."

"What!" screamed Woora, glaring at Lord. "This is no Kaji? Didn't you tell me you were bringing a Kaji?"

"We captured him near the headwaters of the Mafa, O Woora; and what other kind of man would be there but a Kaji?"

"He is no Kaji, fool," said Woora. "I guessed as much the moment I looked into his eyes. He is not as other men. My putrid brother could have no power over this one. You are a fool, Lord; and I have no wish to breed more fools among the Zuli—there are enough already. You will be destroyed. Take his weapons from him, Lorro. He is a prisoner."

Then he turned to the ape-man. "What were you doing in the country of the Zuli?" he demanded.

"Searching for one of my people who is lost."

"You expected to find him here?"

"No, I was not coming here. I was going into the country of the Kaji."

"You are lying," snapped Woora. "You could not come to the headwaters of the Mafa without coming through the country of the Kaji; there is no other way."

"I came another way," replied Tarzan.

"No man could cross the mountains and gorges that surround Kaji and Zuli; there is no trail except that up the Mafa River," insisted Woora.

"I crossed the mountains and the gorges," said Tarzan.

"I see it all!" exclaimed Woora. "You are no Kaji; but you are in the service of my loathsome brother, Mafka. He has sent you here to murder me."

"Well," he laughed mockingly, "we shall see who is more powerful, Mafka or I. We shall see if he can save his servant from the wrath of Woora. And we'll give him time." He turned to Lorro. "Take him away with the other prisoner," he directed, "and see that neither of them escapes—especially this one; he is a dangerous man. But he will die even as Lord will."

5

The Black Panther

ARZAN AND LORD were confined in a room on the second floor of the palace of Woora. It was a small room with a single window heavily barred with wooden bars. The door was thick and solid, and secured upon the outside with heavy bars.

When the guard had closed and bolted the door and departed, Tarzan walked to the window and looked out. The moon had risen and the light clouds that had overcast the sky earlier in the night had disappeared.

In the soft glow of the night light, the ape-man saw a walled compound directly beneath the window; and in the shadow of the wall something that was unrecognizable by sight, yet Tarzan knew what it was from the scent that rose to his nostrils. He took hold of the bars and tested them; then he turned back and faced Lord.

"If you had asked me," he said, "I should have told you that I was not a Kaji; then you wouldn't have been in this mess."

Lord shook his head. "It was only an excuse to kill me," he said. "Woora has been waiting for one. He is afraid of me. The men are more important here than they are in the Kaji country. We are allowed to bear arms and be warriors. That is because Woora knows that we cannot escape, as the only route to the outer world lies through the country of the Kaji. They would make slaves of us or kill us.

"Woora has heard that some of the men have banded together for the purpose of escaping. The plan included assassinating Woora and stealing the great emerald, which is supposed to be the source of his magic power. With this emerald, which Mafka craves more than anything in the world, we hoped to bribe our way through and out of the Kaji country.

"Woora believes that I am the instigator of the plot, and so he wants to destroy me. Of course, he could do that at any time he wishes, but he is a wily old devil and is trying to hide the fact that he has any suspicions. In this way he hopes to trap all of the plotters eventually, killing them one by one on one pretext or another."

"How can you know so much of his plans?" demanded the ape-man.

"Even in this land of horror and iniquity there is some-times love," replied Lord, "and there is always lust. A woman close to Woora is honestly in love with one of us. Woora has talked too much to her—that is all. He is supposed to be above temptations of the flesh, but he is not.

"But now everything is spoiled. The others will be afraid. They will stay on until they die."

"You are an Englishman, aren't you?" asked Tarzan.

Lord nodded. "Yes," he said; "I was an Englishman, but God only knows what I am now. I've been here twenty years —here and in Kaji. The Kaji caught me originally; then the Zuli got me in one of their raids."

"I thought Woora killed the Kaji he caught," said the ape-man. "He was going to have me killed because he thought I was a Kaji, or at least I assumed he was from what I heard after we reached the city."

"Yes, he kills them all now because we have all the men we need; but in those days there were not enough men. We can only support a limited number of people. There's plenty of meat, for game is plentiful; but fruits and vegetables are scarce. As it is, we breed more than enough to keep up the population—in fact, too many. Most of the babies are killed. Then, too, the women are pretty white. That is what they have been breeding for for God knows how many genera-tions; so there isn't much need for new white blood. It's very rare now that a baby is born with Negroid character-istics, but of course occasionally there is a throwback."

"Why do they want to be white?" asked Tarzan.

"The Lord only knows. They never see anyone but them-selves and never will. The original reason is lost in the past —dead with those who conceived it. Unless, perhaps, Woora and Mafka know. It is said they have been here forever—that they are deathless; but of course that is not true.

"I have a theory about them that is based upon various snatches of information that I have picked up during the past twenty years. They are identical twins who came from Columbia many years ago bringing with them the great emerald, which they probably stole. How they came into possession of the Gonfal of the Kaji, I don't know. Doubtless they murdered someone who was trying to get out of the country with it.

"That they have uncanny occult powers there is no doubt, and the very fact that they believe these dependent upon the great diamond of the Kaji and the emerald of the Zuli may very probably have caused this to be true; so if either Mafka or Woora were deprived of his stone his power would be lost. But killing them would make it surer. We were taking no chances; we were going to kill Woora. But now, as far as I am concerned, the dream is over. I'll go to the lions; you'll be tortured to death."

"Why the difference?" asked Tarzan.

"I'll furnish sport for Woora in the lion yard, but he won't risk you. They might tear you to pieces, head and all; and Woora wants your brain. I'm sure of that."

"Why does he want it?"

"You had him guessing; I could see that, and he figures that any one who can do that must have a pretty good brain; so he wants it."

"But why?" insisted the ape-man.

"To eat."

"Oh, I see," said Tarzan. "He believes that if one eats the part in which another excels one acquires a measure of this excellence. I have seen it before, often. A warrior eats the heart of a brave enemy to increase his own courage, or the soles of the feet of a swift runner to accelerate his own speed, or the palms of the hands of a clever artisan."

"It is all rot," said Lord.

"I do not know," admitted Tarzan. "I have lived in Africa all my life, and there are many things that I have learned not to deny simply because I do not understand them. But there is one thing that I guess."

"What is that?"

"That Woora will not eat my brain; nor will you go to the lions if you care to escape."

"Escape!" scoffed Lord. "There is no escape."

"Perhaps not," admitted the ape-man. "I said only that I guessed; I did not say that I knew."

"How can we escape?" demanded Lord. "Look at that door; see the bars on that window, and below the window——"

"The panther," Tarzan concluded for him.

"How did you know a panther was there?" Lord's tone bespoke incredulity.

"The scent of Sheeta is strong," replied the ape-man. "I noticed it the instant I came into this room, and when I went to the window I knew that he was in the compound beneath—a male panther."

Lord shook his head. "Well, I don't know how you did it; but you're right."

Tarzan walked to the window and examined the bars and the casing in which they were set.

"Stupid," he said.

"What is stupid?" asked Lord.

"Whoever designed this. Look." He seized two of the bars close to the sill and surged backward with all his strength and all his weight. There was a rending of wood as the entire window frame was torn from its seat; then he laid the frame with all its bars upon the floor of the room.

Lord whistled. "Man!" he exclaimed. "You're strong as a bull; but don't forget the panther, and the noise'll probably bring the guard."

"We'll be ready for them," Tarzan assured him. He had seized the window frame again, and a moment later he had torn it apart. The bars fell from their sockets. Tarzan picked up two of them and handed one to Lord. "These will make fair weapons," he said.

They waited in silence for a while, but no guard came. Apparently only the panther had been disturbed. He was growling now; and when they went to the window, they saw him standing in the center of the compound looking up at them. He was a large beast and coal black.

Tarzan turned to his companion. "Could you get away if we got outside the city?" he asked. "Or has Woora the same power to direct the movements of his victims at a distance that Mafka has?"

"There's the rub," admitted Lord. "That's the reason we'd planned on killing him."

"How does he stand with the Zuli? Are they loyal to him?"

"The only hold he has upon them is based on terror. They fear and hate him."

"The women, too?"

"Yes, every one."

"What would happen here if he were dead?" asked Tarzan.

"The blacks and whites who are prisoners and slaves

would combine with the women in an attempt to fight our way out into the outer world. The blacks and whites (they are all men) want to get back to their own homes. The women, the true Zuli, have heard so much about the world they have never seen that they want to get out, too. They know from what the whites have told them that they would be rich from the proceeds of the sale of the great emerald; and while they have no first-hand knowledge of money, they have learned enough from the white men here to understand that it will get them everything their hearts desire—especially more white men. Here, each of the whites is married to anywhere from seven to a dozen Zuli women because there are so few of us; so the height of the ambition of every Zuli is to have a husband of her own."

"Why don't they kill Woora themselves, then?"

"Fear of his supernatural powers. Not only would they not kill him themselves, they would protect his life from others; but when he was once dead, then it would be different."

"Where is he?" asked Tarzan. "Where does he sleep?"

"In a room directly behind his throne," replied Lord. "But why? Why do you ask? You're not——?"

"I am going to kill him. There is no other way."

Lord shook his head. "It can't be done. Man, he is almost as powerful as God and almost as omniscient. But anyway, why are you doing it?"

"One of my countrymen is a prisoner among the Kaji. With the help of the Zuli, I can set him free with all the rest of the Kaji prisoners. I am not so sure that I could do it alone. It would be difficult to get into Mafka's presence. He is more afraid and more careful than Woora."

"You haven't got into Woora's presence yet, except with your hands tied behind you," Lord reminded him.

"Is there any way to get into his room except from the throne-room?"

"There is a way, but you can't get in. Woora's room has a window looking onto this compound below us. The panther is there to guard Woora as well as to keep prisoners from escaping. You would have to pass through the compound to get to the window."

"That is not so good," mused the ape-man. "I'd have to make too much noise. I'd certainly arouse Woora by breaking the bars at his window."

"There are no bars there."

"But the panther! What's to keep him from entering and killing Woora?"

"Woora has even greater power over the panther than he has over us humans. He can control the beast's every act."

"You are sure there are no bars at the window?" demanded Tarzan.

"Absolutely sure, and the window is always open so that Woora can call the panther to him if he is ever in danger of attack."

"Excellent! I'll go in by the window."

"You insist on forgetting the panther."

"I have not forgotten him. Tell me something of Woora's habits. Who is with him? When does he arise? Where does he eat? When does he first go into the throne-room?"

"No one is with him in his sleeping room, ever. No one, as far as we know, has ever been in it, other than himself. His breakfast is handed in to him through a small opening near the floor on the side of the room opposite the throne-room. He gets up shortly after sunrise and eats immediately there-after. He has a suite of three rooms. What he does there, only the Devil knows. Sometimes he has one of the women warriors come into one of his rooms. They never tell what they see there, or what happens. They are too terrified. What would be perhaps an hour after his breakfast, he comes into the throne-room. By this time many of the Zuli have congregated there. Charges are heard, punishments are met-ed out, the business of the day is attended to. That is, hunting parties and raiding parties are sent out; directions are given for the planting, cultivation, or harvesting of crops. Reports and complaints are listened to by Woora. Then he goes back to his apartments and remains there until the evening meal which he takes in the throne-room. That is his day, unless something unforeseen occurs such as the examination of a captive brought in unexpectedly, as you were."

"Good!" exclaimed the ape-man. "Everything can be made to conform to my plan."

"Except the panther," said Lord.

"Perhaps you are right," conceded Tarzan; "we'll see." He stepped to the window. The panther had quieted down and was lying once more in the shade of the compound wall. Tarzan listened. Presently he turned to his companion. "He is asleep," he said; then he threw a leg over the sill.

"You are not going down there!" Lord exclaimed.

"Why not? It is the only avenue to Woora, and the panther sleeps."

"He will not be asleep for long."

"I do not expect him to be. I only ask him to stay asleep until I am squarely on my feet below there."

"It is suicide," said Lord, "and nothing to be gained by it."

"Maybe, but let's wait and see." He threw the other leg over the sill; then he turned upon his belly. In his right hand was one of the heavy bars he had taken from the window. Cautiously, silently, he slipped down until he hung from the sill by one hand.

Lord watched him, breathless. He saw the fingers slip gradually from their hold on the sill; then he looked out. The man had alighted erect and then turned like lightning to face the panther, but the beast had not moved. It still slept.

Tarzan crept toward it, silent as the shadow of Usha the wind. The ape-man had covered half the distance to the panther when the beast awoke; then, before it could gather its wits the man leaped toward it.

In the window above, Lord held his breath. He could not but admire the courage of his fellow prisoner, but he thought him foolhardy. Just then the panther charged.

6

Trapped

OF ALL THE cats none bears so evil a reputation as the panther. His ferocity is proverbial, his wiliness uncanny, the force and fury of his attack demoniacal. But all these things the ape-man knew and was prepared for. He had weighed his chances with the panther against his chances with Woora, and he had chosen the lesser of two evils first in the belief that thus he might rid himself of both. And now in a few seconds his judgment would be vindicated, or he would be dead.

The black beast charged with all the fury of its kind, and it charged in silence. No growls disturbed the deathly still-

ness of the night. A serene moon looked down upon the
village of the Zuli, and beyond the confines of the compound there was no warning of death.

Lord looked down upon the swift tragedy with something of contempt for the stupidity that would permit a
man to throw his life away uselessly, and from another
window two deep-set, glowing eyes watched above snarling
lips—watched from the window of the room that was
Woora's.

Grasping the hardwood rod in both hands, Tarzan swung
it above his head in a great circle that started low at his
right side, timing it to the fraction of a second so that it
met the panther with its full momentum, backed by the
strength of the ape-man's giant thews, at the height of the
beast's speed.

Full upon the fierce, flat skull it fell before the protracted
talons or bared fangs could reach the flesh of the panther's
intended prey. There was the sound of splintering wood and
bone, the thud of the heavy body upon the hard ground,
then silence.

Lord drew in his breath in a quick gasp. Although he had
seen the thing with his own eyes, he could scarcely believe.
The eyes at Woora's window were filled with a sudden fear
—with fear and cunning. They watched intently to see what
the next move of the strange prisoner would be.

Tarzan placed a foot upon the carcass of his kill and
raised his face to Goro the Moon. Just for an instant he
stood thus, but no victory cry of the bull ape shocked the
silence of the night to warn his enemies that he was abroad.
Then he moved in the direction of the window that opened
into the room of Woora, the magician; and as he did so, the
eyes receded into the darkness of the interior.

The ape-man paused at the open window while his ears
and his nostrils searched the dark chamber. His ears heard a
faint rustling sound as of the scuffing of sandaled feet
upon a floor and the almost silent closing of a door. His nostrils caught clearly the scent of Woora.

Placing a hand upon the sill, Tarzan vaulted silently into
the room. He stood in silence, listening, in one hand the
splintered remains of the hardwood rod. He heard no sound,
not even the faintest sound of breathing that his ears would
have detected had there been another in the room. He concluded, then, that Woora had seen him coming and that the
slight noises he had heard had been caused by the magi-

cian's departure. Now he must be doubly on his guard.

Lord had told him that there were three rooms in Woora's suite. There was also the throne-room adjoining. To which room had the man fled? Had he gone to summon help? This was probable, yet Tarzan heard no sound to indicate that anyone was coming.

The faint moonlight dissipated but slightly the darkness of the room, yet it was enough for the keen eyes of the ape-man as they became accustomed to the gloom. He advanced noiselessly into the apartment, and presently he saw a door in the wall before him and another at his right. The latter, he judged, must lead into the throne-room. He approached the other and found the latch.

Noiselessly he pulled the door toward him, keeping partially behind it to shield himself from a surprise blow or a missile. The room was dark as a pocket. He listened intently but heard nothing. His nostrils told him that Woora had been there recently, but his ears assured him that he had gone— probably into the farthest apartment.

He stepped into the room, bent upon searching the next and last. He knew that Woora had come this way and that he would find him beyond the next door. He felt something beneath his feet that felt like cords laid upon the floor. Instantly he was suspicious—the suspicion of the wild animal that senses a trap.

He started to retreat to the room he had just quitted—but too late. Cords sprang up around him. They pulled at him and tripped him, so that he fell. Then he felt them closing and tightening about him. He struggled to escape them, but they were everywhere. He was entangled in a mesh of cords.

The door of the third room opened letting in light. In the doorway stood Woora, a cresset in his hand. His death's head face was contorted in a snarling grin. Behind the magician, Tarzan caught a glimpse of a room that might have been the laboratory of a medieval alchemist but for the grisly array of human heads that depended from the beams of the ceiling.

The apartment was lighted by several cressets, and upon a table in the center lay the great emerald of the Zuli, radiating its weird and baleful light, so that the entire chamber was filled with a seemingly palpable essence that was, in some way, mysteriously malign.

"You court an earlier and more horrible death than we had planned for you," squeaked Woora.

The ape-man made no reply. He was examining the trap

that had caught him. It was a heavy net of rawhide the mouth of which could be pulled from the floor and closed by a cord that ran through a block depending from a ceiling beam and thence through a hole near the ceiling into the room where Woora had waited to snare his prey. It was plain to Tarzan that this room was devoted solely to the purposes of the net, forming the magician's final protection against an assassin who sought his life.

In this he was only partially right, as previously all of its victims had been invited to his innermost sanctum by the magician and, rendered helpless in the net, easily murdered. Tonight it served a new purpose.

Satisfied with the success of his strategy in luring the stranger to this room, Woora was in a pleasant frame of mind. The fear and the anger had left his eyes. He surveyed the ape-man with interest.

"You intrigue me," he said. "I shall keep you here for a while to examine you. Perhaps you will get hungry and thirsty, but one who is shortly to die has no need of food or drink. But you shall watch me eat and drink, and you shall meditate upon the various slow and torturing deaths that man may die. I promise you that I shall select something novel and protracted for you, if only to avenge the killing of my pet—the one creature in all the world that I really loved. You shall die many deaths for that and not a few for seeking to destroy me or steal the great emerald. I do not know which you planned doing, nor do I care. Either warrants the direst punishment of which I can conceive.

"In the meantime, I shall show you that Woora can be kind even to an enemy. It is well for you that I am neither cruel nor vindictive. I would save you from unnecessary suffering, from mental anguish induced by the sight of horrible or suggestive objects. Watch me closely."

As he ceased speaking he stepped into the adjoining room where he busied himself lighting the charcoal in a brazier. It took some time to produce a hot fire; but when this was accomplished, he fetched a long metal rod with a sharpened point and a wooden handle. The point he inserted among the hot coals; then he turned his attention once more to the ape-man.

"The human heads upon the walls of my apartment, the paraphernalia of my profession, the preparations that I must make for your torture and death; the sight of these things would prove most depressing to you and add unnecessarily to your suffering; therefore I am going to burn out your eyes so that you cannot see them!"

And yet the ape-man did not speak. His level gaze remained fixed upon the repulsive figure of the old magician and the weird setting in which he wrought his villanies, all bathed in the unholy green light of the great emerald. What his thoughts were only he knew, but it is safe to assume that they were not of death—not of his own death. Probably they were of escape. He tested the strength of the rawhide net. It gave, but it did not break.

Woora saw him and laughed. "A bull elephant could not break that," he said. With his grotesque head cocked upon one side he stared intently at his victim. The laugh died on his lips, leaving a snarl. He was angry because the ape-man showed no fear. He looked to the iron, muttering and mumbling to himself. It had grown hot; the point glowed.

"Take a last look, my guest," cackled Woora, "for after a moment you will never again see anything." He withdrew the iron from the coals and approached his prisoner.

The strands of the net closed snugly about the ape-man, confining his arms; so that though he could move them, he could move them neither quickly nor far. He would have difficulty in defending himself against the glowing point of the iron rod.

Woora came close and raised the red-hot iron to the level of Tarzan's eyes; then he jabbed suddenly at one of them. The victim warded off the searing point from its intended target. Only his hand was burned. Again and again Woora jabbed; but always Tarzan succeeded in saving his eyes, yet at the expense of his hands and forearms.

At his repeated failures to blind his victim, Woora became convulsed with rage. He screamed and cursed as he danced about, foaming at the mouth; then, quite suddenly, he gained control of himself. He carried the iron back to the brazier and inserted it among the coals; then he stepped to another part of the room that was not in line with the doorway, and therefore outside the range of Tarzan's vision. He was gone for but a moment, and when he returned he carried a rope in his hand.

He was chuckling again as he approached Tarzan. "The iron will be hotter this time," he said, "and this time it will reach your eyes."

He passed the rope around the net and Tarzan and made

a slip noose and drew it tight; then he walked around and around the ape-man, binding his hands and his arms with many coils of rope until Tarzan had no use of them for protection.

Now he went to the brazier and withdrew the iron. It glowed strangely red in the weird green light of the chamber. With it, Woora crept slowly toward his victim as though he were trying to prolong the agony of suspense; but Tarzan gave no evidence of fear. He knew that he was helpless, and he awaited the inevitable with stoic indifference.

Suddenly Woora was seized by another spasm of fury. "You pretend that you are not afraid," he screamed, "but I'll make you shriek for mercy yet. First the right eye!" And he came forward again, holding the red point on a level with the ape-man's eyes.

Tarzan heard the door behind him open. He saw Woora shrink back, a new expression of fury writ upon his face; then a man leaped past him carrying a stout wooden bar in his hand. It was Lord.

Woora turned to flee into the next apartment, but Lord overtook him, striking him a glancing blow on the head with the rod. The magician turned then and sought to defend himself with the hot iron. He screamed for mercy and for help; but there was no mercy in Lord's attack, and no help came.

Wielding the rod in both hands, the Englishman struck the iron from Woora's hand, breaking the arm at the wrist; then he swung it again furiously, crashing full on the grotesque skull; and with a splintering and crushing of bone Woora sank to the floor, dead.

Lord turned to Tarzan. "A close call," he said.

"Yes, a very close call. I shall not forget it."

"I saw you kill the panther," continued Lord. "My word! I'd never have thought it possible. Then I waited. I didn't know just what to do. Presently I commenced to worry; I knew what a wily old devil Woora was; so I followed you, and it was a good thing that I did."

While he talked, the Englishman found a knife and cut the bonds and the net that held the ape-man; then the two men examined the contents of the inner room. There was a small furnace in one corner, several retorts and test tubes on a long table, shelves with bottles and vials stored upon them, a small library of occultism, black magic, voodooism. In a little niche, before which stood a chair, there was a crystal sphere. But, dominating all, the center of everything, was the great emerald.

Lord looked at it, spellbound, fascinated. "It is worth over two million pounds sterling," he said, "and it is ours for the taking! There are still several hours of darkness; and it may be hours more, perhaps days, before anyone discovers that Woora is dead and the emerald gone. They could never overtake us."

"You forget your friends here," Tarzan reminded him.

"Any one of them would do the same if he had the chance," argued Lord. "They will have their freedom. We have given them that. The emerald should be ours."

"You have also forgotten the Kaji. How will you pass through their country?"

Lord gestured his disgust. "There is always something; but you're right—we can't escape except with a large force."

"There is a question whether you can escape Mafka even then," said Tarzan. "I've seen some evidence of his power. By comparison, Woora's didn't amount to much."

"Well, then, what?"

"I'll go ahead and try to dispose of Mafka," said Tarzan.

"Good! I'll go with you."

The ape-man shook his head. "I must go alone. Mafka's occult powers are such that he can control the actions of his victims even at great distances, but for some reason he has no power over me. He might have over you. That is the reason I must go alone; he might sense the presence of another with me and through him learn my plans—his powers are most uncanny."

As he ceased speaking, Tarzan picked up the great emerald, and wrapped it in a bit of cloth he had torn from a hanging on the wall.

Lord's eyes narrowed. "What are you doing that for?" he demanded.

"I'm taking the emerald with me. It will insure my getting an audience with Mafka."

Lord gave a short, ugly laugh. "And you think you can get away with that?" he demanded. "What do you take me for—a fool?"

Tarzan knew the greed of men. That was one of the reasons he liked beasts so well. "If you try to interfere," he said, "I'll know that you are a fool—you saw what I did to the panther and how easily."

"What do you want with two million pounds? Maybe

three million—God alone knows what it's worth. There's plenty for both of us."

"I don't want any of it," replied the ape-man. "I have all the wealth I need. I'm going to use it to get some of my people away from Mafka. When that is done, I won't care what becomes of it."

He tied two cords to the package holding the emerald. One he looped over his head, the other he tied around his waist holding the package close to his body. He picked up the knife that Lord had laid on the table and stuck it in his own scabbard; then he found a long piece of rope which he coiled and slung across a shoulder.

Lord watched him sullenly. He remembered the panther and knew that he was helpless to prevent the stranger taking the emerald.

"I'm going now," said Tarzan. "Wait a day, and then follow with all those who want to get out. No matter whether I'm successful or not you may have to fight your way through the Kaji, but with Mafka out of the way you'll stand a much better chance. If I get through, I'll cache the emerald on the Neubari near the mouth of the Mafa and go on about my business. In about three weeks I shall be back again; then I'll turn the emerald over to the Zuli."

"To the Zuli!" exclaimed Lord. "Where do I come in? The emerald belongs to me, and you're trying to cheat me out of it. Is this what I get for saving your life?"

Tarzan shrugged. "It is none of my business," he said. "I do not care who gets the emerald. You told me there was a plan afoot to take it and with the proceeds finance all the Zuli in their desire to go and live in civilization. I did not know that you planned to betray your comrades."

Lord's eyes could not meet those of the ape-man, and he flushed as he replied. "I'll see that they get theirs," he said, "but I want to control it. What do they know about business? They'd be cheated out of everything in a month."

"On the Neubari in three weeks, then," said the ape-man, as he turned and quit the apartment.

As Tarzan vaulted the sill of the window in the outer room and started across the compound where lay the dead body of the black panther, Lord opened the door leading to the throne-room and hastened at a run to the guard-room, his mind busy with a plan based on the belief that the stranger intended to make off with the great emerald and keep it for himself.

Green Magic

THE GUARDS IN the corridor outside the throne-room were so surprised to see anyone coming from the throne-room at that time in the night that Lord was past them before they recovered their wits. They pursued him, shouting commands to halt, to the doorway of the guard-room where, by this time, all the women warriors were aroused and leaping to arms.

Lorro was the first to recognize the Englishman. "What is it, Lord?" she demanded. "What are you doing here? How did you get out of the cell? What has happened?"

"The great emerald!" cried Lord. "The Kaji has killed Woora and stolen the great emerald."

"Killed Woora!" exclaimed half a dozen of the women in unison. "You mean that Woora is dead?"

"Yes, yes," replied Lord impatiently. "But the emerald's stolen. Can't you understand that?"

"Woora is dead!" screamed the women; as with one accord they rushed for the village street to spread the happy tidings.

Out in the night, a short distance beyond the village, Tarzan heard the commotion, followed by the hoarse notes of a primitive trumpet. He recognized the call to arms to which now was added the throbbing of the war drums, and guessed that Lord had spread the alarm and was organizing a pursuit.

The ape-man increased his speed, moving unerringly along the trail that he had passed over but once before, and that at night; and behind him came the entire tribe of Zuli warrior women with their white men and their black slaves.

Lord had at last succeeded in impressing on the minds of the Zuli that the death of Woora was an empty beneficence without possession of the emerald that was to have given them wealth and independence in the outer world;

so that it was an angry, blood-thirsty mob that pursued the Lord of the Jungle through the soft African night.

Plain to the ears of the ape-man came the sounds of the pursuit, and he guessed the temper of the pursuers. If they overtook him, he could hope for neither victory nor quarter. There were too many of them for the one, and they were too angry and too savage to accord the other. Only the cunning of the wild beast that environment and training had implanted within him could avail him against such odds.

As he trotted along the winding trail that led up the course of the rivulet toward the divide he became acutely aware of a presence that he could not see. His acute senses told him that he was alone, yet the feeling persisted that he was not alone. Something moved with him, clinging as closely as his shadow. He stopped to listen. The thing seemed so near that he should have heard it breathe, but there was no sound. His keen nostrils sought a clew—there was none.

As he trotted on he sought to reason out the mystery. He even tried to convince himself that he was the victim of a delusion; but Tarzan had never had a delusion—he had only heard that others sometimes had them. And always the presence was with him, haunting him like a ghost.

He smiled. Perhaps that was it—the ghost of Woora. And then, quite suddenly the truth dawned upon him. It was the great emerald!

It seemed impossible, yet it could be nothing else. The mysterious stone had some quality in common with life—an aura that was, perhaps, mesmeric. It was conceivable that it was this very thing that had imparted to Woora the occult powers that had made him so feared, so powerful. This would account in part for the care with which the stone had been guarded.

If this were true, then the same conditions might obtain with the Gonfal, the great diamond of the Kaji. Without it, the power of Mafka would be gone. The ape-man wondered. He also wondered if Mafka's power would be doubled if he possessed both the diamond and the emerald.

How would these stones affect the power of others? Did the mere possession of one of them impart to any mortal such powers as those wielded by Woora and Mafka? The idea intrigued Tarzan. He let his mind play with it for a while as he trotted up toward the divide; then he reached a decision.

Turning abruptly to the right, he left the trail and sought a place of concealment. Presently he found a great boulder at the foot of the canyon wall. Behind it he would be hidden from the view of anyone passing along the trail. Always cautious, he looked about for an avenue of retreat, if one became necessary and saw that he could scale the canyon side easily; then he placed himself behind the boulder and waited.

He heard the Zuli coming up the trail. They were making no effort to conceal their presence. It was evident that they were quite sure that the fugitive could not escape them.

Now the head of the column came into view. It was led by Lord. There were over fifty men, mostly white, and three or four hundred warrior-women. Tarzan concentrated his efforts on the latter.

"Turn back! Turn back!" he willed. "Go back to the village and stay there."

The women kept on along the trail, apparently unaffected; yet Tarzan felt the presence of the emerald more strongly than ever. He raised it from his side and tore away the skin in which he had wrapped it. Its polished surface, reflecting the moonlight, gave forth rays that enveloped the ape-man in an unearthly glow.

As his bare hands touched the stone he felt a tingling in his arms, his body, as though a mild electric current were passing through him. He felt a surge of new power— a strange, uncanny power that had never before been his. Again he willed the women to turn back, and now he knew that they would turn, now he knew his own power without question, without a doubt.

The women stopped and turned about.

"What's the matter?" demanded one of the men.

"I am going back," replied a woman.

"Why?"

"I don't know. I only know that I have to go back. I do not believe that Woora is dead. He is calling me back. He is calling us all back."

"Nonsense!" exclaimed Lord. "Woora is dead. I saw him killed. His skull was crushed to a pulp."

"Nevertheless he is calling us back."

The women were already starting back along the trail. The men stood undecided.

Presently Lord said in a low tone, "Let them go," and they all stood watching until after the women had disappeared beyond a turn in the trail.

"There are over fifty of us," said Lord then, "and we do not need the women. There will be fewer to divide with when we get out with the emerald."

"We haven't got it yet," another reminded him.

"It is as good as ours if we overtake the Kaji before he gets back to his own village. He's a tough customer, but fifty of us can kill him."

Tarzan, behind the boulder, heard and smiled—just the shadow of a smile; a grim shadow.

"Come on!" said Lord. "Let's be going," but he did not move. No one moved.

"Well, why don't you start?" demanded one of the others.

Lord paled. He looked frightened. "Why don't you?" he asked.

"I can't," said the man, "and neither can you. You know it. It's the power of Woora. The woman was right—he is not dead. God! How we'll be punished!"

"I tell you he is dead," growled Lord, "dead as a doornail."

"Then it's his ghost," suggested a man. His voice trembled.

"Look!" cried one and pointed.

With one accord they all looked in the direction their companion indicated. One who had been a Catholic crossed himself. Another prayed beneath his breath. Lord cursed.

From behind a large boulder set well back from the trail spread a greenish luminosity, faint, shimmering, sending out tenuous rays of emerald light, challenging the soft brilliance of the moon.

The men stood spellbound, their eyes fixed upon the miracle. Then a man stepped from behind the boulder—a bronzed giant clothed only in a loin-cloth.

"The Kaji!" exclaimed Lord.

"And the great emerald," said another. "Now is our chance." But no one drew a weapon; no one advanced upon the stranger. They could only wish; their wills could not command disobedience to him who possessed the mysterious power of the emerald.

Tarzan came down to them. He stopped and looked them over appraisingly. "There are over fifty of you," he said. "You will come with me to the village of the Kaji. Some of my people are prisoners there. We will free them; then we will all go out of the Kaji country and go our ways."

He did not ask them; he told them; for he and they

both knew that while he possessed the great emerald he did not have to ask.

"But the emerald," said Lord; "you promised to divide that with me."

"When, a few minutes ago, you planned to kill me," replied the ape-man, "you forfeited your right to hold me to that promise. Also, since then, I have discovered the power of the emerald. The stone is dangerous. In the hands of a man such as you, it could do untold harm. When I am through with it, it will go into the Neubari where no man shall ever find it."

Lord gasped. "God, man!" he cried. "You wouldn't do that! You couldn't throw away a fortune of two or three million pounds! No, you're just saying that. You don't want to divide it—that's it. You want to keep it all for yourself."

Tarzan shrugged. "Think what you please," he said; "it makes no difference. Now you will follow me," and thus they started once more along the trail that led across the divide and down into the country of the Kaji.

It was dusk of the following day when, from a slight eminence, Tarzan saw for the first time the city of Kaji and the stronghold of Mafka. It was built at the side of a valley close to the face of a perpendicular limestone cliff. It appeared to be a place considerably larger than the Zuli village from which he had just escaped. He stood gazing at it for a few moments; then he turned to the men grouped behind him.

"We have travelled far and eaten little," he said. "Many of you are tired. It will not be well to approach the city until well after dark; therefore we will rest." He took a spear from one of the men and drew a long line upon the ground with the sharp point. "You cannot cross this line," he said, "not one of you"; then he handed the spear back to its owner, walked a short distance away from the line that he had drawn between them, and lay down. One hand rested upon the gleaming surface of the emerald; thus he slept.

The others, glad of an opportunity to rest, lay down immediately; and soon all were asleep. No, not all. Lord remained awake, his fascinated eyes held by the faint radiance of the jewel that conjured in his mind the fleshpots of civilization its wealth might purchase.

Dusk passed quickly, and night came. The moon had not yet risen, and it was very dark. Only the green luminosity surrounding the ape-man relieved the Stygian blackness. In

its weird radiance Lord could see the man he called the
Kaji. He watched the hand resting upon the emerald—
watched and waited; for Lord knew much of the power of
the great stone and the manner in which it was conferred
upon its possessor.

He made plans; some he discarded. He waited. Tarzan
moved in his sleep; his hand slipped from the face of the
emerald; then Lord arose. He gripped his spear firmly and
crept cautiously toward the sleeping man. Tarzan had not
slept for two days, and he was sunk in the slumber of exhaustion.

At the line Tarzan had drawn upon the ground Lord hesitated a moment; then he stepped across and knew that the
power of the emerald had passed from the stranger as his
hand had slipped from the stone. For many years Lord had
watched Woora, and he knew that always when he would
force his will upon another some part of his body was in
contact with the emerald; but he breathed a sigh of relief
with the confirmation of his hope.

Now he approached the sleeping ape-man, his spear ready
in his hand. He came close and stood silently for an instant
above the unconscious sleeper; then he stooped and gathered
up the emerald.

The plan to kill Tarzan was one of those he had discarded.
He feared the man might make an outcry before he died
and arouse the others; and this did not fit in with Lord's
plan, which was to possess the emerald for himself alone.

Creeping stealthily away, Lord disappeared in the night.

8

The Leopard Pit

THE APE-MAN AWOKE with a start. The moon was shining full upon his face. Instantly he knew that he had
slept too long. He sensed that something was amiss.
He felt for the emerald; and when he did not feel it, he
looked for it. It was gone. He leaped to his feet and ap-

proached the sleeping men. A quick glance confirmed his first suspicion—Lord was gone!

He considered the men. There were fifty of them. Without the emerald he had no power over them; he could not control them. They would be enemies. He turned away and circled the camp until he picked up the scent-spoor of the thief. It was where he had expected to find it—leading down the valley of the Mafa toward the valley of the Neubari.

He did not know how much start Lord had. It might be as much as two hours; but had it been two weeks, it would have been the same. No man could escape the Lord of the Jungle.

Through the night he followed, the scent-spoor strong in his nostrils. The trail gave the city of the Kaji a wide berth. The terrain was open and sloped gently, the moon was bright. Tarzan moved swiftly, far more swiftly than Lord.

He had been following the Englishman for perhaps an hour when he discerned far ahead a faint, greenish light. It was moving a little to the right of a direct line; and Tarzan knew that, having passed the city of the Kaji, Lord was swinging back onto the direct trail. By cutting straight across, the ape-man would gain considerable distance. As he did so, he increased his speed, moving swiftly, with long, easy strides.

He was gaining rapidly when suddenly the ground gave way beneath his feet and he was precipitated into a black hole. He fell on loose earth and slender branches that formed a cushion, breaking the fall; so that he was not injured.

When he regained his feet he found that it was difficult to move about among the branches that gave when he stepped on them or entangled his feet if he endeavored to avoid them. Looking up, he saw the mouth of the pit out of reach above him. He guessed its purpose. It was probably a leopard pit, used by the Kaji to capture the fierce cats alive. And he realized, too, the purpose of the loose earth and branches that had broken his fall; they gave no firm footing from which a leopard could spring to freedom. He looked up again at the pit's rim. It was far above his head. He doubted that a cat could have leaped out of it if there had been no branches on the floor; he was sure that he could not.

There was nothing to do but wait. If this were a new pit, and it looked new, the Kaji would be along within a day or so; then he would be killed or captured. This was about all he had to expect. No leopard would fall in upon him now that the mouth of the pit was no longer concealed by the covering he had broken through.

He thought of Lord and of the harm he could do were he to reach the outside world in possession of the great emerald of the Zuli, but he did not concern himself greatly on account of his failure to overtake the Englishman. What was, was. He had done his best. He never repined; he never worried. He merely awaited the next event in life, composed in the knowledge that whatever it was he would meet it with natural resources beyond those of ordinary men. He was not egotistical; he was merely quite sure of himself.

The night wore on, and he took advantage of it to add to his sleep. His nerves, uncontaminated by dissipation, were not even slightly unstrung by his predicament or by the imminence of capture or death. He slept.

The sun was high in the heavens when he awoke. He listened intently for the sound that had awakened him. It was the sound of footfalls carried to him from a distance through the medium of the earth. They came closer. He heard voices. So, they were coming! They would be surprised when they saw the leopard they had trapped.

They came closer, and he heard them exclaim with satisfaction when they discovered that the covering of the pit had been broken through; then they were at the pit's edge looking down at him. He saw the faces of several warrior women and some men. They were filled with astonishment.

"A fine leopard!" exclaimed one.

"Mafka will be glad to have another recruit."

"But how did he get here? How could he pass the guards at the entrance to the valley?"

"Let's get him up here. Hey, you! Catch this rope and tie it around under your arms." A rope was tossed down to him.

"Hold it," said the ape-man, "and I'll climb out." He had long since decided to go into captivity without a struggle—for two reasons. One was that resistance would doubtless mean certain death; the other, that captivity would bring him closer to Mafka, possibly simplify the rescue of Wood and his friends. It did not occur to Tarzan to take into consideration the fact that he might not be able to affect his own escape. He was not wont to consider any proposition from a premise of failure. Perhaps this in itself accounted to some extent for the fact that he seldom failed in what he attempted.

Those above held the rope while the ape-man swarmed up it with the agility of a monkey. When he stood upon solid ground, he was faced with several spear-points. There were eight women and four men. All were white. The women were armed; the men carried a heavy net.

The women appraised him boldly. "Who are you?" demanded one of them.

"A hunter," replied Tarzan.

"What are you doing here?"

"I was on my way down in search of the Neubari when I fell into your pit."

"You were going out?"

"Yes."

"But how did you get in? There is only one entrance to the country of the Kaji, and that is guarded. How did you get past our warriors?"

Tarzan shrugged. "Evidently I did not come in that way," he said.

"There is no other way, I tell you," insisted the warrior.

"But I came in another way. I entered the mountains several marches from here to hunt; that is the reason I came down from the east. I hunted in the back country, coming down from the north. The going was rough. I was looking for an easier way to the Neubari. Now that I am out of the pit, I'll go on my way."

"Not so fast," said the woman who had first addressed him and who had done most of the talking since. "You are coming with us. You are a prisoner."

"All right," conceded the ape-man. "Have it your own way —you are eight spears, and I am only one knife."

Presently, Tarzan was not even a knife; for they took it away from him. They did not bind his hands behind him, evidencing their contempt for the prowess of men. Some of them marched ahead, some behind Tarzan and the four other men, as they started back toward the city that could be seen in the near distance. At any time the ape-man could have made a break for escape had he wished to, and with the chances greatly in his favor because of his great speed; but it pleased him to go to the city of the Kaji.

His captors talked incessantly among themselves. They discussed other women who were not with them, always disparagingly; they complained of the difficulties they experienced in the dressing of their hair; they compared the cut and fit and quality of the pelts that formed their loincloths; and each of them expatiated upon the merits of some exceptionally rare skin she hoped to acquire in the future.

The four men marching with Tarzan sought to engage him in conversation. One was a Swede, one a Pole, one a German, and one an Englishman. All spoke the strange tongue of the Kaji—a mixture of many tongues. Tarzan could understand them, but he had difficulty in making them understand him unless he spoke in the native tongue of the one he chanced to be talking to or spoke in French, which he had learned from d'Arnot before he acquired a knowledge of English. The Swede alone understood no French, but he spoke broken English, a language the German understood but not the Pole. Thus a general conversation was rendered difficult. He found it easier to talk to the Englishman, whose French was sketchy, in their common language.

He heard this man addressed as Troll, and recalled that Stanley Wood had told him that this was the name of one of their white hunters. The man was short and stalky, with heavy, stooped shoulders and long arms that gave him a gorillaesque appearance. He was powerfully muscled. Tarzan moved closer to him.

"You were with Wood and van Eyk?" he asked.

The man looked up at Tarzan in surprise. "You know them?" he asked.

"I know Wood. They recaptured him?"

Troll nodded. "You can't get away from this damned place. Mafka always drags you back, if he doesn't kill you. Wood nearly got away. A fellow—" He paused. "Say, are you Clayton?"

"Yes."

"Wood told me about you. I ought to have known you right away from his description of you."

"Is he still alive?"

"Yes. Mafka hasn't killed him yet, but he's mighty sore. No one ever came so near escaping before. I guess it made the old duffer shake in his pants—only he don't wear pants. A big expedition of whites could make it hot for him—say a battalion of Tommies. Godamighty! How I'd like to see 'em come marchin' in."

"How about the Gonfal?" inquired Tarzan. "Couldn't he stop them, just as he does others, with the power of the great diamond?"

"No one knows, but we think not. Because if he could, why is he so scared of one of us escaping?"

"Do you think Mafka intends to kill Wood?"

"We're pretty sure of it. He's not only sore about his almost getting away, but he's sorer still because Wood has a crush on Gonfala, the Queen; and it looks like Gonfala was sort of soft on Wood. That'd be too bad, too; because she's a Negress."

"Wood told me she was white."

"She's whiter than you, but look at these dames here. Ain't they white? They look white, but they all got Negro blood in 'em. But don't never remind 'em of it. You remember Kipling's, 'She knifed me one night 'cause I wished she was white'? Well that's it; that's the answer. They want to be white. God only knows why; nobody ever sees 'em but us; and we don't care what color they are. They could be green as far as I'm concerned. I'm married to six of 'em. They make me do all the work while they sit around an' gabble about hair and loincloths. Godamighty! I hate the sight of hair an' loincloths. When they ain't doin' that they're knockin' hell out o' some dame that ain't there.

"I got an old woman back in England. I thought she was bad. I run away from her, an' look what I go into! Six of 'em."

Troll kept up a running fire of conversation all the way to the city. He had more troubles than the exchange desk in a department store.

The city of Kaji was walled with blocks of limestone quarried from the cliff against which it was built. The buildings within the enclosure were of limestone also. They were of one and two stories, except the palace of Mafka, which rose against the cliff to a height of four stories.

The palace and the city gave evidence of having been long in the building, some parts of the palace and some of the buildings below it being far more weather-worn than others. There were black men and white and warrior women in the streets. A few children, all girls, played in the sunshine; milch goats were everywhere under foot. These things and many others the ape-man observed as he was conducted along the main street toward the palace of Mafka.

He heard the women discussing him and appraising him as farmers might discuss a prize bull. One of them remarked that he should bring a good price. But he moved on, apparently totally oblivious of them all.

The interior of the palace reminded him of that of Woora, except that there was more and richer stuff here. Mafka was nearer the source of supply. Here was the loot of many safaris. Tarzan wondered how Woora had obtained anything.

The four men had been dismissed within the city; only the eight women accompanied Tarzan into the palace. They had been halted at the heavily guarded entrance and had waited there while word was carried into the interior; then with a number of the guard as escort, they had been led into the palace.

Down a long corridor to another guarded doorway they proceeded; then they were ushered into a large chamber. At the far end, a figure crouched upon a throne. At sight of him, Tarzan was almost surprised into a show of emotion— it was Woora!

Beside him, on another throne-chair, sat a beautiful girl. Tarzan assumed that this must be Gonfala, the Queen. But Woora! He had seen the man killed before his own eyes. Did magic go as far as this, that it could resurrect the dead?

As he was led forward and halted before the thrones he waited for Woora to recognize him, to show the resentment he must feel because he had been thwarted and the great emerald stolen from him; but the man gave no indication that he ever had seen Tarzan before.

He listened to the report of the leader of the party that had captured the ape-man, but all the time his eyes were upon the prisoner. They seemed to be boring through him, yet there was no sign of recognition. When the report had been completed, the magician shook his head impatiently. He appeared baffled and troubled.

"Who are you?" he demanded.

"I am an Englishman. I was hunting."

"For what?"

"Food."

While the magician questioned Tarzan he kept a hand upon an immense diamond that rested on a stand beside him. It was the Gonfal, the great diamond of the Kaji, that endowed its possessor with the same mysterious powers that were inherent in the great emerald of the Zuli.

The girl upon the second throne-chair sat silent and sullen, her eyes always on the ape-man. She wore breastplates of virgin gold and a stomacher covered with gold sequins. Her skirt was of the skins of unborn leopards, soft and clinging. Dainty sandals shod her, and upon her upper arms and her

wrists and her ankles were many bands of copper and gold.
A light crown rested upon her blond head. She was the
symbol of power; but Tarzan knew that the real power lay
in the grotesque and hideous figure at her side, clothed only
in an old and dirty loincloth.

Finally the man motioned impatiently. "Take him away,"
he commanded.

"Am I not to choose wives for him?" demanded Gonfala.
"The women would pay well for this one."

"Not yet," replied her companion. "There are reasons
why I should observe him for a while. It will probably be
better to destroy him than give him to the women. Take
him away!"

The guard took the ape-man to an upper floor and put
him in a large chamber. There they left him alone, bolting
the door behind them as they departed. The apartment was
absolutely bare except for two benches. Several small windows in the wall overlooking the city gave light and ventila-
tion. In the opposite wall was an enormous fireplace in
which, apparently, no fire had ever been built.

Tarzan investigated his prison. He found the windows too
high above the ground to offer an avenue of escape without
the aid of a rope, and he had no rope. The fireplace was
the only other feature of the apartment that might arouse any
interest whatsoever. It was unusually large, so deep that it
resembled a cave; and when he stepped into it he did not
have to stoop. He wondered why such an enormous fireplace
should be built and then never used.

Entering it, he looked up the flue, thinking that here he
might find a way out if the flue were built in size propor-
tionate to the fire chamber. However, he was doomed to
disappointment; not the faintest glimmer of light shone down
to indicate an opening that led to the outside.

Could it be possible that the fireplace had been built
merely as an architectural adornment to the chamber—that
it was false? This seemed highly improbable, since the room
had no other embellishment; nor was the fireplace itself of
any architectural beauty, being nothing more than an opening
in the wall.

What then could its purpose have been? The question intrigued the active imagination of the Lord of the Jungle.
It was, of course, possible that there was a flue but that it
had been closed; and this would have been the obvious explanation had the fireplace shown any indication of ever

having been used. However, it did not; there was not the slightest discoloration of the interior—no fire had ever burned within it.

Tarzan reached upward as far as he could but felt no ceiling; then he ran his fingers up the rear wall of the fire chamber. Just at his finger tips he felt a ledge. Raising himself on his toes, he gripped the ledge firmly with the fingers of both hands; then he raised himself slowly upward. Even when his arms were straight and he had raised himself as far as he could his head touched no ceiling. He inclined his body slowly forward until at length he lay prone upon the ledge. The recess, then, was at least several feet deep.

He drew his legs up and then rose slowly to his feet. He raised a hand above his head, and a foot above he felt the stone of a ceiling—there was plenty of headroom. Laterally, the opening was about three feet wide.

He reached ahead to discover its depth, but his hand touched nothing; then he moved forward slowly a few steps —still nothing. Moving cautiously, he groped his way forward. Soon he was convinced of what he had suspected— he was in a corridor, and the secret of the "fireplace" was partially revealed. But where did the corridor lead?

It was very dark. He might be on the verge of a pitfall without suspecting it. If there were branching corridors he might become hopelessly lost in a minute or two; so he kept his left hand constantly in contact with the wall on that side; he moved slowly, feeling forward with each foot before he threw his weight upon it, and his right hand was always extended before him.

Thus he moved along for a considerable distance, the corridor turning gradually to the left until he was moving at right angles to his original course. Presently he saw a faint light ahead, coming apparently from the floor of the corridor. When he approached it more closely, he saw that it came from an opening in the floor. He stopped at the brink of the opening and looked down. Some seven feet below he saw stone flagging—it was the floor of a fireplace. Evidently this secret passage led from one false fireplace to another.

He listened intently but could hear nothing other than what might have been very soft breathing—almost too faint a sound to register even upon the keen ears of the ape-man; but his nostrils caught the faint aroma of a woman.

For a moment Tarzan hesitated; then he dropped softly

to the floor of the fireplace. He made no sound. Before him lay a chamber of barbarous luxury. At a window in the opposite wall, looking down upon the city, stood a golden-haired girl, her back toward the fireplace.

Tarzan did not have to see her face to know that it was Gonfala.

9

The End of the Corridor

NOISELESSLY HE STEPPED into the chamber and moved toward the end of the room, nearer to the doorway. He sought to reach the door before she discovered him. He would rather that she did not know how he gained entrance to the room. A heavy wooden bolt fastened the door from the inside. He reached the door without attracting the girl's attention and laid a hand upon the bolt.

He slipped it back quietly; then he moved away from the door toward the window where the girl still stood absorbed in her daydream. He could see her profile. She no longer looked sullen but, rather, ineffably sad.

The man was quite close to her before she became aware of his presence. She had not heard him. She was just conscious, suddenly, that she was not alone; and she turned slowly from the window. Only a slight widening of the eyes and a little intake of her breath revealed her surprise. She did not scream; she did not exclaim.

"Don't be afraid," he said; "I'm not here to harm you."

"I am not afraid," she replied; "I have many warriors within call. But how did you get here?" She glanced at the door and saw that the bolt was not shot. "I must have forgotten to bolt the door, but I can't understand how you got by the guard. It is still there, isn't it?"

Tarzan did not answer. He stood looking at her, marvelling at the subtle change that had taken place in her since he had seen her in the throne room just a short time before. She was no longer the queen, but a girl, soft and sweet, appealing.

"Where is Stanley Wood?" he asked.

"What do you know of Stanley Wood?" she demanded.

"I am his friend. Where is he? What are they going to do with him?"

"You are his friend?" she asked, wonderingly, her eyes wide. "But no, it can make no difference—no matter how many friends he has, nothing can save him."

"You would like to see him saved?"

"Yes."

"Then why don't you help me? You have the power."

"No, I can't. You don't understand. I am queen. It is I who must sentence him to death."

"You helped him escape once," Tarzan reminded her.

"Hush! Not so loud," she cautioned. "Mafka suspects that already. If he knew, I don't know what he would do to him and to me. But I know he suspects. That is the reason I am kept in this room with a heavy guard. He says it is for my protection, but I know better."

"Where is this Makfa? I'd like to see him."

"You have seen him. You were just brought before him in the throne room."

"That was Woora," objected Tarzan.

She shook her head. "No. What put that idea in your head? Woora is with the Zuli."

"So that was Mafka!" said the ape-man, and then he recalled Lord's theory that Mafka and Woora were identical twins. "But I thought no one was allowed to see Mafka."

"Stanley Wood told you that," she said. "That is what he thought; that is what he was told. Mafka was very ill for a long time. He dared not let it be known. He was afraid some one would take advantage of it to kill him. But he wanted to see you. He wished to see a man who could get into our country and so close to the city as you did without his knowing it. I do not understand it myself, and I could see that he was disturbed when he talked with you. Who are you? What are you? How did you get into my apartment? Have you such powers as Mafka has?"

"Perhaps," he said. It would do no harm if she thought he possessed such powers. He spoke in a low tone now and watched her closely. "You'd like to see Stanley Wood escape; you'd like to go with him. Why don't you help me?"

She looked at him eagerly. He could read the longing in her eyes. "How can I help you?" she asked.

"Help me to see Mafka—alone. Tell me where I can find him."

She trembled, and the fear that was in her was reflected in her expression.

"Yes," she said, "I can tell you. If you—" She paused. Her expression changed; her body stiffened. Her eyes became hard and cold—cruel. Her mouth sagged into the sullen expression it had worn when he had first seen her in the throne room. He recalled Wood's statement that she was sometimes an angel, sometimes a she-devil. The metamorphosis had occurred before his eyes. But what caused it? It was possible, of course, that she suffered from some form of insanity; yet he doubted it. He believed there was some other explanation.

"Well?" he queried. "You were saying——"

"The guard! The guard!" she cried. "Help!"

Tarzan sprang to the door and shot the bolt. Gonfala whipped a dagger from her girdle and leaped toward him. Before she could strike, the ape-man seized her wrist and wrenched the weapon from her.

The guard were pounding upon the door and shouting for admittance. The ape-man seized Gonfala by the arm; he held her dagger ready to strike. "Tell them you are all right," he whispered. "Tell them to go away."

She snarled and tried to bite his hand. Then she screamed louder than ever for help.

On the opposite side of the room from the door where the guard sought entrance was a second door, bolted upon the inside like the other. Toward this the ape-man dragged the screaming Gonfala. Slipping the bolt, he pushed the door open. Beyond it was another chamber upon the opposite side of which he saw a third door. Here was a series of chambers that it might be well to remember.

He pushed Gonfala into the first chamber and closed and bolted the door. The warriors of the guard were battering now in earnest. It was evident that they would soon have the door down and gain entrance to the apartment.

Tarzan crossed to the fireplace and leaped to the mouth of the secret passage just as the door crashed in and the warriors of the guard entered the room. He waited where he was—listening. He could hear Gonfala screaming in the adjoining room and pounding on the door, which was now quickly opened.

"Where is he?" she demanded. "Have you got him?"

"Who? There is no one here," replied a member of the guard.

"The man—the prisoner that was brought today."

"There was no one here," insisted a warrior.

"Go at once and notify Mafka that he has escaped," she commanded. "Some of you go to the room in which he was imprisoned and find out how he got out. Hurry! Don't stand there like idiots. Don't you suppose I know what I saw? I tell you he was here. He took my dagger from me and shoved me into that room. Now go! But some of you stay here. He may come back."

Tarzan waited to hear no more, but retraced his steps through the passage to the room in which he had been imprisoned. He left Gonfala's dagger on the high ledge inside the fireplace, and had barely seated himself on one of the benches in the room when he heard footsteps in the corridor outside; then the door was swung open and half a dozen warrior women pushed their way in.

They showed their surprise when they saw him sitting quietly in his cell.

"Where have you been?" demanded one.

"Where could I go?" countered the ape-man.

"You were in the apartment of Gonfala, the Queen."

"But how could I have been?" demanded Tarzan.

"That is what we want to know."

Tarzan shrugged. "Some one is crazy," he said, "but it is not I. If you think I was there why don't you go ask the queen."

The warriors shook their heads. "What is the use?" demanded one. "He is here; that is all we have to know. Let Mafka solve the riddle." Then they left the room.

An hour passed during which Tarzan heard nothing; then the door was opened and a warrior woman ordered him to come out. Escorted by a dozen warriors, he was taken through a long corridor to an apartment on the same floor of the palace. His sense of direction told him that the room was one of the suite which adjoined the Queen's.

Mafka was there. He stood behind a table on which rested something covered with a cloth. Also on the table was the great diamond of Kaji, the Gonfal. Mafka's left hand rested upon it.

The ape-man's keen nostrils scented blood, and his eyes saw that the cloth that covered the object on the table was stained with blood. Whose blood? Something told him that whatever was beneath the blood-stained cloth he had been brought to see.

He stood before the magician, his arms folded across his deep chest, his level, unwavering gaze fixed upon the grotesque figure facing him. For minutes the two stood there in silence, waging a strange battle of minds. Mafka was attempting to plumb that of his prisoner; and Tarzan knew it, but his defense was passive. He was sure that the other could not control him.

Mafka was annoyed. To be frustrated was a new experience. The mind of the man before him was a sealed book. He felt a little bit afraid of him, but curiosity compelled him to see him. It kept him from ordering his destruction. He wished to fathom him; he wished to break the seal. Inside that book was something strange and new. Mafka was determined to learn what it was.

"How did you get to the apartment of the queen?" he demanded suddenly.

"If I were in the apartment of the queen, who should know it better than Mafka?" demanded Tarzan. "If I were there, who should know better than Mafka how I got there?"

The magician appeared discomfitted. He shook his head angrily. "How did you get there?" he demanded.

"How do you know I was there?" countered the ape-man.

"Gonfala saw you."

"Was she sure that it was I in person, or only a figment of her imagination? Would it not have been possible for the great Mafka to make her think that I was there when I was not?"

"But I didn't," growled the magician.

"Perhaps some one else did," suggested Tarzan. He was positive now that Mafka was ignorant of the existence of the secret passage through which he had gained entrance to the apartment of Gonfala. Possibly this part of the palace belonged to a period that antedated Mafka, but why had no one investigated the fireplaces that were obviously not intended to hold fires? There was one in this very room where Mafka was and doubtless had been many times before. Tarzan wondered if it, too, opened into a corridor and where the corridor led; but he had little time for conjecture, as Mafka shot another question at him.

"Who has that power but Mafka?" demanded the magician superciliously, but there was a suggestion of incertitude in his manner. It was more a challenge to uncertainty than a declaration of fact.

Tarzan did not reply; and Mafka seemed to have forgotten that he had put a question, as he continued to study the ape-man intently. The latter, indifferent, swept the interior of the room with a leisurely glance that missed nothing. Through open doors leading to other apartments he saw a bedchamber and a workshop. The latter was similar to that which he had seen in the palace of Woora. It was obvious that this was the private suite of Mafka.

Suddenly the magician shot another question. "How did you get to Zuli without my sentries seeing you?"

"Who said I had been in Zuli?" demanded Tarzan.

"You killed my brother. You stole the great emerald of the Zuli. You were coming here to kill me. You ask who said you had been in Zuli. The same man who told me these other things. This man!" And he snatched the cloth from the thing upon the table.

Glaring at the ape-man with staring eyes was the bloody head of the Englishman, Lord; and beside it was the great emerald of the Zuli.

Mafka watched his prisoner intently to note the reaction to this startling and dramatic climax to the interview, but he reaped scant satisfaction. The expression on Tarzan's face underwent no change.

For a moment there was silence; then Mafka spoke. "Thus die the enemies of Mafka," he said. "Thus will you die and the others who have brought intrigue and discontent to Kaji." He turned to the captain of the guard. "Take him away. Place him again in the south chamber with the other troublemakers who are to die with him. It was an evil day that brought them to Kaji."

Heavily guarded, Tarzan was returned to the room in which he had been confined. From Mafka's instructions to the captain of the guard, he had expected to find other prisoners here on his return; but he was alone. He wondered idly who his future companions were to be, and then he crossed to one of the windows and looked out across the city and the broad valley of the Kaji.

He stood there for a long time trying to formulate some plan by which he might contact Wood and discuss means by which the escape of the American could be assured. He had a plan of his own, but he needed the greater knowledge that Wood possessed of certain matters connected with Mafka and the Kaji before he could feel reasonably certain of its success.

As he stood there pondering the advisability of returning to Gonfala's apartment and seeking again the cooperation that he knew she had been on the point of according him when the sudden Jekyll and Hyde transformation had wrought the amazing change in her, he heard footsteps outside the door of his prison; then the bolt was drawn and the door swung open, and four men were pushed roughly in. Behind them, the door was slammed and bolted.

One of the four men was Stanley Wood. At sight of Tarzan he voiced an exclamation of astonishment. "Clayton!" he cried. "Where did you come from? What in the world are you doing here?"

"The same thing that you are—waiting to be killed."

"How did he get you? I thought you were immune—that he couldn't control you."

Tarzan explained about the misadventure of the leopard pit; then Wood introduced the other three to him. They were Robert van Eyk, Wood's associate, and Troll and Spike, the two white hunters who had accompanied their safari. Troll he had already met.

"I ain't had a chance to tell Wood about seeing you," explained Troll. "This is the first time I've seen him. He was in the cooler, and I was just arrested. I don't even know what for, or what they're goin' to do to me."

"I can tell you what they plan on doing to you," said Tarzan. "We're all to be killed. Mafka just told me. He says you are all troublemakers."

"He wouldn't have to be a psychoanalyst to figure that out," remarked van Eyk. "If we'd had half a break we'd 've shown him something in the trouble line, but what you going to do up against a bird like that? He knows what you're thinking before you think it."

"We wouldn't have been in this mess if it hadn't been for Wood messin' around with that Gonfala dame," growled Spike. "I never knew it to fail that you didn't get into trouble with any bunch of heathen if you started mixin' up with their women folk—especially niggers. But a guy's got it comin' to him that plays around with a nigger wench."

"Shut that dirty trap of yours," snapped Wood, "or I'll shut it for you." He took a quick step toward Spike and swung a vicious right for the other man's jaw. Spike stepped back and van Eyk jumped between them.

"Cut it!" he ordered. "We got enough grief without fighting among ourselves."

"You're dead right," agreed Troll. "We'll punch the head of the next guy that starts anything like that again."

"That's all right, too," said Wood; "but Spike's got to apologize or I'll kill him for that the first chance I get. He's got to take it back."

"You'd better apologize, Spike," advised van Eyk.

The hunter looked sullenly from beneath lowering brows. Troll went over and whispered to him. "All right," said Spike, finally; "I take it back. I didn't mean nothin'."

Wood nodded. "Very well," he said, "I accept your apology," and turned and joined Tarzan, who had been standing by a window a silent spectator of what had transpired.

He stood for a time in silence; then he shook his head dejectedly. "The trouble is," he said in low tones, "I know Spike is right. She must have Negro blood in her—they all have; but it doesn't seem to make any difference to me—I'm just plain crazy about her, and that's all there is to it. If you could only see her, you'd understand."

"I have seen her," said the ape-man.

"What!" exclaimed Wood. "You've seen her? When?"

"Shortly after I was brought here," said Tarzan.

"You mean she came here to see you?"

"She was on the throne with Mafka when I was taken before him," explained Tarzan.

"Oh, yes; I see. I thought maybe you'd talked with her."

"I did—afterward, in her apartment. I found a way to get there."

"What did she say? How was she? I haven't seen her since I got back. I was afraid something had happened to her."

"Mafka suspects her of helping you to escape. He keeps her locked up under guard."

"Did she say anything about me?" demanded Wood, eagerly.

"Yes; she wants to help you. At first she was eager and friendly; then, quite abruptly and seemingly with no reason, she became sullen and dangerous, screaming for her guard."

"Yes, she was like that—sweet and lovely one moment; and the next, a regular she-devil. I never could understand it. Do you suppose she's—well, not quite right mentally?"

The ape-man shook his head. "No," he said, "I don't think that. I believe there is another explanation. But that is neither here nor there now. There is just one matter that should concern us—getting out of here. We don't know when Mafka plans on putting us out of the way nor how. Whatever we are going to do we should do immediately—take him by surprise."

"How are we going to surprise him—locked up here in a room, under guard?" demanded Wood.

"You'd be surprised," replied Tarzan, smiling faintly; "so will Mafka. Tell me, can we count on any help beyond what we can do ourselves—the five of us? How about the other prisoners? Will they join with us?"

"Yes, practically all of them—if they can. But what can any of us do against Mafka? We're beaten before we start. If we could only get hold of the Gonfal! I think that's the source of all his power over us."

"We might do that, too," said Wood.

"Impossible," said Wood. "What do you think, Bob?" he asked van Eyk, who had just joined them.

"Not a chance in a million," replied van Eyk. "He keeps the old rock in his own apartment at night, or in fact wherever he is the Gonfal is with him. His apartment is always locked and guarded—warriors at the door all the time. No, we never could get it."

Tarzan turned to Wood. "I thought you told me once that they seemed very careless of the Gonfal—that you had handled it."

Wood grinned. "I thought I had, but since I came back I learned differently. One of the women told me. It seems that Mafka is something of a chemist. He has a regular lab and plays around in it a lot—ordinary chemistry as well as his main line of black magic. Well, he learned how to make phony diamonds; so he makes an imitation of the Gonfal, and that's what I handled. They say he leaves the phony out where it can be seen and hides the real Gonfal at night when he goes to bed; so that if, by any chance, some one was able to get into his room to steal it they'd get the wrong stone. But he has to keep the Gonfal near him just the same, or he'd be more or less helpless against an enemy."

"The only chance to get it would be to get into Mafka's apartment at night," said van Eyk, "and that just can't be done."

"Do his apartments connect with Gonfala's?" asked Tarzan.

"Yes, but the old boy keeps the door between them locked

at night. He isn't taking any chances—not even with Gonfala."

"I think we can get into Mafka's apartment," said the apeman. "I'm going now to find out."

"Going!" exclaimed Wood. "I'd like to know how."

"Don't let anyone follow me," cautioned the ape-man. "I'll be back."

The two Americans shook their heads skeptically as Tarzan turned away and crossed the room; then they saw him enter the fireplace and disappear.

"Well I'll be damned!" exclaimed van Eyk. "Who is that guy, anyway?"

"An Englishman named Clayton," replied Wood. "At least that's all I know about him, and that came direct from him."

"If there were such a bird as Tarzan of the Apes, I'd say this was he," said van Eyk.

"That's what I thought when I first met him. Say, he flits through the trees like a regular Tarzan, kills his meat with a bow and arrow, and packs it back to camp on his shoulder through the trees."

"And now look what he's done! Up the flue like a—a—well, like something, whatever it is goes up a flue."

"Smoke," suggested Wood; "only he's coming back, and smoke doesn't—except occasionally."

Tarzan followed the corridor as he had before until he came to the opening into Gonfala's chamber; then he retraced his steps a short distance and felt his way back again with his right hand touching the side of the passageway instead of his left as before; nor was he surprised to discover that the tunnel ran on past the apartment of Gonfala. It was what he had expected—what he had been banking his hopes upon.

Now, past the opening that led to Gonfala's room, he touched the left-hand wall again and, pacing off the distance roughly, came to another opening that he judged would be about opposite the center of the next apartment, which was one of Mafka's suite. He did not stop here, but went on until he had located three more openings. Here the corridor ended.

He stepped to the edge of the flue and looked down into the fireplace. It was night now, but a faint illumination came from the opening below him. It was a greenish glow, now all too familiar.

He listened. He heard the snores of a heavy sleeper. Was

there another in the apartment below, or was the sleeper alone? His sensitive nostrils sought an answer.

With the dagger of Gonfala in one hand, Tarzan dropped lightly to the floor of the fireplace that opened into the room where the sleeper lay.

10

Toward Freedom

BEFORE HIM WAS a large chamber with a single door, heavily bolted upon the inside. He who slept there quite evidently slept in fear. It was Mafka. He lay upon a narrow cot. Upon a table at one side rested the Gonfal and the great emerald of the Zuli and beside them a cutlass and a dagger. Similar weapons lay on a table at the other side of the cot. All were within easy reach of the sleeper. A single cresset burned upon one of the tables.

Tarzan crossed noiselessly to the side of the cot and removed the weapons; first upon one side; then the other. Next, he carried the great emerald and the Gonfal to the fireplace and put them upon the ledge at the mouth of the corridor; then he returned to the side of the cot. Mafka slept on, for the ape-man moved as silently as a ghost in the night.

He laid a hand upon the shoulder of the magician and shook him lightly. Mafka awoke with a start.

"Keep still and you will not be harmed." Tarzan's voice was low, but it was the voice of authority that knew its power.

Mafka looked wildly about the apartment as though searching for help, but there was none.

"What do you want?" His voice trembled. "Tell me what you want and it is yours, if you will not kill me."

"I do not kill old men or women or children unless they force me to. As long as my life is safe, yours is."

"Then why have you come here? What do you want?"

"Nothing that you can give me. What I want, I take."

He turned Mafka over on his stomach and bound his wrists, his ankles, and his knees with strips torn from the bedding;

then he gagged him so that he could not raise an alarm. He also blindfolded him that he might not see how entrance had been gained to his apartment.

These things done, he returned to the corridor and groped his way back to Gonfala's apartment, leaving the two great gems where he had first placed them. He was confident they would never be found by another than himself, so sure was he that these corridors were entirely unknown to the present occupants of the palace.

At the entrance to Gonfala's apartment he listened again, but his senses detected no presence in the room below. As he entered it, a quick glance assured him that it was vacant. A single small cresset lighted it dimly. A door at the far end of the room was ajar. He went to it and pushed it open.

As he did so, Gonfala sat up in her couch near the center of the room and faced him. "You have come back! I hoped you would. You have chosen a good time."

"I thought so—he sleeps."

"Then you know?"

"I guessed."

"But why have you come back?"

"Wood and his three friends are prisoners. They are all to be killed."

"Yes, I know. It is by my orders." A qualm of pain and self-disgust was registered in her expression.

"You can help them to escape. Will you?"

"It would do no good. He would only drag them back, and their punishment would be even worse than they can expect now. It is hopeless."

"If Mafka did not interfere would the women obey you?"

"Yes."

"And if you had the opportunity you would like to escape from Kaji?"

"Yes."

"Where would you go?"

"To England."

"Why to England?"

"One who was always good to me, but who is dead now, told me to go to England if ever I escaped. He gave me a letter to take with me."

"Well, get your letter and get ready. You are going to escape. We will be back for you in a little while—Wood and his friends and I. But you will have to help. You will have to give the necessary orders to the women to let us all pass."

She shook her head emphatically. "It will do no good, I tell you. He will get us all."

"Don't worry about that. Just give me your promise that you will do as I ask."

"I'll promise, but it will mean death for me as well as for you."

"Get ready, then; I'll be back with the others in a few minutes."

He left her room, closing the door after him, and went at once to the corridor. A moment later he dropped into the room where Wood and his companions were imprisoned. It was very dark. He spoke to them in low tones, directing them to follow him. Soon they were all in the corridor.

Tarzan led the way to Mafka's room, the glow from the great gems lighting their way as they approached the end of the corridor.

Spike drew in his breath in astonishment. "Cripes! The big rock!" he exclaimed.

Troll halted before the radiant stones and gazed at them in fascinated silence for a moment. "This other—it must be the great emerald of the Zuli. Both of 'em! Lord! They must be worth millions." He started to touch them, but drew back in terror. He knew the power that lay in them, and feared it.

Tarzan dropped over the ledge into the fireplace then, and the others followed him. As they gathered around Mafka's couch, Wood and his companions were speechless with astonishment when they saw the old magician lying bound and helpless.

"How did you do it?" exclaimed Wood.

"I took the gems away from him first. I think all his power lies in them. If I am right, we can get away from here. If I'm wrong—" The ape-man shrugged.

Van Eyk nodded. "I think you're right. What are we going to do with this old devil?"

Troll seized one of the cutlasses that lay beside the cot. "I'll show you what we're going to do with him!"

Tarzan grasped the man's wrist. "Not so fast. You are taking orders from me."

"Who said so?"

Tarzan wrenched the weapon from Troll's hand and slapped the man across the side of the face with an open palm. The blow sent him reeling across the room to fall in a heap against the wall.

Troll staggered to his feet, feeling his jaw. "I'll get you for this." His voice trembled with rage.

"Shut up and do as you're told." The ape-man's voice showed no emotion. It was, however, a voice that commanded obedience. Then he turned to Wood. "You and van Eyk get the gems. Troll and Spike will carry Mafka."

"Where are we going?" Van Eyk put the question apprehensively. He knew that there was a guard of warrior-women in the corridor outside Mafka's suite.

"We are going first to Gonfala's apartments. They adjoin Mafka's."

"She'll give the alarm, and we'll have the whole bloomin' bunch of 'em on us," objected Spike.

"Don't worry about Gonfala; just do as I say. However, you may as well take these weapons. Something might happen, of course."

Wood and van Eyk got the great emerald and the Gonfal from the ledge in the fireplace; then Troll and Spike picked up Mafka, who was trembling in terror; and all followed Tarzan to the door of the apartment. They passed through the adjoining room and the next, coming then to the door leading into Gonfala's suite. Like the other doors, it was barred on the inside. Slipping the bars, the ape-man pushed the door open.

Gonfala was standing in the center of the room as the party entered. She was clothed as for a journey, with a long robe of leopard skins and heavy sandals. A narrow fillet of beaded doeskin bound her golden hair. At sight of Mafka, bound, gagged, and blindfolded, she gasped and shrank away. Then she saw Wood and ran to him.

He put an arm about her. "Don't be afraid, Gonfala. We're going to take you away. That is, if you want to come with us."

"Yes; anywhere—with you. But him! What are you going to do with him?" She pointed at Mafka. "He'll drag us all back, no matter where we go, and kill us; or he'll kill us there. He kills them all, who escape."

Spike spat venomously. "We'd ought to kill him now."

Van Eyk looked at Tarzan. "I agree with Spike. Why shouldn't we, when it's his life or ours?"

The ape-man shook his head. "We don't know the temper of the Kaji women. This man must be something of a deity to them. He represents their power—he *is* their power. Without him, they would be just a tribe of women upon which any other tribe could prey. He means most to us alive, as a hostage."

Wood nodded. "I think Clayton's right."

The discussion was interrupted by a commotion in the outer corridor upon which the apartments of Mafka and Gonfala opened. There was pounding upon the door of Mafka's apartment and loud cries for the magician.

Tarzan turned to Gonfala. "Call some warrior in authority and see what they want. We'll wait in the next room. Come!" He motioned the others to follow him, and led the way into the adjoining apartment.

Gonfala crossed the room and struck a drum that stood upon the floor near the doorway leading into the corridor. Three times she struck it; then she drew the bolt that secured the door upon the inside. A moment later the door was swung open, and a warrior-woman entered the apartment. She bent to one knee before the queen.

"What is the meaning of the noise in the corridor? Why are they calling Mafka at this hour of the morning?"

"The Zuli are coming, Gonfala. They are coming to make war upon us. They sent a slave to demand the return of their great emerald. There are many of them. We invoke the power of Mafka to make the Zuli weak so that we can kill many of them and drive them away."

"They have no power. Woora is dead, and we have the great emerald. Tell the warriors that I, Gonfala the Queen, command them to go out and slay the Zuli."

"The Zuli are already at the gates of the city. Our warriors are afraid, for they have no power from Mafka. Where is Mafka? Why does he not answer the prayers of the Kaji?"

Gonfala stamped her foot. "Do as I command. You are not here to ask questions. Go to the gate and defend the city. I, Gonfala, will give my warriors power to defeat the Zuli."

"Let us see Mafka," insisted the woman sullenly.

Gonfala reached a quick decision. "Very well. See that my orders for the defense of the city are obeyed; then come to the throne room, and you shall see Mafka. Bring the captains with you."

The woman withdrew, and the door was closed. Immediately, Tarzan stepped into the room. "I overheard. What is your plan?"

"Merely to gain time."

"Then you didn't intend to have Mafka in the throne room to meet them?"

"No. That would be fatal. If we took him in bound, gagged, and blindfolded they might kill us all. If we gave him his freedom, he would kill us."

"Nevertheless, I think it a good plan. We'll do it." A grim smile touched the lips of the ape-man.

"You are mad."

"Perhaps; but if we try to leave now, we can't get out of Kaji without a fight; and I do not relish fighting women. I think there is another way. Do you know where the imitation Gonfal is kept?"

"Yes."

"Get it, and bring it here at once. Wrap a skin around it so that no one can see it. Tell no one. Only you and I must know."

"What are you going to do?"

"Wait and see. Do as I tell you."

"You forget that I am queen." She drew herself up proudly.

"I know only that you are a woman who would like to escape from Kaji with the man she loves."

Gonfala flushed, but she made no reply. Instead, she quit the room at once, going into the apartments of Mafka.

She was gone but a few moments. When she returned she carried a bundle wrapped in a skin.

Tarzan took it from her. "We are ready now. Lead the way to the throne room." He summoned the others from the adjoining apartment; then he turned again to the queen. "Is there a private way to the throne room?"

Gonfala nodded. "This way. Follow me."

She led them into Mafka's apartments where she opened a small door revealing a flight of steps, and they followed her down these to another door that opened upon the dais where the throne chairs stood.

The throne room was empty. The captains had not yet arrived. At Tarzan's direction, Wood placed the Gonfal on the stand beside the throne; Troll and Spike seated Mafka, still bound, gagged, and blindfolded, in his chair; Gonfala seated herself in the other. Tarzan stood beside the table bearing the Gonfal. The others stood behind the chairs. Van Eyk concealed the great emerald of the Zuli beneath a skin he took from the floor of the dais.

In silence they waited. All but Tarzan were tense with nervousness. Presently they heard approaching footfalls in the corridor leading to the throne room. The doors were swung open, and the captains of the Kaji filed in.

They came with heads bent in reverence for their queen and the great power of their magician. When they looked up they were close to the dais. At sight of Mafka they gave vent to cries of astonishment and anger. They looked at the strangers on the dais; then their eyes centered upon the queen.

One of them stepped forward. "What is the meaning of this, Gonfala?" Her tones were menacing.

It was Tarzan who answered. "It means that the power of Mafka is gone. All your lives he has held you in the hollow of his hand. He has made you fight for him. He has taken the best fruits of your conquests. He has held you prisoners here. You feared and hated him, but most of all you feared him."

"He has given us power," answered the warrior. "If that power is gone, we are lost."

"It is not gone, but Mafka no longer wields it."

"Kill them!" cried one of the captains.

The cry arose from many throats. "Kill them! Kill them!" With savage yells they pushed forward toward the dais.

Tarzan laid a hand upon the Gonfal. "Stop! Kneel before your queen!" His voice was low. In the din of their shouting it probably reached the ears of few if any of the warriors, but as one they stopped and knelt.

Again the ape-man spoke. "Stand up! Go to the gates and bring in the captains of the Zuli. They will come. The fighting will stop." The warriors turned and filed out of the chamber.

Tarzan turned toward his companions. "It worked. I thought it would. Whatever this strange power is, it is inherent in the Gonfal. The great emerald has the same mystic power. In the hands of vicious men it is bad. Perhaps, though, it may be used for good."

Gonfala was listening intently. The sounds of the battle ceased; then came echoing footfalls in the long corridor leading to the palace entrance. "They come!" she whispered.

Fifty warrior women entered the throne room of the queen of the Kaji. Half of them were Kaji and half Zuli. They were a savage company. Many of them were bleeding from wounds. They looked sullenly at one another and at the little company upon the dais.

Tarzan faced them. "You are free now from the rule of Woora and Mafka. Woora is dead. I shall turn Mafka over to you presently to do with as you wish. His power is gone if you keep the Gonfal from him. We are leaving your country. Gonfala is going with us. As many prisoners and slaves as wish to accompany us may come. When we are safely out we will hand the Gonfal back to one of your warriors, who may accompany us with three companions— no more. It is dawn. We leave at once. Here is Mafka." He lifted the old magician in his arms and handed him down to the warrior women.

Amidst deathly silence the little company of white men filed out of the throne room with Gonfala the queen of the Kaji. Tarzan carried the Gonfal so that all might see it. Van Eyk bore the great emerald of the Zuli concealed beneath a wrapping of skin.

In the main street of the city a little group of black men and white awaited them, summoned by Tarzan through the necromancy of the Gonfal. They were the slaves and prisoners of the Kaji.

"We are leaving this country," he told them; "any who wish to may accompany us."

"Mafka will kill us," objected one.

Shrill screams issued from the interior of the palace only to be drowned by savage yells of rage and hatred.

"Mafka will never kill again," said the ape-man.

11

Treachery

IN PEACE THEY marched through the country of the Kaji under the protection of Tarzan and the Gonfal. Those who had been prisoners and slaves for years were filled with nervous apprehension. They could not believe this miracle that had seemingly snatched them from the clutches of the old magician who had dominated and terrorized them

for so long. Momentarily they expected to be killed or dragged
back to certain torture and death; but nothing happened,
and they came at last to the valley of the Neubari.

"I'll leave you here," said Tarzan. "You will be going
south. I go north." He handed the Gonfal to van Eyk. "Keep
it until morning; then give it to one of these women." He
indicated the three warrior women who had accompanied
them from Kaji; then he turned to them. "Take the stone
back; and if any among you can use it, use it for good and
not for evil.

"Wood, take the great emerald of the Zuli in trust for
Gonfala. I hope it will bring her happiness, but the chances
are that it will not. At least, however, she need never want."

"Where do we come in?" demanded Spike.

The ape-man shook his head. "You don't; you go out—
you go out with your lives. That's a lot more than you
could have hoped for a few days ago."

"You mean to say you're goin' to give the big rock back
to the niggers and we don't get no split? It ain't fair. Look
what we been through. You can't do it."

"It's already done."

Spike turned toward the others. "Are you fellows goin' to
stand for this?" he shouted angrily. "Them two rocks belongs
to all of us. We ought to take 'em back to London and sell
'em and divide up equal."

"I'm glad enough to get out with my life," said van Eyk. "I
think Gonfala has a right to one of the stones; the other will
be plenty for both the Kaji and the Zuli to carry out their
plans to go out into the world. They'll be cheated out of
most of it anyway, but they'll get their wish."

"I think they ought to be divided," said Troll. "We ought
to get something out of this."

Some of the white men who had been liberated agreed
with him. Others said they only wanted to get home alive
and the sooner they saw the last of the two stones the better they'd be satisfied.

"They're evil," said one of the men. "They'll bring no good
to anyone."

"I'd take the chance," growled Spike.

Tarzan regarded him coldly. "You won't get it. I've told
you all what to do; see that you do it. I'll be travelling south
again before you get out of the country. I'll know if you've
pulled anything crooked. See that you don't."

Night had fallen. The little band of fugitives, perhaps a

hundred strong, were making camp, such as it was, and preparing the food they had brought from Kaji. The blacks, who had been slaves, fell naturally into positions of porters and personal servants to the whites. There had been some slight attempt toward organization, Wood and van Eyk acting as lieutenants to the man they knew only as Clayton, who had assumed the leadership as naturally as the others had accepted the arrangement.

He stood among them now noting the preparations for the night; then he turned to Wood. "You and van Eyk will take charge. You will have no trouble unless it be from Spike. Watch him. Three marches to the south you will find friendly villages. After that it will be easy."

That was all. He turned and was gone into the night. There were no farewells, long-drawn and useless.

"Well," said van Eyk, "that was casual enough."

Wood shrugged. "He is like that."

Gonfala strained her eyes out into the darkness. "He has gone? You think he will not come back?"

"When he finishes whatever business he is on, perhaps. By that time we may be out of the country."

"I felt so safe when he was with us." The girl came and stood close to Wood. "I feel safe with you, too, Stanlee; but him—he seemed a part of Africa."

The man nodded and put an arm about her. "We'll take care of you, dear; but I know how you feel. I felt the same way when he was around. I had no sense of responsibility at all, not even for my own welfare. I just took it for granted that he'd look after everything."

"I often wonder about him," said van Eyk musingly—"who he is, where he comes from, what he is doing in Africa. I wonder—I wonder if there could be—if——"

"If what?"

"If there could be a Tarzan."

Wood laughed. "You know, the same thought came to me. Of course, there is no such person; but this fellow, Clayton, sure would fill the bill."

The black boy who was cooking for them called them then to the evening meal. It was not much, and they decided that Spike and Troll would have to do some hunting the following day.

Suddenly Wood laughed—a bit ruefully. "What with?" he demanded. "We've got spears and knives. What could any of us kill with those?"

Van Eyk nodded. "You're right. What are we going to do? We've got to have meat. All the way to those first friendly villages we've got to depend on game. There won't be anything else."

"If we raise any game, we'll have to send out beaters and chase it toward the spears. We ought to get something that way."

Van Eyk grinned. "If we're lucky enough to raise something with *angina pectoris*, the excitement might kill it."

"Well, they do kill big game with spears," insisted Wood.

Van Eyk's face brightened. He snapped his fingers. "I've got it! Bows and arrows! Some of our blacks must be good at making them and using them. Hey, Kamudi! Come here!"

One of the black boys arose from the two calloused black heels he had been squatting upon and approached. "Yes, Bwana—you call?"

"Say, can any of you boys kill game with a bow and arrow?"

Kamudi grinned. "Yes, Bwana."

"How about making them? Can any of you make bows and arrows?"

"Yes, Bwana—all can make."

"Fine! Any of the stuff you use grow around here?" Van Eyk's tones were both eager and apprehensive.

"Down by the river—plenty."

"Gee! That's bully. When the boys have finished supper take 'em down there and get enough stuff to make bows for every one and lots of arrows. Make a few tonight. If we don't have 'em, we don't eat tomorrow. Sabe?"

"Yes, Bwana—after supper."

The night was velvet soft. A full moon shone down upon the camp, paling the embers of dying fires where the men had cooked their simple meal. The blacks were busy fashioning crude bows and arrows, roughly hewn but adequate.

The whites were gathered in little groups. A shelter had been fashioned for Gonfala; and before this she and Wood and van Eyk lay upon skins that had been brought from Kaji and talked of the future. Gonfala of the wonders that awaited her in unknown civilization, for she was going to London. The men spoke of America, of their families, and old friends, who must long ago have given them up as dead.

"With the proceeds from the great emerald of the Zuli you will be a very rich woman, Gonfala." Wood spoke a little regretfully. "You will have a beautiful home, wonderful gowns and furs, automobiles, and many servants; and there will be men—oh, lots of men."

"Why should I have men? I do not want but just one."

"But they will want you, for yourself and for your money." The thought seemed to sadden Wood.

"You will have to be very careful," said van Eyk. "Some of those chaps will be very fascinating."

The girl shrugged. "I am not afraid. Stanlee will take care of me. Won't you, Stanlee?"

"If you'll let me, but——"

" 'But' what?"

"Well, you see you have never known men such as you are going to meet. You may find someone who—" Wood hesitated.

" 'Someone who' what?" she demanded.

"Whom you'll like better than you do me."

Gonfala laughed. "I am not worrying."

"But I am."

"You needn't." The girl's eyes swam with the moisture of adulation.

"You are so young and naive and inexperienced. You haven't the slightest idea what you are going to be up against or the types of men there are in the world—especially in the civilized world."

"Are they as bad as Mafka?"

"In a different way they are worse."

Van Eyk stood up and stretched. "I'm going to get some sleep," he said. "You two'd better do the same thing. Good night."

They said good night to him and watched him go; then the girl turned to Wood. "I am not afraid," she said, "and you must not be. We shall have each other, and as far as I am concerned, no one else in the world counts."

He took her hand and stroked it. "I hope you will always feel that way, dear. It is the way I feel—it is the way I always shall."

"Nothing will ever come between us then." She turned her palm beneath his and pressed his fingers.

For a little time longer they talked and planned as lovers have from time immemorial; and then he went to lie down at a little distance, and Gonfala to her shelter; but she could not sleep. She was too happy. It seemed to her that she could not waste a moment of that happiness in sleep, lose minutes of rapture that she could not ever recall.

After a moment she got up and went into the night. The camp slept. The moon had dropped into the west, and the girl walked in the dense shadow of the ancient trees against which the camp had been made. She moved slowly and silently in the state of beatific rapture that was engendered not alone by her love but by the hitherto unknown sense of freedom that had come to her with release from the domination of Mafka.

No longer was she subject to the hated seizures of cruelty and vindictiveness that she now realized were no true characteristics of her own but states that had been imposed upon her by the hypnotic powers of the old magician.

She shuddered as she recalled him. Perhaps he was her father, but what of it? What of a father's love and tenderness had he ever given her? She tried to forgive him; she tried to think a kindly thought of him; but no, she could not. She had hated him in life; in death she still hated his memory.

With an effort she shook these depressing recollections from her and sought to center her thoughts on the happiness that was now hers and that would be through a long future.

Suddenly she became aware of voices near her. "The bloke's balmy. The nerve of him, givin' the Gonfal back to them niggers. We ort to have it an' the emerald, too. Think of it, Troll—nearly five million pounds! That's wot them two together would have brought in London or Paris."

"An he gives the emerald to that damn nigger wench. Wot'll she do with it? The American'll get it. She thinks he's soft on her, thinks he's goin' to marry her; but whoever heard of an American marryin' a nigger. You're right, Spike; it's all wrong. Why——"

The girl did not wait to hear more. She turned and fled silently through the darkness—her dream shattered, her happiness blasted.

*   *   *

Wood awakened early and called Kamudi. "Wake the boys," he directed; "we're making an early start." Then he called van Eyk, and the two busied themselves directing the preparations for the day's march. "We'll let Gonfala sleep as long as we can," he said; "this may be a hard day."

Van Eyk was groping around in the dim light of early dawn, feeling through the grasses on which he had made his bed. Suddenly he ripped out an oath.

"What's the matter?" demanded Wood.

"Stan, the Gonfal is gone! It was right under the edge of these skins last night."

Wood made a hurried search about his own bed; then another, more carefully. When he spoke he seemed stunned, shocked. "The emerald's gone, too, Bob. Who could have———"

"The Kaji!" Van Eyk's voice rang with conviction.

Together the two men hurried to the part of the camp where the warrior-women had bedded down for the night; and there, just rising from the skins upon which they had slept, were the three.

Without preliminaries, explanation, or apology the two men searched the beds where the women had lain.

"What are you looking for?" demanded one of them.

"The Gonfal," replied van Eyk.

"You have it," said the woman, "not we."

The brief equatorial dawn had given way to the full light of day as Wood and van Eyk completed a search of the camp and realized that Spike and Troll were missing.

Wood looked crestfallen and hopeless. "We might have guessed it right off," he said. "Those two were sore as pups when Clayton gave the Gonfal back to the Kaji and the emerald to Gonfala."

"What'll we do?" asked van Eyk.

"We'll have to follow them, of course; but that's not what's worrying me right now—it's telling Gonfala. She'd been banking a lot on the sale of the emerald ever since we kept harping on the wonderful things she could buy and what she could do with so much money. Poor kid! Of course, I've got enough for us to live on, and she can have every cent of it. But it won't be quite the same to her, because she wanted so much to be independent and not be a burden to me—as though she ever could be a burden."

"Well, you've got to tell her; and you might as well get it off your chest now as any time. If we're going after those birds, we want to get started *pronto*."

"O.K." He walked to Gonfala's shelter and called her. There was no response. He called again louder; and then again and again, but with no results. Then he entered. Gonfala was not there.

He came out, white and shaken. "They must have taken her, too, Bob."

The other shook his head. "That would have been impossible without disturbing us—if she had tried to arouse us."

Wood bridled angrily. "You mean——?"

Van Eyk interrupted and put a hand on the other's shoulder. "I don't know any more about it than you, Stan. I'm just stating a self-evident fact. You know it as well as I."

"But the inference."

"I can't help the inference either. They couldn't have taken Gonfala by force without waking us; therefore either she went with them willingly, or she didn't go with them at all."

"The latter's out of the question. Gonfala would never run away from me. Why only last night we were planning on the future, after we got married."

Van Eyk shook his head. "Have you ever really stopped to think about what that would mean, Stan? What it would mean to you both in the future—in America? I'm thinking just as much of her happiness as yours, old man. I'm thinking of the Hell on earth that would be your lot—hers and yours. You know as well as I what one drop of colored blood does for a man or woman in the great democracy of the U.S.A. You'd both be ostracized by the blacks as well as the whites. I'm not speaking from any personal prejudice; I'm just stating a fact. It's hard and cruel and terrible, but it still remains a fact."

Wood nodded in sad acquiescence. There was no anger in his voice as he replied. "I know it as well as you, but I'd go through Hell for her. I'd live in Hell for her, and thank God for the opportunity. I love her that much."

"Then there's nothing more to be said. If you feel that way about it, I'm for you. I'll never mention it again, and if you ever do marry it'll never change me toward either of you."

"Thanks, old man; I'm sure of it. And now let's get busy and start after them."

"You still think they took her?"

"I have a theory. They have both the Gonfal and the great emerald of the Zuli. You saw how Clayton used that mysterious power to bend the Kaji and Zuli to his will. They used it to compel Gonfala to accompany them without making any disturbance. You know the experience I had. Mafka dragged me away from Clayton in the same way."

"I guess you're right. I hadn't thought of that, but why did they want Gonfala?"

Van Eyk looked uncomfortable, and the other noticed it. "You don't mean—?" he exclaimed.

Van Eyk shrugged helplessly. "They are men," he said, "and not very high types."

"We've got to find her—we've got to hurry!" Wood was almost frantic.

Some of the blacks picked up the trail of the two men, leading toward the south; and the manhunt was on.

12

Reunion

TWO WEEKS ROLLED by. Tarzan was returning from the north with the information he sought. Sometimes he thought of the two Americans and Gonfala and the prisoners he had released from the Kaji and wondered how they fared. There had been enough of them to make their way in safety to the friendly tribes, and after that it would have been very simple to reach the outposts of civilization. He imagined that they were well on their way by this time with a good safari of trained bearers and ample provisions. He knew that the Americans were amply able to bear the expense even if they were unable to finance themselves on the security of the great emerald of the Zuli.

It was late afternoon as the Lord of the Jungle swung along a game trail at the edge of a forest. A light wind was blowing in his face, waving his black hair. It brought to his nostrils evidence of things unseen that lay ahead. Presently it brought the acrid scent of Numa the lion. It was an old lion, for the odor was stronger than that of a cub or a young lion in its prime.

To Tarzan it was just another lion. He gave it little thought until the wind brought faintly to his nostrils another scent—the scent spoor of a Tarmangani, a she—a white woman. This scent came from the same direction as that of Numa. The two, in conjunction, spelled tragedy.

Tarzan took to the trees. Game trails are winding. Through the trees he could move in a straight line, shortening the distance to his destination; and through the trees he could move with incredible swiftness. They had been his natural element since infancy when he had been borne swiftly from danger by his foster mother, Kala the she-ape.

The woman, haggard, unkempt, starving, exhausted, moved slowly and hopelessly along the trail. Her senses were dulled by fatigue and suffering. She heard nothing, yet some inner sense prompted her to turn a backward glance along the trail; then she saw the lion. He was moving softly and slowly after her. When he saw that he was discovered, he bared his fangs and growled.

The woman stopped and faced him. She had not the strength to climb a tree to safety. She knew that flight was useless. She just stood there, wide-eyed and hopeless, waiting for the end. She did not care. She had nothing to live for. She only prayed that death might come with merciful quickness.

When she had stopped, the lion had stopped. He stood glaring at her, his eyes blazing. Suddenly he started toward her at a trot. A few steps and he would charge—that swift, merciless charge of the king of beasts that is the culmination of ferocity.

He seemed to crouch lower, almost flattening himself against the ground; and now a horrid roar burst from his savage throat as he sprang forward!

The woman's eyes went wide, first in horror and then in surprise; for as the lion charged, an almost naked man dropped from an overhanging limb full upon the beast's back. She heard the roars and growls of the man mingling with those of the beast, and she shuddered. She saw a knife flash in the air, once, twice again. Then, with a final hideous roar, the lion slumped to the ground, dead.

The man leaped to his feet. It was then that she recognized him, and a feeling of relief and a sense of security possessed her. They endured for but a moment to be blasted by the hideous victory cry of the bull ape as Tarzan placed a foot upon the carcass of his kill and voiced the weird scream that had echoed so many times through other forests and jungles, deserts and plains.

Then his eyes dropped to the woman. "Gonfala! What has happened? What are you doing here alone?"

She told him a little—just that she felt that she would bring unhappiness into Wood's life and so had run away. She had

come north because she knew that he was going south. She
had hoped to find some village where they would take her
in; but she had found nothing; and so she had turned back
intending to return to Kaji and the only people that she knew
as her own.

"You can't go back there," Tarzan told her. "Without
Mafka's protection, they would kill you."

"Yes, I suppose they would; but where else may I go?"

"You are coming with me. Wood will save the emerald for
you. You will have all the money you will ever need. You
can live then where you wish in safety and comfort."

It was weeks before the ape-man brought the girl to his
home—to the commodious bungalow where his wife welcomed and comforted her. All that time they had sought for
word of Wood and van Eyk and their party but had had none.
Their total disappearance seemed a mystery to Tarzan,
and he planned to set out presently to solve it. Time, however, means little to the ape-man. There were other things to
be done, and days passed. Yet time itself was bringing the
solution nearer.

Two white men with a small safari trekked through a grim
forest—damp, dark, depressing. It seemed endless.

"If ever two people were thoroughly and completely lost,
we are they." Wood had stopped and removed his sun helmet
to wipe the perspiration from his forehead.

"We're no more lost than our guides," van Eyk reminded
him.

"If we keep on going east we ought to strike some village
where we can get guides."

"All right, let's get going."

Within half a mile they emerged from the forest at the
edge of a wide, rolling plain.

"What a relief!" exclaimed van Eyk. "A little more of that
forest and I'd have gone nuts."

"Look!" Wood seized his companion by the arm and
pointed. "Men!"

"Looks like a war party. See those plumes? Maybe we'd
better lay low."

"Well, the responsibility is no longer ours. They've seen us.
Here they come."

The two men stood watching a party of a dozen warriors
approaching them.

"Gee, they're a good-looking bunch," commented Wood.

"I hope they're also good."

The blacks halted a dozen paces from the white men; then one who was evidently their leader approached closer.

"What are the bwanas doing in this country?" he asked in good English. "Are they hunting?"

"We're lost," explained Wood. "We want to get guides to get us out of here."

"Come," said the black. "I take you to the Big Bwana."

"What's his name?" asked van Eyk. "Perhaps we know him."

"He is Tarzan."

The two whites looked at one another in astonishment.

"You don't mean to tell me there really is a Tarzan?" demanded Wood.

"Who ever tells you there isn't does not speak true words. In an hour you shall see him."

"What is your name?"

"Muviro, bwana."

"Well, lead on, Muviro; we're ready."

An hour later the two men stood on the broad verandah of a sprawling bungalow waiting the coming of their host.

"Tarzan!" muttered van Eyk. "It doesn't seem possible. This must be he coming. They heard footsteps approaching from the interior of the house, and a moment later a man stepped onto the verandah and faced them.

"Clayton!" they both exclaimed in unison.

"I am glad to see you," said Tarzan. "I hadn't been able to get any word of you, and I was worried. Where have you been?"

"The night you left, Spike and Troll stole the Gonfal and the great emerald and beat it. They took Gonfala with them. We have been hunting for them. The very first day we lost their trail in some rocky country. We never found it again. Some of our blacks thought they had gone to the south and west. We searched in that direction and got lost ourselves."

"The Gonfal and the great emerald are both gone? Well, perhaps it is just as well. They would have brought more unhappiness than anything else. Riches usually do."

"Hang the stones!" exclaimed Wood. "It is Gonfala I want to find. I don't give a tinker's damn for either of the rocks."

"I think we shall find her. It is not difficult for me to find anyone in Africa. But now I will have you shown to your rooms. You will find a bath and clean clothes; among them something that will fit you, I'm sure. When you are ready, come to the patio; you will find us there."

Van Eyk was the first to enter the patio, a flowering paradise around which the house was built. A golden haired girl lay on a reed chaise lounge, a copy of the Illustrated London News in her hand. Hearing him, she turned. Her eyes went wide in astonishment.

"Bob!" she gasped as she sprang to her feet.

"Gonfala!"

"Where is he? Is he all right?"

"Yes; he is here. How did you escape from Spike and Troll?"

"Escape from Spike and Troll? I was never with them."

"You went away alone? Why did you go?"

She told him then what she had overheard Spike and Troll say. "I knew then that I would spoil Stanlee's life. I knew that he loved me. I never thought that he wanted me just for the emerald. And I loved him. I loved him too much to let him marry me. Perhaps, when he had time to think it over, he was glad that I went away."

Van Eyk shook his head. "No, you are very wrong. I spoke to him of the matter; and here is what he said, as nearly as I can recall his words: 'I'd go through Hell for her. I'd live in Hell for her, and thank God for the opportunity. That is how much I love her.' I think those were about his very words."

Tears came to the girl's eyes. "May I see him soon?"

"He'll be out in a minute. Here he comes now. I'll go." She looked her thanks.

When Wood came into the patio and saw her, he just stood and looked at her for a moment, devouring her with his eyes. He never said a word or asked a question—just crossed to her and took her in his arms. Their voices were too full of tears of happiness for words.

After a while, when they could speak, each had the other's story. After that they knew that nothing could ever come between them.

In the evening, with the others, they were discussing their plans for the future. Wood said they would be married and go at once to America.

"I must go to London first," said Gonfala. "I have a letter to take to the Colonial Office there. You know, I told you about it. Let me get it. I cannot read it. I was never taught to read."

She went to her room and presently returned with the letter. It was yellow with age. She handed it to Tarzan. "Please read it aloud," she said.

Tarzan opened the single sheet and read:

"To Whom it May Concern:

"I am giving this letter to my daughter to take to London to identify her if she is ever fortunate enough to escape from the Kaji. They killed her mother shortly after she was born and raised her to be queen of the Kaji. They call her Gonfala. I have never dared to tell her that she is my daughter, as Mafka has threatened to kill her if she ever learns that he is not her father.

"Mountford."

13

Cannibals

A LOW SUN POINTED LONG shadows toward the east; the tired day was preparing to lay aside its burdens. Far away, a lion roared. It was the prelude to another African night, majestic as the king of beasts and as savage.

A party of eight men laid down their few belongings and made camp beside a water hole. Two of the men were white. Like their black companions they were armed with bows and arrows and short spears; there was not a firearm among them all.

Some of the men carried meat from the last kill, and there were two packages wrapped in skins. Beside their weapons, that was all. It was a poorly equipped safari, if it could be said to have been equipped at all.

The blacks were quiet, speaking in whispers as they cooked the meat for their evening meal. The white men were glum and scowling.

One of them nodded toward the blacks. "The beggars are scairt stiff."

The other nodded. "Cannibal country, and they know it."

His companion sat scowling down at the two skin

wrapped packages for a long period of silence. "I'm a-scairt myself, Troll," he said finally. "Scairt o' these things. I think they's a curse on 'em."

Troll shrugged. "I could take a lot o' cursin' for six million pun."

"Yeh; if we get out alive."

"I ain't worrit about that. What I'm worrit about is runnin' into that bloke, Clayton. He'll take the rocks away from us."

"He went north."

"But he said he was comin' back, an' he said he'd know if we'd pulled anything crooked. I don't like that bloke."

They lapsed into silence, chewing on the half cooked meat of a tough old boar the blacks had killed the day before. From the forest, a spur of which ran down almost to the water hole, eyes watched them. Again the lion roared.

"The beggar's gettin' closer," remarked Spike. "I hopes he ain't no man-eater."

Troll fidgeted. "Shut up!" he growled. "Can't you think of somethin' pleasant for a change?"

"Bein' way out here without no gun'd make any bloke nervous. Look at them damn things!" He kicked his bow and bundle of arrows that lay at his feet. "I might kill a rabbit with 'em—if I could hit 'im; but I couldn't hit a elephant if he stood still at ten paces—and you know wot kind of a target a lion makes when he charges."

"Oh, fer cripe's sake, shut up!"

Again they lapsed into silence. The shadow of the forest covered them and stretched out across the plain, for the sun had all but set. Suddenly there was a frightened cry of, "Bwana! Look!" One of the blacks was pointing toward the forest.

The white men wheeled as they rose to their feet. Coming toward them were a dozen black warriors. Spike stooped to pick up his bow and arrows.

"Lay off!" warned Troll. "They ain't enough of us—an' anyways they may be friendly." Spike stood erect again with empty hands. One by one the blacks of their party rose slowly to their feet.

The strangers were approaching cautiously, their weapons ready. They halted a dozen paces from the camp, their grim visaged leader in advance of the others. He surveyed the two white men and their six bearers arrogantly, contemptuously. Troll made the sign of peace.

The leader strode forward followed by his warriors. "What you do here in the country of the Bantango?" he demanded.

"We look for guides," replied Troll in the same dialect. "Big safari behind us—many guns—they come soon; then we go. We wait here they come."

"You lie," said the chief. "My man one he follow you two days; then he come me. No big safari. No guns. You lie."

"Wot did I tell you?" demanded Spike. "They's a curse on us—an' look at them filed teeth. You know what them filed teeth mean."

"I told you it was cannibal country," observed Troll, lamely.

"Gawdamighty, I'd give both them rocks for a gun," moaned Spike.

"The rocks!" exclaimed Troll. "That's it! Why didn't we think o' that before?"

"Think o' what?"

"The Gonfal. We can use it like old Mafka did, just put a hand on it an' make any bloke do wotever you wants him to do."

"Blime! That's a idea. Make 'em get out o' here." He stopped and started to unwrap the Gonfal, the great diamond of the Kaji.

The chief took a step forward. "What you got?" he demanded.

"Big medicine," said Troll. "You like see?"

The chief nodded. "Me like, me take."

The swift equatorial night had fallen. Only the cooking fires of the little camp illuminated the tense scene. From the deep shadows a great lion watched.

Spike undid the thongs that bound the wrappings to the Gonfal, and with trembling hands threw back the skin revealing the great stone shimmering and scintillating in the dancing lights of the cooking fires. The chief recoiled with a short gasp of astonishment. He did not know what the stone was, but its brilliance awed him.

Troll dropped to one knee beside the Gonfal and laid a hand on it. "Go away!" he said to the chief. "Lay down your weapons, all of you; and go away!"

The chief and his warriors stood looking at the Gonfal and at Troll. They did not lay down their weapons and they did not go away. As nothing happened, they regained confidence.

"No lay down weapons; no go away," said the chief. "We

stay. Me take." He pointed at Gonfal. "You come our village. You b'long me."

"You better go away," insisted Troll. He tried to make his voice sound commanding, but it did not.

"Wot's wrong with the Gonfal?" demanded Spike.

"It won't work."

"Le'me try it." Spike stooped and placed a palm on the stone. "You blokes drop your weapons an' beat it before our big medicine kills you," he shouted threateningly.

The chief stepped forward and kicked Spike in the face, bowling him over on his back. His warriors rushed in with loud war cries, brandishing their weapons. And then from the outer darkness came a thunderous roar that shook the earth, and a great lion charged into the savage melee.

He leaped over the prostrate Spike and brushed past Troll, falling upon the terrified chief and his warriors.

Troll was quick to grasp the opportunity for escape. He gathered up the great diamond, and shouted to Spike and the bearers to follow him and bring the other stone; then he ran for the forest.

A few screams, mingled with savage growls, rang in their ears for brief moments; then silence.

All night they followed close to the edge of the forest, nor did they stop until they came upon a small stream shortly after daylight. Then they threw themselves upon the ground, exhausted.

As they chewed once more upon the flesh of the old boar their spirits revived, and they spoke for the first time for hours.

"I guess we don't know how to work the rock," ventured Troll.

"Who says 'we'?" demanded Spike. "I worked it."

"You?"

"Sure. Didn't I tell 'em they'd get killed if they didn't beat it? And wot happens? The Gonfal calls the old man-eater. You remember that lamp that bloke used to rub—I forget his name—but this works just the same for me. I rubs it and wishes—and there you are!"

"Rats!"

"A'right; didn't I do it?"

"No. That lion was comin' long before you touched the rock. He smelled meat—that was wot brought him, not you and your bloody rock."

"I'll show you. Here, give it to me."

Spike took the diamond from Troll, uncovered it, and placed a palm on its gleaming surface. He glowered fixedly at his companion.

"Sit down!" he commanded.

Troll grinned derisively and advised Spike to "Go to 'ell." The latter scratched his head in momentary confusion; then he brightened. " 'Ere," he exclaimed; "I got a better idea." He scratched a line on the ground with a bit of stick. "I says now that you can't cross that line—and you can't."

"Who says I can't?" demanded Troll, stepping across the line.

"I guess maybe there's something I don't understand about this," admitted Spike. "That Clayton bloke worked it on the Kaji and the Zuli. You seen him yourself."

"Gonfala was there," reminded Troll. "Maybe that's the answer. Maybe it won't work without her."

"Maybe," admitted Spike; "but the Zuli medicine man done the same work with the emerald, an' he didn't have no Gonfala."

"Well, try the emerald, then."

"Le'me have it."

"I ain't got it."

"One of the boys must have it."

"I told you to bring it."

"One of the boys always carries it," insisted Spike, turning to the bearers sprawled on the ground. "Hey, you! W'ich one o' you 's got the green rock?" They looked at him blankly; then they looked at one another.

"No got," said one. "No bring."

"Hell!" ejaculated Troll. "You're a rare un, you are, aleavin' maybe a three million pun stone back there in the cannibal country!"

T IRED?" ASKED WOOD.
Gonfala shook her head. "Not a bit."

"You're doing pretty well for a girl who never had to do anything more strenuous than sit on a throne," laughed van Eyk.

"You'd be surprised. I can probably out-run and out-last either of you. You see I used to hunt with the Kaji. Mafka insisted on it—lots of exercise. He was a great believer in exercise for every one but Mafka."

"I'm glad," said Wood, "for we've got two long marches between this camp and railhead. I'll be glad when it's over. To tell you the truth, I'm fed up on Africa. I hope I never see it again."

"I don't blame you, Stanlee; you came near staying here a long time."

"Yes; eternity is rather a long time." Wood grimaced. "It's hard to realize, even now, that we escaped."

"It's incredible," agreed Gonfala. "We're the first persons ever to escape from Mafka; and he'd been there, oh, no one knows how long—the Kaji said always. They believed that he created the world."

The three were camped at the end of a day's march on their way out toward civilization. They had a dependable, well equipped safari furnished by Tarzan. The men planned on devoting one day to hunting, as they were in excellent game country; then they would cover the two long marches to railhead. The delay for hunting was Wood's concession to van Eyk, an indefatigable Nimrod, who had obtained permission from the Lord of the Jungle to take out a few trophies for his collection.

As night fell, the light of their beast fire cast dancing shadows through the camp and shone far out into the night, both attracting and repelling the great carnivores upon whose domain they trespassed; for this was lion country. It attracted also other eyes a mile or more to the north.

"I wonder what that might be," said Spike.

"A fire," growled Troll; "what you think it was—a iceberg?"

"Funny, ain't you?"

"Not as funny as a bloke what runs off an leaves three million puns worth o' emerald with a bunch of cannibals."

"Fer cripe's sake quit chewin' about that; I didn't leave it any more 'n you did. What I mean is, there must be men over by that fire; I wonders who they might be."

"Natives, perhaps."

"Or white hunters."

"What difference does it make?" asked Troll.

"They might put us on the right trail."

"An' tell that Clayton bloke where we are? You're balmy."

"How do you know he's around here? Maybe they never even heard of him."

"He's everywhere. Everybody's heard of him. He said he'd know it if we double-crossed Stanley. After I seen what he done in the Kaji country, I wouldn't put nothin' past him—he's omnivirous."

"Whatever that means."

"You're igorant."

"Well, just the same, I think we'd ourghter find out who made that fire. If they're one thing, we'd better light out of here; if they're the other, we can ask 'em to set us on the right trail."

"Maybe you said something intelligent at last. It wouldn't do no harm to go have a look-see."

"That fire may be a long ways off, and——"

"And what?"

"This is lion country."

"You scared?"

"Sure I'm scared. So are you, unless you're a bigger fool than I think. Nobody but a fool wouldn't be scared in lion country at night without a gun."

"We'll take a couple of the smokes with us. They say lions like dark meat."

"All right; let's get goin'."

Guided by the fire, the four men approached the Wood-van Eyke camp; and after reconnoitering made their way to the concealment of a clump of bushes where they could see and not be seen.

"Cripes!" whispered Spike. "Look who's there!"

"Gonfala!" breathed Troll.

"An' Wood an' van Eyk."

"T'ell with them! If we only had the girl!"

"Wot do we want of her?"

"You get less brains every minute. Wot do we want of 'er! If we had her we could make the diamond do its stuff just like Mafka did—just like Clayton did. We'd be safe; nothin' nor nobody couldn't hurt us."

"Well, we ain't got her."

"Shut up! Listen to wot they're sayin'."

The voices of the three whites by the campfire came clearly to Troll and Spike. Van Eyk was making plans for the morrow's hunt.

"I really think Gonfala ought to stay in camp and rest; but as long as she insists on coming along, you and she can go together. If there were three men, now, we could spread out farther and cover more ground."

"I can do whatever a man can do," insisted Gonfala. "You can assume that you have three men."

"But, Gonfala——"

"Don't be foolish, Stanlee. I am not as the women you have known in your civilized countries. From what you have told me, I shall be as helpless and afraid there as they would be here; but here I am not afraid. So I hunt tomorrow as the third man, and now I am going to bed. Good night, Stanlee. Good night, Bob."

"Well, I guess that settles it," remarked Wood, with a wry smile; "but when I get you back in God's country you'll have to mind me. Good night."

"Perhaps," said Gonfala.

*   *   *

The chill of night still hung like a vapor below the new sun as the three hunters set out from their camp for the day's sport, and although the hunt had been van Eyk's idea primarily, each of the others was keen to bag a lion. Over their breakfast coffee they had laid wagers as to which would be the lucky one to bring down the first trophy, with the result that not a little friendly rivalry had been engendered. That each might, seemed entirely possible; as the night had been filled with the continual roaring of the great carnivores.

Shortly after leaving camp the three separated, van Eyk keeping straight ahead toward the east, Wood diverging toward the south, and Gonfala to the north; each was accompanied by a gunbearer; and some of the members of the safari followed along after van Eyk and Wood, either believing that one of the men would be more likely to get a lion than would the girl, or, perhaps, feeling safer behind the guns of the men.

From behind an outcropping of rock at the summit of a low hill northwest of the Wood-van Eyk camp Spike and Troll watched their departure; while below them, concealed from sight, the six men of their safari waited. The two whites watched Gonfala and her gunbearer approaching across the open plain. The direction that she was taking suggested that she would pass a little to the east of them, but that she would then still be in sight of van Eyk and possibly Wood also.

The latter was not at all happy about the arrangements for the day; he did not like the idea of Gonfala going out on her own after lion with only a gunbearer, but the girl had overridden his every objection. He had insisted, however, upon sending as gunbearer a man of known courage who was also a good shot; and him he had instructed to be always ready with the second rifle in the event that Gonfala got into a tight place and, regardless of custom, to shoot a charging lion himself.

While Gonfala had had little previous experience of firearms prior to a few weeks ago, it gave him some consolation to reflect that she had, even in that short time, developed into an excellent shot; and insofar as her nerve was concerned he had no cause for anxiety. What he could not have known, of course, was the far greater menace of the two men who watched her from their rocky concealment upon the hilltop.

Gonfala passed the hill beneath the eyes of Spike and Troll and then crossed a low rise that was a continuation of the hill running down into the plain, and from then on she was hidden from the sight of either van Eyk or Wood. The country she now entered was broken by gullies and outcroppings of rock, by low bushes and occasional trees; so that it was comparatively easy for Spike and Troll to follow her without danger of being discovered; and this they did, keeping well to the rear of her and catching only an occasional glimpse of her during the ensuing hour.

Quite unsuspecting the fact that eight men followed upon her trail, Gonfala continued her seemingly fruitless search for lion, bearing constantly a little to the west because of a range of low hills that lay to the right of her and thus constantly increasing the distance between herself and her two companions. She had about come to the conclusion that the lions had all left the country when she heard, faint and far toward the east, the report of two rifle shots.

"Some one else had the luck," she said to her gunbearer; "I guess we came in the wrong direction."

"No, Memsahib," he whispered, pointing; "look! Simba!"

She looked quickly in the direction he indicated; and there among the grasses beneath a tree she saw the head of a lion, the yellow-green eyes gazing unblinkingly at her. The beast was about a hundred yards distant; he was lying down, and as only his head was visible he offered a poor target. A frontal shot, she knew, would only tend to infuriate him and precipitate a charge.

"Pay no attention to him," she whispered; "we'll try to get closer and to one side."

She moved forward then, not directly toward the lion but as though to pass a little to the right of him; and always his eyes followed them, but neither she nor the gunbearer gave any indication that they were aware of his presence. When she had approached to within about fifty yards she stopped and faced him, but he only lay quietly regarding her. But when she took a few steps straight toward him, he bared his great fangs and growled.

Topping a rise behind her, Spike took in the situation at a glance. He motioned to his men to halt, and beckoned Troll to his side. Together they watched the tense scene below them.

"I wish he'd get up," said Gonfala.

The gunbearer picked up a stone and hurled it at the lion. The result was immediate and electrical. With an angry roar the lion leaped to its feet and charged.

"Shoot, Memsahib!"

Gonfala dropped to one knee and fired. The lion leaped high into the air, its angry roars shattering the silence. It was hit, but it was not stopped; for although it rolled over on its back it was up again in an instant and bearing down on them at terrific speed. Gonfala fired again and missed. Then the gunbearer took aim and pressed the trigger of his gun. There was only a futile click. The cartridge misfired.

The lion was almost upon Gonfala when the gunbearer, unnerved by the failure of his gun, turned and fled. Unwittingly he had saved Gonfala's life, for at sight of the man in flight the lion, already rising over Gonfala, followed a natural instinct that has saved the life of many a hunter and pursued the fleeing man. Gonfala fired again, and again scored a hit; but it did not stop the infuriated beast as it rose upon its hind feet and seized the gunbearer, the great fangs closing upon his head until they met in the center of his brain.

The girl was aghast as she stood helplessly by while the huge cat mauled its victim for a moment; then it sagged upon the body of the man and died.

"That," said Troll, "is wot I call a bit o' luck. We not only gets the girl, but we gets two guns."

"And no witness," added Spike. "Come on!" He motioned the others to follow him, and started down the declivity toward Gonfala.

She saw them almost immediately and for a moment thought her companions were coming, but presently she recognized them. She knew that they were bad men who had stolen the great diamond and the emerald, but she had no reason to believe that she was in any danger from them.

They came up to her smiling and friendly. "You sure had a narrow squeak," said Spike. "We seen it from the top of that rise, but we couldn't have done nothing to help you even if we'd had guns—we was too far away."

"What are you doing here?" she asked.

"We was tryin' to find our way to railhead," explained Spike. "We been lost fer weeks."

Troll was recovering the gun and ammunition from the dead gunbearer, and Spike was eyeing the splendid rifle that Gonfala carried.

"We're on our way to railhead," she explained. "You can come back to camp with me and go on to railhead with us."

"Won't that be nice!" exclaimed Spike. "Say, that's a fine gun you got there. Lemme see it a minute." Thoughtlessly, she handed the weapon over to him; then she stepped over to the body of the dead gunbearer.

"He's quite dead," she said. "It's too bad. Your men can carry him back to camp."

"We ain't goin' back to your camp," said Spike.

"Oh," she exclaimed. "Well, what am I to do? I can't take him back alone."

"You ain't goin' back neither."

"What do you mean?"

"Just wot I says: You ain't goin' back to your camp. You're comin' with us."

"Oh, no I'm not."

"Listen, Gonfala," said Spike. "We don't want no trouble with you. We don't want to hurt you none; so you might as well come along peaceful like. We need you."

"What for?" Her voice was brave, but her heart sank within her.

"We got the Gonfal, but we can't make it work without you."

"Work?"

"Yes, work. We're goin' to set ourselves up like Mafka did and be kings—just as soon as we find a piece o' country we like. We'll live like kings, too, off the fat of the land. You can be queen—have everything you want. Maybe, even, I'll marry you." He grinned.

"The hell you will," snapped Troll. "She belongs to me as much as she does to you."

Gonfala cringed. "I belong to neither of you. You are both fools. If you take me away, you will be followed and killed; or, at the least, both I and the Gonfal will be taken from you. If you have any sense you will let me go; then you can take the Gonfal to Europe. They tell me that there the money that it would bring would buy you anything that you wanted all the rest of your lives."

"A fat chance we'd have gettin' rid o' that rock in Europe," said Troll. "No, sister, we got it all figgered out. You're comin' with us, an' that's that."

15

Clews

VAN EYK DROPPED his lion with the second shot, and a few minutes later he heard the three shots fired by Gonfala. Wood, having had no luck and attracted by the report of van Eyk's gun, joined him. He was still apprehensive concerning Gonfala's safety; and now that van Eyk had his trophy, he suggested that they send the carcass back to camp while they joined Gonfala. Van Eyk agreed, and they set out in the direction from which they had heard the shots.

They searched for two hours without result, often calling her name and occasionally discharging their rifles; then, more by chance than design, they stumbled upon the little swale where Gonfala had come upon her lion. There it lay upon the body of the dead gunbearer, but Gonfala was nowhere to be seen.

The ground was hard and stony, giving no indication to the untrained eyes of the white men that others beside Gonfala and her gunbearer had been there; so they assumed that, having no one to cut off or carry the head of the lion back to camp, the girl had returned there herself alone; and that, having come from another direction, they had missed her. They were, therefore, not unduly apprehensive until after they reached the camp and discovered that she had not returned.

By that time it was late in the afternoon; but Wood insisted upon taking up the search at once, and van Eyk seconded the suggestion. They divided the safari into three sections. Van Eyk and Wood each heading one set out on slightly diverging trails in the general direction that Gonfala had taken in the morning, while the third, under a headman, was ordered to remain in camp, keeping a large fire burning and occasionally discharging a rifle to guide Gonfala if she should return toward camp without meeting either Wood or van Eyk. And all during the night Gonfala and her captors heard the faint report of rifles far to the south.

It was around noon of the following day that, exhausted and disheartened, Wood and van Eyk returned to camp.

"I'm afraid it's no use, old man," said the latter, sympathetically; "if she'd been alive she'd have heard our rifles and replied."

"I can't believe that she's dead," said Wood; "I won't believe it!"

Van Eyk shook his head. "I know it's tough, but you've got to face facts and reason. She couldn't be alive in this lion country now."

"But she had two guns," insisted Wood. "You saw that she took the gun and ammunition from the gunbearer after he was killed. If she'd been attacked by a lion, she'd have fired at least once; and we never heard a shot."

"She might have been taken unaware—stalked after dark and struck down before she knew a lion was near. You've seen 'em charge; you know it's all over in a second if you aren't ready for 'em."

Wood nodded. "Yes, I know. I suppose you're right, but I won't give up—not yet."

"Well, Stan, I've got to get back home. If I thought there was the slightest chance I'd stay, but I know there's not. You'd better come along and try to forget it as soon as you can. You might never, here; but back home it'll be different."

"There's no use, Van; you go along. I'm going to stay."

"But what can you do alone?"

"I won't try to do anything alone. I'm going back and find Tarzan; he'll help me. If any one can find her or where she was killed it's he."

*   *   *

Ten days later Wood plodded wearily into the camp that he had not left except in daily fruitless searches for his Gonfala. He had not gone back to enlist Tarzan's aid; but had, instead, sent a long letter to the ape-man by a runner. Every day for ten days he had combed the country for miles around, and each day he had become more convinced that Gonfala was not dead. He had found no trace of a human kill by lions, no shred of clothing, no sign of the two guns or the ammunition that Gonfala had had with her; though he had found plenty of lion kills—zebra, antelope, wildebeest. But he had found something else that gave support to his belief that Gonfala might be alive—the camp of Spike and Troll. It lay only a short distance north from his own camp. Gonfala must have pressed close to it the morning that she started out to hunt. What type of men had camped there, he could not know; but he assumed that they were natives; for there were no signs of white men—no empty tins, no discarded scrap of clothing, no indications that a tent had been pitched.

Perhaps, then, Gonfala's fate had been worse than the merciful death the king of beasts would have accorded her. That thought goaded him to desperation, and filled his mind with red imaginings of vengeance. Such were his thoughts as he threw himself upon his cot in hopeless bafflement to reproach himself as he had a thousand thousand times for having permitted Gonfala to hunt alone that day—how long ago it seemed, how many ages of bitter suffering!

A figure darkened the doorway of the tent, and Wood turned to look. Wood sprang to his feet. "Tarzan! God, I thought you'd never come."

"I came as soon as I got your letter. You have been searching, of course; what have you found?"

Wood told him of his failure to find any evidence that Gonfala had fallen prey to lions but that he had found a camp in which there had been men recently.

"That is interesting," commented Tarzan. "It is too late now to investigate that today; tomorrow I'll have a look at it."

Early the next morning Wood and the ape-man were at the camp from which Spike and Troll had been attracted by the campfire that had led them to the discovery of the presence of Gonfala. Tarzan examined the ground and the surroundings minutely. His lifetime of experience, his trained powers of observation, his sensitive nostrils revealed facts that were a sealed book to the American. The charred wood in the dead fires, the crushed grass, the refuse each told him something.

"It was a poor camp," he said finally. "Perhaps ten or a dozen men camped here. They had very little food and their packs were few. They did have packs, and that indicates that there were white men—perhaps one, perhaps two; the rest were natives. Their food was poor. That would suggest that they had no firearms, for this is a good game country; so perhaps there were no white men at all. Yet I am sure there were. They had only the meat of an old boar to eat. Some of the bones were split and the marrow extracted. That suggests natives. Other bones were not split, and that suggests white men."

"How do you know they had packs?" asked Wood, who could see no evidence to suggest anything more than that some one had been there and built fires and eaten food. He could see the discarded bones of their repast.

"If you look carefully you will see where they lay on the ground. It has been ten days at least; and the signs are faint, but they are there. The grasses are pressed down and the marks of the cords that bound the packs are still visible."

"I see nothing," admitted Wood after close scrutiny.

Tarzan smiled one of his rare smiles. "Now we shall see

which way they went," he said. "The spoor of so many men should be plain."

They followed toward the north the freshest spoor that led from the camp, only to lose it where a great herd of grazing game had obliterated it; then Tarzan picked it up again beyond. Eventually it led to the spot where the bodies of the gunbearer and the lion had lain.

"Your theory seems to have been correct," said the ape-man. "Gonfala, apparently, was captured by this party."

"That was eleven days ago," mused Wood despairingly. "There is no telling where they are now, or what they have done to her. We must lose no time in following."

"Not we," replied Tarzan. "You will return to your camp and start tomorrow for my place. When I have definitely located Gonfala, if I cannot rescue her without help" (Again he smiled) "I'll send word by a runner, and you can come with an escort of Waziri."

"But can't I go along with you?" demanded Wood.

"I can travel much faster alone. You will do as I say. That is all."

And that *was* all. Wood stood watching the magnificent figure of the ape-man until it disappeared beyond a rise in the rolling plain; then he turned dejectedly back toward camp. He knew that Tarzan was right, that a man whose senses were dulled by generations of non-use would prove only a drag on the alert ape-man.

For two days Tarzan followed the trail in a northerly direction; then an unseasonable rain obliterated it forever. He was now in the country of the Bantangos, a warlike tribe of cannibals and hereditary enemies of his Waziri. He knew that if the captors of Gonfala had come this way it might be because they were themselves Bantangos, and so he determined to investigate thoroughly before searching farther. If they had not been Bantangos, it was very possible that they had been captured by this tribe; for he knew that they were a small and poorly equipped company.

In any event it seemed best to have a look into the village of the chief, to which, unquestionably, important captives would have been taken; but where the village lay, the ape-man did not know. To the east of him a range of low hills stretched way into the north, and to these he made his way. As he ascended them he commenced to glimpse villages to the west and north, and finally from the summit of one of the higher hills he obtained a view of a considerable extent

of country containing many villages. The majority of these
were mean and small—just a handful of huts surrounded
by flimsy palisades of poles.

The valley in which the villages lay was dotted with trees,
and on the west abutted upon a forest. It was a scene of
peace and loveliness that lent a certain picturesqueness to
even the squalid kraals of the Bantangos and belied the
savagery and bestiality of the inhabitants. The beauty of the
aspect was not lost upon the ape-man, whose appreciation of
the loveliness or grandeur of nature, undulled by familiarity,
was one of the chief sources of his joy of living. In con-
templating the death that he knew must come to him as to
all living things his keenest regret lay in the fact that he
would never again be able to look upon the hills and valleys
and forests of his beloved Africa; and so today, as he lay
like a great lion low upon the summit of a hill, stalking his
prey, he was still sensible of the natural beauties that lay
spread before him. Nor was he unmindful of a large village
that lay toward the center of the valley, the largest, by far,
of any of the villages. This, he knew, must be the village of
the chief of the Bantangos.

The moonless night descended, a black shroud that enveloped the forest, the trees, and the villages, concealing
them from the eyes of the watcher; then the Lord of the
Jungle arose, stretching himself. So like a lion's were all his
movements that one might have expected the roar of the
hunting beast to rumble from his great chest. Silently he
moved down toward the village of the chief. Little lights
shone now about the valley, marking the various villages by
their cooking fires. Toward the fires of the largest strode an
English lord, naked but for a G string.

From the hills he was quitting a lion roared. He too was
coming down to the villages where the natives had gathered their little flocks within the flimsy enclosures of their
kraals. The ape-man stopped and raised his face toward the
heavens. From his deep chest rose the savage, answering
challenge of the bull-ape. The savages in the villages fell
silent, looking questioningly at one another, wide eyed in
terror. The warriors seized their weapons, the women hud-
dled their children closer.

"A demon," whispered one.

"Once before I heard that cry," said the chief of the
Bantangos. "It is the cry of the devil-god of the Waziri."

"Why would he come here?" demanded a warrior. "The

rains have come many times since we raided in the country
of the Waziri."

"If it is not he," said the chief, "then it is another devil-
god."

"When I was a boy," said an old man, "I went once with
a raiding party far toward the place where the sun sleeps, to
a great forest where the hairy tree-men live. They make a
loud cry like that, a cry that stops the heart and turns the
skin cold. Perhaps it is one of the hairy tree-men. We
were gone a long time. The rains were just over when we left
our village; they came again before we returned. I was a great
warrior. I killed many warriors on that raid. I ate their
hearts; that is what makes me so brave." No one paid any
attention to him, but he rambled on. The others were listening
intently for a repetition of the weird cry or for any sound
that might presage the approach of an enemy.

Tarzan approached the palisade that surrounded the village
of the chief. A tree within the enclosure spread its branches
across the top. The ape-man came close and investigated.
Through the interstices between the poles that formed the
palisade he watched the natives. Gradually their tense nerves
relaxed as there was no repetition of the cry that had alarmed
them; and they returned to their normal pursuits, the women
to their cooking, the men to the immemorial custom of the
lords of creation—to doing nothing.

Tarzan wished to scale the palisade and gain the branches
of the tree that spread above him; but he wished to do it
without attracting the attention of the Bantangos, and because
of the frail construction of the palisade, he knew that that
would be impossible during the quiet that prevailed
within the village at the supper hour. He must wait. Perhaps
the opportunity he sought would present itself later. With
the patience of the wild beast that stalks its prey, the ape-
man waited. He could, if necessary, wait an hour, a day,
a week. Time meant as little to him as it had to the apes
that raised him, his contacts with civilization not having as
yet enslaved him to the fetish of time.

Nothing that he could see within the restricted limits of
his vision, a section of the village visible between two huts
just within the palisade, indicated that the Bantangos held
white prisoners; but he knew that if such were the case they
might be confined within a hut; and it was this, among other
things, that he must know before continuing his search elsewhere.

The evening meal concluded, the blacks lapsed into som-
nolence. The quiet of the African night was broken only by
the occasional roars of the hunting lion, coming closer
and closer, a sound so familiar that it aroused the interest of
neither the blacks within the village nor the watcher without.

An hour passed. The lion ceased his roaring, evidence
that he was now approaching his prey and stalking. The
blacks stirred with awakening interest with the passing of the
phenomenon of digestion and became motivated by the same
primitive urge that fills El Morocco and other late spots
with dancers after the theater. A dusky maestro gathered his
players with their primitive instruments, and the dancing
began. It was the moment for which Tarzan had been await-
ing. Amidst the din of the drums and the shouts of the
dancers he swarmed to the top of the palisade and swung into
the tree above.

From a convenient limb he surveyed the scene below. He
could see the chief's hut now and the chief himself. The old
fellow sat upon a stool watching the dancers, but in neither
the chief nor the dancers did the ape-man discover a focus
for his interest—that was riveted upon something that lay
at the chief's feet—the Great Emerald of the Zuli.

There could be no mistake. There could be but one such
stone, and its presence here induced a train of deductive
reasoning in the alert mind of the ape-man that led to
definite conclusions—that Spike and Troll had been in the
vicinity and that it was logical to assume that it must have
been they who abducted Gonfala. Were they here now, in
this village of the Bantangos? Tarzan doubted it; there was
nothing to indicate that there were any prisoners in the
village, but he must know definitely; so he waited on with the
infinite patience that was one of the heritages of his upbring-
ing.

The night wore on; and at last the dancers tired, and the
village street was deserted. Sounds of slumber arose from the
dark huts, unlovely sounds, fitting bed-fellows of unlovely
odors. Here and there a child fretted or an infant wailed.
Beyond the palisade a lion coughed.

The ape-man dropped silently into the empty street. Like a
shadow he passed from hut to hut, his keen nostrils searching
out the scents that would tell him, as surely as might his eyes
could he have seen within, whether a white lay prisoner
there. No one heard him; not even a sleeping cur was disturbed. When he had made the rounds he knew that those

he sought were not there, but he must know more. He returned to the chief's hut. On the ground before it, like worth-
less trash, lay the Great Emerald of the Zuli. Its weird green
light cast a soft radiance over the bronzed body of the jungle
lord, tinged the chief's hut palely green, accentuated the
blackness of the low entrance way.

The ape-man paused a moment, listening; then he stooped
and entered the hut. He listened to the breathing of the
inmates. By their breathing he located the women and the
children and the one man—that one would be the chief.
To his side he stepped and kneeled, stooping low. Steel
thewed fingers closed lightly upon the throat of the sleeper.
The touch awakened him.

"Make no sound," whispered the ape-man, "if you would
live."

"Who are you?" demanded the chief in a whisper. "What
do you want?"

"I am the devil-god," replied Tarzan. "Where are the two
white men and the white woman?"

"I have seen no white woman," replied the chief.

"Do not speak lies—I have seen the green stone."

"The two white men left it behind them when they ran
away," insisted the chief, "but there was no white woman
with them. The sun has risen from his bed as many times
as I have fingers on my two hands and toes on one foot
since the white men were here."

"Why did they run away?" demanded the ape-man.

"We were at their camp. A lion came and attacked us;
the white men ran away, leaving the green stone behind."

A woman awoke and sat up. "Who speaks?" she demanded.

"Tell her to be quiet," cautioned Tarzan.

"Shut up," snapped the chief at the woman, "if you do not
wish to die—it is the devil-god!"

The woman stifled a scream and lay down, burying her
face in the dirty reeds that formed her bed.

"Which way did the white men go?" asked the ape-man.

"They came from the north. When they ran away they
went into the forest to the west. We did not follow them. The
lion had killed two of my warriors and mauled others."

"Were there many in the safari of the white men?"

"Only six, beside themselves. It was a poor safari. They
had little food and no guns. They were very poor." His tone
was contemptuous. "I have told you all I know. I did not

harm the white men or their men. Now go away. I know no more."

"You stole the green stone from them," accused Tarzan.

"No. They were frightened and ran away, forgetting it; but they took the white stone with them."

"The white stone?"

"Yes, the white stone. One of them held it in his hands and told us to put down our weapons and go away. He said it was big medicine and that it would kill us if we did not go away; but we stayed, and it did not kill us."

In the darkness the ape-man smiled. "Has a white woman passed through your country lately? If you lie to me I shall come back and kill you."

"I have never seen a white woman," replied the chief. "If one had passed through my country I should know it."

Tarzan slipped from the hut as silently as he had come. As he went, he gathered up the Great Emerald and swung into the tree that overhung the palisade. The chief breathed a choking sigh of relief and broke into a cold sweat.

Strong in the nostrils of the ape-man was the scent of Numa the lion. He knew that the great cat was stalking close to the palisade. He had no quarrel with Numa this night and no wish to tempt a hungry hunting lion; so he made himself comfortable in the tree above the cannibal village to wait until Numa had taken himself elsewhere.

16

Tantor

WEARY DAY AFTER weary day Gonfala had trudged north with Spike and Troll. They had made a wide detour to avoid the country of the Bantangos, for although they had both the Gonfal and Gonfala they lacked the courage of their convictions relative to this combination that previously had seemed all-powerful to them.

Gonfala's safety, so far, had lain in the men's jealousy of one another. Neither would leave her alone with the other. Because of her, they had ceased to speak except when absolutely necessary; and each was constantly afraid that the other would murder him. To assure her own safety, the girl watched over the safety of each of the others as though she loved them both.

One of the blacks carried the great diamond, nor did either of the white men attempt to touch it without arousing the savage objections of the other; for now that Gonfala was with them each feared that the other might use the magical power of the stone to destroy him.

Spike was in search of a district which he had passed through on safari several years before.

"It's a regular garden, Miss," he explained to Gonfala; "and game! S'elp me, it's lousy with game; and that gentle, from not bein' hunted none, that you can walk right up to 'em an' bat 'em over the head, if you'd a mind to. We could live like kings and with plenty of servants, too; for the natives is peaceablelike, and not many of 'em. I mean not too many. We could rule 'em easy what with our havin' the Gonfal and you."

"I don't know that the Gonfal would do you much good," said the girl.

"Wy not?" demanded Troll.

"You don't know how to use it. One must have certain mental powers to succeed with the Gonfal."

"Have you got 'em?" asked Spike.

"I could use it unless Mafka desired to prevent me. He could do that, for his mind could control mine. I have never tried to use these powers since Mafka died."

"But you think you can?" Spike's voice reflected the fear that was in him. He had banked heavily on the power of the Gonfal. All his future plans were dependent upon his being able to control the acts of others through the mysterious powers of the great diamond, and now there was doubt. It haunted him day and night.

"I think so," replied Gonfala, "but I shall not use it to help either of you unless I am absolutely assured that neither one of you will harm me."

"I wouldn't think of hurtin' you, Miss," Spike assured her.

"Me neither, but you better not trust him," said Troll.

Spike took a step toward Troll, his fist clenched. "You dirty crook," he shouted, "you're the one needs watchin', but you won't need it much longer. I'm goin' to break your neck for you right now."

Troll jumped back and picked up his rifle. "Come any

closer and I'll let you have it," he threatened, holding the muzzle of the weapon aimed at Spike's belly.

"You'd better not," Spike admonished him. "You may need another gun in some of the country we got to go through. You'd never get through alone with just six niggers."

"That goes for you, too," growled Troll.

"Then let's call it quits, and quit our rowin'—it ain't gettin' us nothin'."

"It won't ever get either one of you me," said Gonfala, "and that's what's been the trouble between you. You stole me from my friends, and some day they're going to catch up with you. When they do, it'll be better for you if you haven't harmed me. Stanlee Wood will never give up until he finds me; and when he tells Tarzan I have been stolen, you can rest assured I'll be found and you will be punished."

"Tarzan!" exclaimed Spike. "What's Tarzan got to do with it?"

"You know who he is?" demanded Gonfala.

"Sure—everybody's heard of him; but I ain't never seen him. I always thought maybe he was just somethin' somebody made up. What do you know about him? Have you ever seen him?"

"Yes, and so have you."

"Not us," said Troll.

"You remember Clayton?" asked the girl.

"Sure, I remember Clayton. That bloke was as good as two—Say! You don't mean——?"

"Yes, I do. Clayton is Tarzan."

Troll looked worried. Spike scowled; then he shrugged. "Wot if he is?" he demanded. "He couldn't never find us—not where we're goin'; and even if he did, wot could he do against the Gonfal? We could do what we pleased with him."

"Sure," agreed Troll; "we could snuff him out like that." He snapped his fingers.

"Oh, no you couldn't," said Gonfala.

"An' wy couldn't we?"

"Because I wouldn't let you. You can't use the Gonfal without my help, and when Tarzan and Stanlee come I shall help them. You see, with the Gonfal, I can snuff *you* out."

The two men looked at one another. Presently Spike walked away and called to Troll to accompany him. When he was out of earshot of Gonfala he stopped. "Listen," he said; "that dame's got us to rights. If she ever gets her paws on that rock our lives won't be worth nothin'."

"Looks like the Gonfal ain't goin' to do us much good," said Troll. "We can't make it work without her; and if we let her get her hands on it, she'll kill us. Wot are we goin' to do?"

"In the first place we got to see that she doesn't get to touch it. One of us has got to carry it—she might get the nigger to let her touch it some time when we weren't around. You can carry it if you want to."

"That's wot I been sayin' for a long time," Troll reminded him.

"Well, it's different now," Spike explained. "Neither one of us can get it to work, an' neither one of us dares let her touch it; so we're safe as long as one of us has it."

"But wot good is the stone goin' to do us, then?"

"Wait 'til we get up in that country I been tellin' you about. We can make the dame be good then. All we got to do is tell her to work the stone the way we say or we'll croak her. She'll have to do it, too; for where I'm takin' her she couldn't never find her way out after she'd killed us; so it wouldn't do her no good."

Troll shook his head. "Maybe she'd kill us any way, just to get even with us."

"Well, there ain't nothin' we can do about it now, anyway," said Spike; "so let's get goin'. Come on, you niggers! Come on, Gonfala! we're trekkin'—the sun's been up an hour."

As they broke camp far to the north of him, Tarzan stopped at the edge of the forest that bordered the valley of the Bantangos on the west. He looked about him, carefully taking his bearings; then with the tip of his spear he loosened the earth in the center of a triangle formed by three trees and with his hands scooped out the earth until he had a hole about a foot deep. Into this he dropped the Great Emerald of the Zuli. When he had refilled the hole and covered it with the fallen leaves and twigs that he had carefully scraped away, no human eye could have detected the hiding place. With his knife he blazed a tree fifteen paces from one of the three trees that formed the triangle. Only Tarzan could ever find the place again. Should he never return, the ransom of a dozen kings would lie there to the end of time, undiscovered.

Unable to find the trail that the storm had obliterated, the ape-man attempted to deduce from his knowledge of the two men he was now positive were the abductors of Gonfala and from his knowledge of events leading up to the present moment the logical destination for which they were headed.

He knew that they were familiar with the miraculous powers of the Gonfal and that they had been unable to call these powers into being themselves. The chief of the Bantangos had told him of their failure to demonstrate the value of their big medicine. Either by accident or intent they had found Gonfala, and what more natural than that they would assume that with her aid they could command the wonders of the Gonfal? And where would be the best place to utilize these powers? Why, the country of the Kaji, naturally; for there they would be safer from detection than almost anywhere on earth, and there they would find a tribe accustomed to the domination of the stone. There they would find women; and Tarzan felt that if he were any judge of men, that circumstance would have considerable bearing with Troll and Spike. So Tarzan travelled toward the north on a trail parallel to that taken by Spike and Troll but some distance to the west of it.

For two days Tarzan moved toward the north, and still there was no sign of those whom he sought. He made his kills and ate and slept, and swung on tirelessly through forest or across plains.

As he was passing through a strip of forest along the shoulder of a range of hills thick with bamboo he heard a sound that brought him to halt, listening. It was repeated—the weak trumpeting of an elephant in distress. The ape-man turned aside from the direction he had been travelling and moved cautiously through the bamboo thicket. He was moving down wind; so he made a wide circuit in order to pick up the scent spoor of what lay ahead. There might be something beside an elephant. The caution of the beast aided and abetted the reasoning powers of the man.

Presently the scent of Tantor the elephant told him that he had circled his quarry, and even stronger was the rank odor of Dango the hyena; then, harsh and raucous, came the hideous laughing cry of the unclean beast followed by the plaintive help-cry of the elephant. Tantor was in trouble, and the ape-man pushed forward to learn the cause.

Almost as old as Tarzan was the friendship of Tarzan and Tantor. Perhaps he had never seen this elephant before; but still, to Tarzan, he would be Tantor—the name and the friendship belonged to all elephants.

As he came closer, he moved more cautiously—beastlike, always scenting a trap. For those of the jungle, eternal vigilance is the price of life. At last he came close enough so that by parting the bamboo he could see that for which he had been searching. The top of Tantor's back was just visible in an elephant pit. Snapping and growling at the edge of the pit were a pair of hyenas, circling above was Ska the vulture; and from these omens the ape-man knew that Tantor was near death.

Parting the bamboo, Tarzan stepped into the little clearing that the builders of the pit had made, an enlargement of a wide elephant trail. Instantly the hyenas transferred their attention from the elephant to the ape-man, and with bared fangs faced him. But as the man advanced, they retreated snarling. He paid no attention to them; for he knew that ordinarily Dango would not attack any but a helpless man.

As he approached the pit Tantor saw him and trumpeted a feeble warning. The elephant's skin hung loosely on its great frame, evidencing that it had been long without food or water. It had fallen into a pit that must have been dug and then abandoned, either because the tribe that dug it had moved away or because no elephant having fallen into it, they had ceased to visit it.

Tarzan spoke to Tantor in the strange language that he used with the beasts of the jungle. Perhaps Tantor did not understand the words—who may know?—but something, the tone perhaps, carried the idea that the ape-man wished to convey, that he was a friend; but Tantor needed something beside kind words, and so Tarzan set about cutting the bamboo that bore the tenderest shoots and carrying them to the imprisoned beast.

Tantor ate with avidity, the water content of the shoots furnishing at least some of the moisture that his great frame required even more than it required food; then Tarzan set to work with spear and knife and hands upon the seemingly Herculean task of excavating a ramp up which Tantor could walk to liberty. It was the work not of an hour but of many hours, and it was not completed until the following day; then, weak and staggering, the great pachyderm climbed slowly from the pit. He was a huge beast, one of the largest old bulls Tarzan had ever seen. One tusk, by some peculiar freak of nature, was much darker than the other; and this, with his great size, must have marked him among his fellows as a bull of distinction.

As he came out of the pit, his sensitive trunk passed over the body of the ape-man in what was almost a caress; then, as Tarzan took his way once more toward the north, Tantor turned and moved slowly along the elephant trail toward the east and the nearest water.

Days passed. Stanley Wood, waiting at Tarzan's estate, grew more and more frantic as no news came of the whereabouts of Tarzan. He plead with Muviro, headman of the Waziri, to furnish him with an escort and let him set out in search of Gonfala; and at last Muviro yielded to his importunities and sent him away with half a dozen warriors as an escort.

Wood took up the search at the point at which Tarzan had left him, where the clean picked bones of the lion Gonfala had killed lay bleaching in the sun. He knew only that those he sought had started north at that spot. It was a blind and seemingly hopeless search; but it meant action; and anything was preferable to sitting idly, his mind torn by fears and doubts as to the fate of Gonfala.

As they approached the Bantango country, the Waziri, knowing the nature and temper of the inhabitants, counseled making a detour to avoid them; and entirely by chance they selected an easterly route—the route that Spike and Troll had chosen for the same reason. Thus it happened that a week later they received definite proof that they were on the right trail. At a village of friendly blacks they were told that a safari of nine that included two white men and a white girl had stopped overnight with the tribe. The chief had furnished them with guides to the next friendly village to the north.

Wood talked to these men and learned that the chief of the village to which they had guided the safari had also furnished them guides for the next stage of their journey, and for the first time in weeks the young American found hope rekindled in his bosom. He had learned that up to this point Gonfala had been alive and well; and that, from what the villagers had seen, there was no indication that she was being ill-treated.

All the marvelous tracking skill of the Lord of the Jungle had been nullified by a heavy rain, and then chance had set in and sent him upon the wrong trail and Stanley Wood upon the right one.

Through such a trivial vagary of fate lives were jeopardized and men died.

17

Strangers

SPIKE AND TROLL were holding palaver with the chief of a northern tribe. They had come far, guided from village to village by friendly natives. Luck had been with them, but now this good fortune seemed to be at an end. They were trying to persuade the old chief to furnish them with guides to the next village.

"No more villages," he said. He did not like these white men. He held them in contempt because their safari was small and poor, too poor even to rob. They had nothing but two rifles—and the girl. He had been thinking about her. He was also thinking of a black sultan to the east to whom she might be sold, but he put this thought from him. He did not wish any trouble with the white men. Native soldiers had come to his village once under white officers and punished him for ill-treating the safari of some white hunters. They had come from a great distance just to do that, and the incident had given him vast respect for the power and the long arm of the white man.

"What is north?" asked Spike.

"Mountains," replied the chief.

"That," said Spike to Troll, "is like the country where my valley is. It is surrounded by mountains." He tried to explain to the chief the valley for which they were searching and the tribe that inhabited it.

A cunning look came into the eyes of the chief. He wished to be rid of these men, and he saw how he might do it. "I know the valley," he said. "Tomorrow I will give you guides."

"I guess maybe we ain't lucky," gloated Spike, as he and Troll came from their palaver with the chief and sat down beside Gonfala. The girl did not inquire why; but Spike

explained, nevertheless. "It won't be long now," he said, "before we're safe and sound in my valley."

"You won't be safe," said Gonfala. "Tarzan and Stanlee
Wood will come soon—very soon now."

"They won't never find us where we're goin'."

"The natives will guide them from village to village just
as they have guided you," she reminded him. "It will be
very easy to follow you."

"Yes," admitted Spike, "they can follow us up to where
these people will guide us."

"But there we will stop. They will find you there."

"We don't stop there," said Spike. "I guess I ain't nobody's
fool. The valley these people are takin' us to, ain't my valley;
but once I get in this here first valley, I can find the other. I
passed through it comin' out of my valley. It's about two
marches east of where we want to go. When we get to this
first valley, we won't need no guides the rest of the way;
so, when we leave this here first valley, we'll tell 'em we're
goin' to the coast, an' start off to the east; then we'll swing
around back way to the north of 'em an' go west to my valley.
And there won't nobody never find us."

"Tarzan and Stanlee Wood will find you."

"I wisht you'd shut up about this here Tarzan and Stanlee Wood. I'm sick of hearin' of 'em. It's gettin' on my
nerves."

Troll sat staring at Gonfala through half closed lids. He
had not spoken much all day, but he had looked much at
Gonfala. Always when she caught his glance he turned his
eyes away.

They had been able to sustain themselves this far by killing game and trading the meat to natives for other articles
of food, principally vegetables and corn. Tonight they
feasted royally and went to their beds early. Gonfala occupied a hut by herself; the two men had another near by.
They had had a hard day's trek, and tired muscles combined
with a heavy meal to induce early slumber. Gonfala and
Spike were asleep almost as soon as they had stretched themselves on their sleeping mats.

Not so Troll. He remained very much awake—thinking.
He listened to the heavy breathing of Spike that denoted
that he slept soundly. He listened to the sounds in the village.
Gradually they died out—the village slept. Troll thought how
easy it would be to kill Spike, but he was afraid of Spike.
Even when the man slept, he was afraid of him. That

made Troll hate him all the more, but it was not hate alone that made him wish to kill him. Troll had been day-dreaming —very pleasant dreams. Spike stood in the way of their fulfillment, yet he could not muster the courage to kill the sleeping man—not yet. "Later," he thought.

He crawled to the doorway of the hut and looked out. There was no sign of waking life in the village. The silence was almost oppressive; it extended out into the black void of night beyond the village. As Troll rose to his feet outside the hut he stumbled over a cooking pot; the noise, against the background of silence, seemed terrific. Cursing under his breath, the man stood motionless, listening.

Spike, disturbed but not fully awakened, moved in his sleep and turned over; the first dead slumber of early night was broken. Thereafter he would be more restless and more easily awakened. Troll did not hear him move, and after a moment of listening he tip-toed away. Stealthily he approached the hut in which Gonfala slept.

The girl, restless and wakeful, lay wide-eyed staring out into the lesser darkness framed by the doorway of her hut. She heard footsteps approaching. Would they pass, or were they coming here for her? Weeks of danger, weeks of suspicion, weeks of being constantly on guard had wrought upon her until she sensed menace in the most ordinary occurrences; so now she felt, intuitively, she believed, that someone was coming to her hut. And for what purpose, other than evil, should one come thus stealthily by night?

Raising herself upon her hands, she crouched, waiting. Every muscle tense, she scarcely breathed. Whatever it was, it was coming closer, closer. Suddenly a darker blotch loomed in the low opening that was the doorway. An animal or a man on all fours was creeping in!

"Who are you? What do you want?" It was a muffled scream of terror.

"Shut up! It's me. Don't make no noise. I want to talk to you."

She recognized the voice, but it did not allay her fears. The man crept closer to her. He was by her side now. She could hear his labored breathing.

"Go away," she said. "We can talk tomorrow."

"Listen!" he said. "You don't want to go to that there valley and spend the rest of your life with Spike an' a bunch o' niggers, do you? When he gets us there, he'll kill me an' have you all to himself. I knows him—he's that kind of a rat. Be good to me an' I'll take you away. Me an' you'll beat it with the diamond. We'll go to Europe, to Paris."

"I don't want to go anywhere with you. Go away! Get out of here, before I call Spike."

"One squawk out of you, an' I'll wring your neck. You're goin' to be good to me whether you want to or not." He reached out in the darkness and seized her, feeling for her throat.

Before he found it she had time to voice a single scream and cry out once, "Spike!" Then Troll closed choking fingers upon her throat and bore her down beneath his weight. She struggled and fought, striking him in the face, tearing at the fingers at her throat.

Awakened by the scream, Spike raised upon an elbow. "Troll!" he called. "Did you hear anything?" There was no response. "Troll!" He reached out to the mat where Troll should have been. He was not there. Instantly his suspicions were aroused and, because of his own evil mind, they centered unquestioningly upon the truth.

In a dozen strides he was at Gonfala's hut; and as he scrambled through the doorway, Troll met him with an oath and a snarl. Clinching, the two men rolled upon the floor, biting, gouging, striking, kicking; occasionally a lurid oath or a scream of pain punctuated their heavy breathing. Gonfala crouched at the back of the hut, terrified for fear that one of them would kill the other, removing the only factor of safety she possessed.

They rolled closer to her; and she edged to one side, out of their way. Her new position was nearer the doorway. It suggested the possibility of temporary escape, of which she was quick to take advantage. In the open, she commenced to worry again for fear that one of the men would be killed.

She saw that some of the natives, aroused by the commotion within her hut, had come from theirs. She ran to them, begging them to stop the fight. The chief was there, and he was very angry because he had been disturbed. He ordered several warriors to go and separate the men. They hesitated, but finally approached the hut. As they did so, the sounds of conflict ended; and a moment later Spike crawled into the open and staggered to his feet.

Gonfala feared that the worst had happened. Of the two men, she had feared Spike the more; for while both were equally brutal and devoid of decency, Troll was not as courageous as his fellow. Him she might have circumvented through his cowardice. At least, that she had thought until tonight; now she was not so sure. But she was sure that Spike was always the more dangerous. Her one thought now was to escape him, if only temporarily. Inflamed by his fight, secure in the knowledge that Troll was dead, what might he not do? To a far corner of the village she ran and hid herself between a hut and the palisade. Each moment she expected to hear Spike hunting for her, but he did not come. He did not even know that she had left her hut where he thought he had left her with the dead Troll, and he had gone to his own hut to nurse his wounds.

But Troll was not dead. In the morning Spike found him bloody and dazed squatting in the village street staring at the ground. Much to the former's disgust, Troll was not even badly injured. He looked up as Spike approached.

"Wot happened?" he asked.

Spike looked at him suspiciously for a moment; then his expression turned to puzzlement. "A bloomin' lorry ran over you," he said.

" 'A bloomin' lorry,' " Troll repeated. "I never even seen it."

Gonfala, looking around a corner of the hut behind which she had been hiding, saw the two men and breathed a sigh of relief. Troll was not dead; she was not to be left alone with Spike. She came toward them. Troll glanced up at her.

" 'Ose the dame?" he asked.

Gonfala and Spike looked at one another, and the latter tapped his forehead. "A bit balmy," he explained.

"She don't look balmy," said Troll. "She looks like my sister—my sister—sister." He continued to stare at her, dully.

"We better get some grub an' be on our way," interrupted Spike. He seemed nervous and ill at ease in the presence of Troll. It is one thing to kill a man, quite another to have done this thing to him.

It was a silent, preoccupied trio that moved off behind two guides in a northeasterly direction after the morning meal had been eaten. Spike walked ahead, Troll kept close to Gonfala. He was often looking at her, a puzzled expression in his eyes.

"Wot's your name?" he asked.

Gonfala had a sudden inspiration. Perhaps it was madness to hope that it might succeed, but her straits were desperate.

"Don't tell me you don't remember your sister's name," she exclaimed.

Troll stared at her, his face expressionless. "Wot *is* your name?" he asked. "Everything is sort o' blurrylike in my memory."

"Gonfala," she said. "You remember, don't you—your sister?"

"Gonfala; oh, yes—my sister."

"I'm glad you're here," she said; "for now you won't let anyone harm me, will you?"

"Harm you? They better not try it," he exclaimed belligerently.

The safari had halted, and they caught up with Spike who was talking with the two guides.

"The beggars won't go no farther," he explained. "We ain't made more'n five miles an' they quits us, quits us cold."

"Why?" asked Gonfala.

"They say the country ahead is taboo. They say they's white men up ahead that'll catch 'em an' make slaves out of 'em an' feed 'em to lions. They've went an' put the fear o' God into our boys, too."

"Let's turn back," suggested the girl. "What's the use anyway, Spike? If you get killed the Gonfal won't do you any good. If you turn around and take me back safely to my friends, I'll do my best to get them to give you the Gonfal and let you go. I give you my word that I will, and I know that Stanlee Wood will do anything that I ask."

Spike shook his head. "Nothin' doin'! I'm goin' where I'm goin', an' you're goin' with me." He bent close and stared boldly into her eyes. "If I had to give up one or t'other, I'd give up the Gonfal before I would you—but I'm not goin' to give up neither."

The girl shrugged. "I've given you your chance," she said. "You are a fool not to take it."

So they pushed on without guides farther and farther into the uncharted wilderness; and each new day Spike was confident that this day he would stumble upon the enchanted valley of his dreams, and each night he prophesied for the morrow.

Troll's mental condition remained unchanged. He thought that Gonfala was his sister, and he showed her what little consideration there was in his gross philosophy of life to accord any one. The protective instinct of the brutal male was stimulated in her behalf; and for this she was grate-

ful, not to Troll but to fate. Where he had been, where he
was going he appeared not to know or to care. He trudged
on day after day in dumb silence, asking no question, show-
ing no interest in any thing or anyone other than Gonfala.
He was obsessed by a belief that she was in danger, and
so he constantly carried one of the rifles the better to protect her.

For many days they had been in mountainous country
searching for the elusive valley, and at the end of a hard
trek they made camp on the shoulder of a mountain beside
a little spring of clear water. As night fell the western sky
was tinged with the golden red of a dying sunset. Long
after the natural phenomenon should have faded into the
blackness of the night the red glow persisted.

Gonfala sat gazing at it, dreamily fascinated. Spike
watched it, too, with growing excitement. The blacks watched
it with fear. Troll sat crosslegged, staring at the ground.

Spike sat down beside Gonfala. "You know wot that is,
girlie?" he asked. "You know it ain't no sunset, don't you?"

"It looks like a fire—a forest fire," she said.

"It's a fire all right. I ain't never been there, but I've
seen that light before. I figure it's from the inside of one
of them volcanoes, but I'll tell you wot it means to us—it
means we found our valley. When I was in that valley I
seen that light to the south at night. All we got to do now
is trek along a little west o' north, an' in maybe four or
five marches we orter be there; then, girlie, you an' me's
goin' to settle down to housekeepin'."

The girl made no reply. She was no longer afraid; for
she knew that Troll would kill Spike if she asked him to;
and now she had no reason to fear being alone with Troll,
other than the waning possibility that he might regain his
memory.

The new day found Spike almost jovial, so jubilant was
he at the prospect of soon finding his valley; but his jovi-
ality disappeared when he discovered that two of his six
men had deserted during the night. He was in a cold sweat
until he found that they had not taken the Gonfal with
them. After that, he determined, he would sleep with the
great stone at his side, taking no more chances. He could
do this now without arousing the suspicions of Troll, for
Troll had no suspicions. He paid no attention to the Gonfal nor ever mentioned it.

Toward noon a great valley opened before them, the

length of which ran in the direction Spike wished to travel; and so they dropped down into it to easy travelling after their long days in the mountains.

The valley was partially forested, the trees growing more profusely along the course of a river that wound down from the upper end of the valley, crossed it diagonally, and disappeared in a cleft in the hills to the west; but considerable areas were open and covered with lush grasses, while on the east side of the valley was a veritable forest of bamboo.

Spike, not knowing if the valley were inhabited; nor, if it were, the nature or temper of its inhabitants, chose to follow the wooded strip that bordered the river, taking advantage of the cover it afforded. Along the river he found a wide elephant trail, and here they were making excellent speed when one of the blacks stopped suddenly, listened intently, and pointed ahead.

"What's the matter?" demanded Spike.

"Men, Bwana—coming," replied the black.

"I don't hear nothin'," said Spike. "Do you?" he turned to Gonfala.

She nodded. "Yes, I hear voices."

"Then we better get off the trail and hide—at least until we see who they are. Here, all of you! Here's a little trail leadin' off here."

Spike herded the party off to the left of the main trail along a little winding path through rather heavy underbrush, but they had covered little more than a hundred yards when they came out onto the open plain. Here they stopped at the edge of the wood, waiting and listening. Presently the voices of men came plainly to their ears, constantly closer and closer, until suddenly it dawned on them all that the men they heard were approaching along the little trail through which they had sought to escape.

Spike looked for a place of concealment, but there was none. The thick underbrush was almost impenetrable behind them, while on the other hand the plain stretched away across the valley to the hills upon the west. As a last resort he turned north along the edge of the wood, urging the others to haste until all were running.

Glancing back, Gonfala saw the party that had alarmed them debouching onto the plain. First came a dozen huge Negroes, each pair of whom held a lion in leash. Following these were six white men strangely garbed. Even at a dis-

tance she could see that their trappings were gorgeous.
Behind them followed a score or more of other white men.
They were similarly dressed but in quieter raiment. They
carried spears as well as swords. One of the warriors carried something dangling at his side which, even at a distance, could not have been mistaken for other than it was
—a bloody human head.

"They're white men," Gonfala called to Spike. "Maybe
they'd be friendly."

"They don't look like it to me," he replied. "I ain't
takin' no chances after wot I been through gettin' you an'
the Gonfal this far."

"Anyone would be better than you," said the girl, and
stopped.

"Come on, you fool!" he cried; and, coming back, seized
her and sought to drag her with him.

"Troll!" she cried. "Help!"

Troll was ahead of them, but now he turned; and, seeing
Spike and the girl scuffling, he ran back. His face was
white and distorted with rage. "Le' go her," he bellowed.
"Le' go my sister!" Then he was upon Spike; and the two
went down, striking, kicking, and biting.

For an instant Gonfala hesitated, undecided. She looked
at the two beasts upon the ground, and then she turned
in the direction of the strange warriors. No one, she
reasoned, could be more of a menace to her than Spike;
but she soon saw that the decision had already been made
for her—the entire party was moving in their direction.
She stood and waited as they approached.

They had covered about half the distance when a warrior
in the lead halted and pointed up the valley. For an instant they hesitated; then they turned and started off across
the valley at a run, the lions tugging at their leashes and
dragging their keepers after them, the warriors keeping in
formation behind them.

The girl, wondering at their sudden flight, looked up the
valley in the direction in which the warrior had pointed.
The sight that met her eyes filled her with amazement. A
herd of perhaps a hundred elephants carrying warriors on
their backs was moving rapidly down upon them. On the
ground at her feet Spike and Troll still bit and gouged
and kicked.

STANLEY WOOD HAD no difficulty following the trail of
Gonfala's abductors to the point at which their guides
had deserted them, and from there the trained Waziri
trackers carried on until the trail was lost at the edge of a
wood where it had been obliterated by the shuffling pads of
a herd of elephants. Search as they would they could not
pick up the trail again. To Wood, the mystery was complete;
he was baffled, disheartened.

Wearily he pushed on up the valley. If only Tarzan were
here! He, of all men, could find an answer to the riddle.

"Look, Bwana!" cried one of the Waziri. "A city!"

Wood looked ahead, amazed; for there lay a city indeed.
No native village of thatched huts was this, but a walled city
of white, its domes of gold and azure rising above its gleaming wall.

"What city is it?" he asked.

The Waziri shook their heads and looked at one another.

"I do not know, Bwana," said one. "I have never been in
this country before."

"Perhaps the memsahib is there," suggested a warrior.

"Perhaps," agreed Wood. "If the people here are unfriendly they will take us all prisoners," he mused, half
aloud; "and then no one will know where we are, where
Gonfala probably is. We must not all be taken prisoners."

"No," agreed Waranji, "we must not all be taken prisoners."

"That is a big city," said Wood; "there must be many
warriors there. If they are unfriendly they could easily take
us all or kill us all. Is that not so?"

"We are Waziri," said Waranji, proudly.

"Yes, I know; and you're great fighters. I know that too;
but, holy mackerel! seven of us can't lick an army, even
though six of us are Waziri."

Waranji shook his head. "We could try," he said. "We
are not afraid."

Wood laid a hand on the ebony shoulder. "You're great guys, Waranji; and I know you'd walk right plumb into Hell for any friend of the Big Bwana, but I'm not goin' to sacrifice you. If those people are friendly, one man will be as safe as seven; if they're not, seven men won't be any better off than one; so I'm goin' to send you boys home. Tell Muviro we couldn't find Tarzan. Tell him we think we've found where the memsahib is. We don't know for sure, but it seems reasonable. If you meet Tarzan, or he's back home, he'll know what to do. If you don't see him, Muviro will have to use his own judgment. Now, go along; and good luck to you!"

Waranji shook his head. "We cannot leave the bwana alone," he said. "Let me send one warrior back with a message; the rest of us will stay with you."

"No, Waranji. You've heard my orders. Go on back."

Reluctantly they left him. He watched them until they passed out of sight in the wood; then he turned his steps toward the mysterious city in the distance.

*   *   *

Once again Tarzan of the Apes stood upon the edge of the high plateau at the western rim of the valley of Onthar and looked down upon Cathne, the city of gold. The white houses, the golden domes, the splendid Bridge of Gold that spanned the river before the city's gates gleamed and sparkled in the sunlight. The first time he had looked upon it the day had been dark and gloomy; and he had seen the city as a city of enemies; because then his companion had been Valthor of Athne, the City of Ivory, whose people were hereditary enemies of the Cathneans. But today, ablaze in the sunshine, the city offered him only friendship.

Nemone, the queen who would have killed him, was dead. Alextar, her brother, had been taken from the dungeon in which she had kept him and been made king by the men who were Tarzan's fast friends—Thudos, Phordos, Gemnon, and the others of the loyal band whom Tarzan knew would welcome him back to Cathne. Tomos, who had ruled under Nemone as her chief advisor, must have been either killed or imprisoned. He would be no longer a menace to the ape-man.

With pleasant anticipation, Tarzan clambered down the steep gully to the floor of the valley and swung off across the

Field of the Lions toward the city of gold. Field of the Lions! What memories it conjured! The trip to Xarator, the holy volcano, into whose fiery pit the kings and queens of Cathne had cast their enemies since time immemorial; the games in the arena; the wild lions which roved the valley of Onthar, giving it its other name—Field of the Lions. Such were the memories that the name inspired.

Boldly the ape-man crossed the valley until he stood before the Bridge of Gold and the two heroic golden lions that flanked its approach. The guard had been watching his progress across the valley for some time.

"It is Tarzan," one of them had said while the ape-man was still half a mile away; and when he stopped before the gates they all came and welcomed him.

The captain of the guard, a noble whom Tarzan knew well, escorted him to the palace. "Alextar will be glad to know that you have returned," he said. "Had it not been for you, he might not now be king—or alive. Wait here in this anteroom until I get word to Alextar."

The room and its furnishings were of a type common in the palaces of the king and nobles of Cathne. The low ceiling was supported by a series of engaged columns, carved doors inlaid in mosaics of gold and ivory gave to the corridor and an adjoining apartment, on the stone floor lay some lion skins and several heavy woolen rugs of simple design, mural decorations depicted battle scenes between the lion men of Cathne and the elephant men of Athne, and above the murals was a frieze of mounted heads—lions, leopards, one huge elephant's head, and several human heads—the heads of warriors, beautifully cured and wearing the ivory head ornaments of nobles of Athne—trophies of the chase and of war.

It was a long time before the captain of the guard returned; and when he did, his face was flushed and troubled and twenty warriors accompanied him. "I am sorry, Tarzan," he said; "but I have orders to arrest you."

The ape-man looked at the twenty spears surrounding him and shrugged. If he were either surprised or hurt, he did not show it. Once again he was the wild beast trapped by his hereditary enemy, man; and he would not give man the satisfaction of even being asked to explain. They took his weapons from him and led him to a room on the second floor of the palace directly above the guardroom. It was a better cell than that he had first occupied in Cathne when he had been incarcerated in a dark hole with Phobeg, the temple guard who had stepped on god's tail and thus merited death; for this room was large and well lighted by two barred windows.

When they had left him and bolted the door, Tarzan walked to one of the windows and looked down upon one of the palace courtyards for a moment; then he went to the bench that stood against one wall and lay down. Seemingly unconscious of danger, or perhaps contemptuous of it, he slept.

It was dark when he was awakened by the opening of the door of his cell. A man bearing a lighted torch stood in the doorway. The ape-man arose as the other entered, closing the door behind him.

"Tarzan!" he exclaimed; and, crossing the room, he placed a hand on the other's shoulder—the Cathnean gesture of greeting, of friendship, and loyalty.

"I am glad to see you, Gemnon," said the ape-man; "tell me, are Doria and her father and mother well? and your father, Phordos?"

"They are well, but none too happy. Things here are bad again, as you must have conjectured from the treatment accorded you."

"I knew that something must be wrong," admitted the ape-man; "but what it was, I didn't know—and don't."

"You soon shall," said Gemnon. "Ours is indeed an unhappy country."

"All countries are unhappy where there are men," observed the ape-man. "Men are the stupidest of beasts. But what has happened here? I thought that with the death of Nemone all your troubles were over."

"So did we, but we were wrong. Alextar has proved to be weak, cowardly, ungrateful. Almost immediately after ascending the throne he fell under the influence of Tomos and his clique; and you know what that means. We are all in disfavor. Tomos is virtually ruler of Cathne, but as yet he has not dared to destroy us. The warriors and the people hate him, and he knows it. If he goes too far they will rise, and that will be the end of Tomos.

"But tell me about yourself. What brings you again to Cathne?"

"It is a very long story," replied Tarzan. "In the end a young woman was stolen by two white men. She and the man whom she was to marry were under my protection. I am searching for her. Several days ago I came upon two blacks who had been with the safari of the men who abducted the girl. They described the country in which the safari had been when they deserted. It lay to the southeast of Xarator. That is why I am here. I am going into the country southeast of Xarator in an effort to pick up the trail."

"I think you will not have to search long," said Gemnon. "I believe that I know where your young woman is—not that it will do you or her much good now that you are a prisoner of Tomos. As you must know, he has no love for you."

"What makes you think that you know where she is?" asked the ape-man.

"Alextar sends me often to the valley of Thenar to raid the Athneans. It is, of course, the work of Tomos, who hopes that I shall be killed. Very recently I was there. The raid was not very successful, as we were too few. Tomos always sends too few, and they are always nobles he fears and would be rid of. We took only one head. On the way out we saw a small party of people who were not Athneans. There were four or five slaves, two white men, and a white woman. The white men were fighting. The woman ran toward us, which made us think she wished to escape the two men she was with. We were going to meet her and take the entire party prisoners when we saw a large body of Athneans coming down the valley on their war elephants. We were too few to engage them; so we ran for the Pass of the Warriors and escaped. I naturally assume that the Athneans captured the young woman and those with her and that she is now in the City of Ivory; but, as I said before, the knowledge won't help you much now—Tomos has you."

"And what do you think he will do with me? Has he another Phobeg?"

Gemnon laughed. "I shall never forget how you tossed 'the strongest man in Cathne' about and finally threw him bodily into the laps of the audience. Tomos lost his last obol on that fight—another good reason why he has no love for you. No, I don't think he'll pit you against a man this time —probably a lion. It may even be poison or a dagger—they are surer. But what I am here for tonight is to try to save you. The only trouble is, I have no plan. A friend of mine is captain of the guard tonight. That is how I was able to reach you, but if I were to leave your door unbarred and you escaped his life would not be worth an obol. Perhaps you can think of a plan."

Tarzan shook his head. "I shall have to know Tomos' plan first. Right now the only plan I have is for you to leave before you get caught in here."

"Isn't there anything that I can do, after all that you did for me? There must be something."

"You might leave your dagger with me. It might come in handy. I can hide it under my loin cloth."

They talked for a short time then before Gemnon left, and within a few minutes thereafter Tarzan was asleep. He did not pace his cell, fretting and worrying. His was more the temperament of the wild animal than the man.

19

Retribution

THE SUN IS an impartial old devil. He shines with equal brilliance upon the just and the banker, upon the day of a man's wedding, or upon the day of his death. The great African sun, which, after all, is the same sun that shines on Medicine Hat, shone brilliantly on this new day upon which Tarzan was to die. He was to die because Alextar had decreed it—the suggestion had been Tomos'. The sun even shone upon Tomos; but then the sun is ninety-three million miles away, and that is a long way to see what one is shining on.

They came about eleven o'clock in the morning and took Tarzan from his cell. They did not even bother to bring him food or water. What need has a man who is about to die for food or drink? He was very thirsty; and perhaps, if he had asked, the guards would have given him water; for after all they were common soldiers and not a king's favorites, and therefore more inclined to be generous and humane. The ape-man, however, asked for nothing. It was not because he was consciously too proud; his pride was something instinctive—it inhibited even a suggestion that he might ask a favor of an enemy.

When he was brought out of the palace grounds onto the avenue, the sight that met his eyes apprised him of the fate

that had been decreed for him. There was the procession of
nobles and warriors, the lion drawn chariot of the king, and
a single great lion held in leash by eight stalwart blacks.
Tarzan had seen all this before, that time that he had been
the quarry in the Queen's Hunt. Today he was to be the
quarry in the King's Hunt, but today he could expect no
such miracle as had saved him from the mighty jaws of
Belthar upon that other occasion.

The same crowds of citizens lined the sides of the avenue;
and when the procession moved toward the Bridge of Gold
and out toward the Field of the Lions, the crowds moved
with it. It was a good natured crowd, such as one might see
milling toward the gates at a Cub-Giant game or the Army-
Navy "classic." It was no more bloody minded than those
who throng to see Man Mountain Dean and the Honorable
Mr. Detton or a professional ice hockey game at Madison
Square Garden, and who would be so unkind as to suggest
that these are looking for trouble and blood? Perish the
thought!

They had taken no chances when they brought Tarzan
from his cell. Twenty spearmen betokened the respect in
which they held him. Now they chained him to Alextar's
chariot, and the triumph was under way.

Out upon the Field of the Lions the procession halted, and
the long gantlet of warriors was formed down which the
quarry was to be pursued by the lion. The ape-man was un-
chained, the wagers were being laid as to the point in the
gantlet at which the lion would overtake and drag down its
victim, and the hunting lion was being brought up to scent
the quarry. Tomos was gloating. Alextar appeared nervous—
he was afraid of lions. He would never have gone on a hunt
of his own volition. Tarzan watched him. He saw a young
man in his late twenties with nervous, roving eyes, a weak
chin, and a cruel mouth. There was nothing about him to remind one that he was the brother of the gorgeous Nemone.
He looked at Tarzan, but his eyes fell before the steady gaze
of the ape-man.

"Hurry!" he snapped querulously. "We are bored."

They did hurry, and in their haste it happened. In a fraction of a second the comparatively peaceful scene was trans-
formed to one of panic and chaos.

By accident one of the blacks that held the hunting lion in
leash slipped the beast's collar, and with an angry roar the
trained killer struck down those nearest him and charged the

line of spearmen standing between him and the crowd of spectators. He was met by a dozen spears while the unarmed citizenry fled in panic, trampling the weaker beneath their feet.

The nobles screamed commands. Alextar stood in his chariot, his knees shaking, and begged some one to save him. "A hundred thousand drachmas to the man who kills the beast!" he cried. "More! Anything he may ask shall be granted!"

No one seemed to pay any attention to him. All who could were looking after their own safety. As a matter of fact, he was in no danger at the time; for the lion was engaged elsewhere.

The jabbing spears further enraged the maddened carnivore, yet for some reason he did not follow up his attack upon the warriors; instead, he wheeled suddenly and then charged straight for the chariot of the king. Now, indeed, did Alextar have reason to be terrified. He would have run, but his knees gave beneath him so that he sat down upon the seat of his golden vehicle. He looked about helplessly. He was practically alone. Some of his noble guard had run to join in the attack upon the lion. Tomos had fled in the opposite direction. Only the quarry remained.

Alextar saw the man whip a dagger from his loin cloth and crouch in the path of the charging lion. He heard savage growls roll from human lips. The lion was upon him. Alextar screamed; but, fascinated, his terror-filled eyes clung to the savage scene before him. He saw the lion rise to make the kill, and then what happened happened so quickly that he could scarcely follow it.

Tarzan stooped and dodged beneath the great forepaws outstretched to seize him; then he closed in and swung to the lion's back, one great arm encircling the shaggy throat. Mingled with the beast's horrid growls were the growls of the man-beast upon his back. Alextar went cold with terror. He tried to run, but he could not. Whether he would or not, he must sit and watch that awful spectacle—he must watch the lion kill the man and then leap upon him. Yet the thing that terrified him most was the growls of the man.

They were rolling upon the ground now in the dust of the Field of the Lions, sometimes the man on top, sometimes the lion; and now and again the dagger of Gemnon flashed in the sunlight, flashed as the blade drove into the side of the frantic beast. The two were ringed now by eager spearmen ready to thrust a point into the heart of the lion, but no chance presented that did not endanger the life of the man. But at last the end came. With a final supreme effort to escape the clutches of the ape-man, the lion collapsed upon the ground. The duel was over.

Tarzan leaped to his feet. For a moment he surveyed the surrounding warriors with the blazing eyes of a beast of prey at bay upon its kill; then he placed a foot upon the carcass of the hunting lion, raised his face to the heavens, and from his great chest rose the challenge of the bull ape.

The warriors shrank away as that weird and hideous cry shattered the brief new silence of the Field of the Lions. Alextar trembled anew. He had feared the lion, but he feared the man more. Had he not had him brought here to be killed by the very lion he had himself dispatched? And he was only a beast. His growls and his terrible cry proved that. What mercy could he expect from a beast? The man would kill him!

"Take him away!" he ordered feebly. "Take him away!"

"What shall we do with him?" asked a noble.

"Kill him! Kill him! Take him away!" Alextar was almost screaming now.

"But he saved your life," the noble reminded.

"Huh? What? Oh, well; take him back to his cell. Later I shall know what to do with him. Can't you see I am tired and don't wish to be bothered?" he demanded querulously.

The noble hung his head in shame as he ordered the guard to escort Tarzan back to his cell; and he walked at Tarzan's side, where a noble does not walk except with one of his own caste.

"What you did," he remarked on the way back to the city, "deserves better reward than this."

"I seem to recall hearing him offer anything he wished to the man who killed the lion," said the ape-man. "That and a hundred thousand drachmas."

"Yes, I heard him."

"He seems to have a short memory."

"What would you have asked him."

"Nothing."

The noble looked at him in surprise. "You would ask for nothing?"

"Nothing."

"Is there nothing that you want?"

"Yes; but I wouldn't ask anything of an enemy."

"I am not your enemy."

Tarzan looked at the man, and a shadow of a smile lit his grim visage. "I have had no water since yesterday, nor any food."

"Well," remarked the noble, laughing, "you'll have them both—and without asking for them."

On their return to the city Tarzan was placed in another cell; this one was on the second floor of a wing of the palace that overlooked the avenue. It was not long before the door was unbolted and a warrior entered with food and water. As he placed them on the end of the bench he looked at Tarzan admiringly.

"I was there and saw you kill the king's hunting lion," he said. "It was such a thing as one may see only once in a lifetime. I saw you fight with Phobeg before Nemone, the queen. That, too, was something to have seen. You spared Phobeg's life when you might have killed him, when all were screaming for the kill. After that he would have died for you."

"Yes, I know," replied the ape-man. "Is Phobeg still alive?"

"Oh, very much; and he is still a temple guard."

"If you see him, tell him that I wish him well."

"That I will," promised the warrior. "I shall see him soon. Now I must be going." He came close to Tarzan then, and spoke in a whisper. "Drink no wine, and whoever comes keep your back to the wall and be prepared to fight." Then he was gone.

" 'Drink no wine,' " mused Tarzan. Wine, he knew, was the medium in which poison was customarily administered in Cathne; and if he kept his back to the wall no one could stab him from behind. Good advice! The advice of a friend who might have overheard something that prompted it. Tarzan knew that he had many friends among the warriors of the City of Gold.

He walked to one of the windows and looked out upon the avenue. He saw a lion striding majestically toward the center of the city, paying no attention to the pedestrians or being noticed by them. It was one of the many tame lions that roam the streets of Cathne by day. Sometimes they fed upon the corpses thrown out to them, but rarely did they attack a living man.

He saw a small gathering of people upon the opposite side of the avenue. They were talking together earnestly, often glancing toward the palace. Pedestrians stopped to listen and

joined the crowd. A warrior came from the palace and
stopped and spoke to them; then they looked up at the window where Tarzan stood. The warrior was he who had
brought food to Tarzan.

When the crowd recognized the ape-man it commenced to
cheer. People were coming from both directions, some of
them running. There were many warriors among them. The
crowd and the tumult grew. When darkness came torches
were brought. A detachment of warriors came from the
palace. It was commanded by a noble who sought to disperse
the gathering.

Some one yelled, "Free Tarzan!" and the whole crowd
took it up, like a chant. A huge man came, bearing a torch.
In its light Tarzan recognized the man as Phobeg, the temple
guard. He waved his torch at Tarzan, and cried, "Shame,
Alextar! Shame!" and the crowd took that cry up and chanted
it in unison.

The noble and the guardsmen sought to quiet and disperse
them, and then a fight ensued in which heads were broken
and men were slashed with swords and run through with
spears. By this time the mob had grown until it filled the
avenue. Its temper was nasty, and when once blood was
spilled it went berserk. Before it the palace guard was helpless, and those who survived were glad to retreat to the
safety of the palace.

Now some one shouted, "Down with Tomos! Death to
Tomos!" and the hoarse voice of the mob seized upon this
new slogan. It seemed to stir the men to new action, for
now in a body they moved down upon the palace gates.

As they hammered and shoved upon the sturdy portals, a
man at the outer fringe of the mob shouted, "The hunting
lions! Alextar has turned his hunting lions upon us! Death
to Alextar!"

Tarzan looked down the avenue toward the royal stables;
and there, indeed, came fully fifty lions, held in leash by
their keepers. Excited by the vast crowd, irritated by the
noise, they tugged at their chains, while the night trembled
to their thunderous roars; but the crowd, aroused now to
demonical madness, was undaunted. Yet what could it do
against this show of savage force? It started to fall back,
slowly, cursing and growling, shouting defiance, calling for
Tarzan's release.

Involuntarily, a low growl came from the chest of the ape-
man, a growl of protest that he was helpless to aid those

who would befriend him. He tested the bars in the window at which he stood. To his strength and his weight they bent inward a little; then he threw all that he had of both upon a single bar. It bent inward and pulled from its sockets in the frame, the soft iron giving to his giant strength. That was enough! One by one in quick succession the remaining bars were dragged out and thrown upon the floor.

Tarzan leaned from the window and looked down. Below him was an enclosed courtyard. It was empty. A wall screened it from the avenue beyond. He glanced into the avenue and saw that the crowd was still falling back, the lions advancing. So intent were all upon the lions that no one saw the ape-man slip through the window and drop into the courtyard. Opposite him was a postern gate, barred upon the inside. Through it he stepped into the avenue just in front of the retreating crowd, between it and the lions.

A dozen saw and recognized him at once; and a great shout went up, a shout of defiance with a new note in it—a note of renewed confidence and elation.

Tarzan seized a torch from one of the citizens. "Bring your torches!" he commanded. "Torches and spears in the front line!" Then he advanced to meet the lions, and the men with the torches and the spears rushed forward to the front line. All that they had needed was a leader.

All wild animals fear fire. The king of beasts is no exception. The hunting lions of Alextar, king of Cathne, shrank back when blazing torches were pushed into their faces. Their keepers, shouting encouragement, cursing, were helpless. One of the lions, his mane ablaze, turned suddenly to one side, fouling another lion, causing him to wheel in terror and confusion and bolt back toward the stables. In doing so, they crossed the leashes of other lions, became entangled in them, and tore them from the hands of the keepers. The freed lions hesitated only long enough to maul the keepers that chanced to be in their way, and then they too galloped back along the avenue toward the stables.

Emboldened by this success, the torch bearers fell upon the remaining lions, beating them with fire until the beasts were mad with terror; and Tarzan, in the forefront, urged them on. Pandemonium reigned. The hoarse shouts of the mob mingled with the roars of the carnivores and the screams of stricken men. By now the lions were frantic with terror. With leashes entangled, keepers down, manes afire, they could stand no more. Those that had not already broken and run, did so now. The mob was for pursuing, but Tarzan stopped them. With raised hand he quieted them after a moment.

"Let the lions go," he counselled. "There is bigger game. I am going after Alextar and Tomos."

"And I am going with you," a big voice boomed beside him.

Tarzan turned and looked at the speaker. It was Phobeg, the temple guard.

"Good!" said the ape-man.

"We are going after Alextar and Tomos!" cried Phobeg.

A roar of approval rose from the crowd. "The gates!" some cried. "To the gates! To the gates!"

"There is an easier way," said Tarzan. "Come!"

They followed him to the postern gate that he knew was unbarred and through it into the palace grounds. Here, Tarzan knew his way well; for he had been here both as a prisoner and a guest of Nemone, the queen.

Alextar and a few of his nobles were dining. The king was frightened; for not only could he hear the shouts of the mob, but he was kept constantly informed of all that was occurring outside the palace, and knew that the hunting lions he had been certain would disperse the rioters had been turned back and were in flight. He had sent every available fighting man in the palace to the gates when the shouts of the crowd indicated that it was about to storm them, and though assured by his nobles that the mob could not hope to overcome his warriors, even if the gates failed to hold against them, he was still terrified.

"It is your fault, Tomos," he whined. "You said to lock the wild-man up, and now look what has happened! The people want to dethrone me. They may even kill me. What shall I do? What can I do?"

Tomos was in no better state of nerves than the king, for he had heard the people calling for his death. He cast about for some plan that might save him, and presently he thought of one.

"Send for the wild-man," he said, "and set him free. Give him money and honors. Send word at once to the gates that you have done this."

"Yes, yes," assented Alextar; and, turning to one of his nobles, "Go at once and fetch the wild-man; and you, go to the gates and tell the people what has been done."

"Later," said Tomos, "we can offer him a cup of wine."

The first noble crossed the room hurriedly and threw open
a door leading into a corridor from which he could ascend to
the second floor where Tarzan had been imprisoned, but he
did not cross the threshold. In dismay he stepped back into
the room.

"Here is Tarzan now!" he cried.

Alextar and Tomos and the others sprang to their feet as
the opened door let in the murmurings of the crowd that followed the ape-man; then Tarzan stepped into the room, and
crowding behind him came Phobeg and the others.

Alextar arose to flee, as did Tomos also; but with a bound
Tarzan crossed the room and seized them. No noble drew a
sword in defense of the king; like rats fleeing a sinking ship
they were ready to desert Alextar. So great was his terror, the
man was in a state of collapse. He went to his knees and
begged for his life.

"You do not understand," he cried. "I had just given orders to release you. I was going to give you money—I will
give you money—I will make you a lion-man—I will give
you a palace, slaves, everything."

"You should have thought of all this on the Field of
the Lions today, now it is too late. Not that I would have
what you offer," the ape-man added, "but it might have
saved your life temporarily and your throne, too, because
then your people would not have grown so angry and dis-
gusted."

"What are you going to do to me?" demanded the king.

"I am going to do nothing to you," replied Tarzan. "What
your people do to you is none of my concern, but if they
don't make Thudos king they are fools."

Now Thudos was the first of the nobles, as Tarzan knew;
and in his veins flowed better blood from an older line than
the king of Cathne could claim. He was a famous old warrior, loved and respected by the people; and when the crowd
in the room heard Tarzan they shouted for Thudos; and those
in the corridor carried it back out into the avenue, and the
word spread through the city.

Alextar heard, and his face went ashen white. He must
have gone quite mad, as his sister before him. He came slowly
to his feet and faced Tomos. "You have done this to me," he
said. "For years you kept me in prison. You ruined my sister's life—you and M'duze. You have ruined my life, and now
you have lost me my throne. But you shall never ruin another life," and with that he drew his sword so quickly that

none could stay him and brought the blade down with all his strength on Tomos's skull, cleaving it to the nose.

As the body slumped to his feet he broke into maniacal laughter, while those in the room stood stunned and silent; then, as quickly as he had done before, he placed the point of his sword at his heart and threw himself forward upon it.

Thus died Alextar, the last of the mad rulers of Cathne.

20

Athne

THE MAIN GATE of Athne, the City of Ivory, looks toward the south; for in that direction runs the trail that leads to Cathne, the City of Gold, the stronghold of the hereditary enemies of the Athneans. In that direction ride the warriors and the nobles of Athne seeking women and heads and other loot; from that direction come the raiding parties from Cathne, also seeking women and heads and other loot; so the main gate of Athne is strong and well guarded. It is surmounted by two squat towers in which warriors watch by day and by night.

Before the gate is a great level plain where the elephants are trained and the warriors of Athne drill upon their mighty mounts. It is dusty, and nothing grows there but a sturdy Cynodon; and even that survives the trampling pads of the pachyderms only in scattered patches. The fields of the Athneans lie north of the city, and there the slaves labor; so one might approach the city from the south without glimpsing a sign of human life.

It was mid afternoon. The hot sun beat down upon the watchtowers. The warriors, languid with the heat, gamed at dice—those who were not on watch. Presently one of the latter spoke.

"A man comes from the south," he said.

"How many?" asked one of the players.

"I said *a* man. I see but one."

"Then we do not have to give the alarm. But who could come alone to Athne? Is it a man from Cathne?"

"There have been deserters come to us before. Perhaps this is one."

"He is yet too far off to see plainly," said the warrior who had discovered the stranger, "but he does not look like a Cathnean. His dress seems strange to me."

He went to the inner side of the tower then and, leaning over the edge of the parapet, called the captain of the guard. An officer came from the interior of the tower and looked up.

"What is it?" he asked.

"Some one is coming from the south," explained the warrior.

The officer nodded and mounted the ladder leading to the tower's top. The warriors stopped their game then, and all went to the southern parapet to have a look at the stranger. He was nearer now, and they could see that he wore garments strange to them.

"He is no Cathnean," said the officer, "but he is either a fool or a brave man to come thus alone to Athne."

As Stanley Wood neared the gates of Athne he saw the warriors in the watchtowers observing him, and when he came quite close they challenged him but in a language he could not understand.

"Friend," he said, and raised his hand in the peace sign.

Presently the gate opened and an officer and several warriors came out. They tried to talk with him, and when they found that neither could understand the other they formed about him and escorted him through the gateway.

He found himself at the end of an avenue lined with low buildings occupied by shops. The warriors who had brought him into the city were white as were most of the people on the avenue, although there were some Negroes. Everyone appeared much interested in him; and he was soon surrounded by a large crowd, all talking at once, pointing, feeling of his clothes and weapons. The latter were soon taken from him by his guard, the officer shouted some commands, and the warriors pushed the people out of the way and started up the avenue with Wood.

He felt very uncomfortable and helpless because of his inability to converse with those about him. There were so many questions he wished to ask. Gonfala might be in this city and yet he might never know it if he could not ask anyone about her who could understand him. He determined that the first thing he must do was to learn the language of these people. He wondered if they would be friendly. The fact that they were white gave him hope.

Who could they be? Their garb, so different from anything modern, gave him no clew. They might have stepped from the pages of ancient history, so archaic were their weapons and their raiment; but he could not place them exactly. Where did they originate, these strange, rather handsome men and women? How and when did they reach this unknown valley in Africa? Could they be descendants of some Atlantean colonists stranded here after the submergence of their continent?

Vain speculations. No matter who they were, they were here; and he was either their prisoner or their guest—the former, he was inclined to believe. One did not usually surround a guest by armed warriors.

As they proceeded along the avenue Wood observed more closely the raiment of his escort and of the people whom they passed. The officer in charge was a handsome, black haired fellow who strode along apparently oblivious of those they passed, yet there was nothing offensive about his manner. If there were social castes here, Wood hazarded a safe guess that this man was of the nobility. The headband that confined his hair supported a carved ivory ornament at the center of his forehead, an ornament that was shaped like a concave, curved trowel, the point of which projected above the top of the man's head and curved forward. He wore wristlets and anklets of long, flat strips of ivory laid close together and fastened around his limbs by leather thongs that were laced through holes piercing the strips near their tops and bottoms. Sandals of elephant hide encasing his feet were supported by leather thongs fastened to the bottoms of his anklets. On each arm, below the shoulder, was an ivory disc upon which was a carved device; about his neck was a band of smaller ivory discs elaborately carved, and from the lowest of these a strap ran down to a leather habergeon, which was also supported by shoulder straps. Depending from each side of his headband was another ivory disc of large size, above which was a smaller disc, the former covering his ears. Heavy, curved, wedge-shaped pieces of ivory were held, one upon each shoulder, by the same straps that supported his habergeon. He was armed with a dagger and a short sword.

The warriors who accompanied him were similarly garbed, but less elaborately in the matter of carved ivory; and their habergeons and sandals were of coarser leather more roughly fabricated. Upon the back of each was a small shield. The common warriors carried short, heavy spears as well as swords and daggers. From their arms, Wood concluded that what he had first supposed to be ivory ornaments were definitely protective armour.

The American was conducted to a large, walled enclosure in the center of the city. Here stood the most elaborate buildings he had seen. There was a large central structure and many smaller buildings, the whole set in a parklike garden of considerable beauty which covered an area of several acres.

Just inside the gate was a small building before which lolled a score of warriors. Within, an officer sat at a table; and to him Wood was taken, and here the officer who had brought him evidently made his report. What passed between them Wood could not, of course, understand; but when the first officer left he realized that he had been delivered into the custody of the other.

While similarly garbed, this second officer did not give the impression of birth or breeding that had been so noticeable in the first. He was a burly, uncouth appearing fellow with much less in his appearance to recommend him than many of the common warriors Wood had seen. When left alone with his prisoner he commenced to shout questions at him; and when he found that Wood could not understand him, or he Wood, he pounded on the table angrily.

Finally he summoned warriors to whom he issued instructions, and once again Wood was taken under escort. This time he was led to an enclosure toward the rear of the grounds not far from a quite large one-storied building with the interior of which he was destined to become well acquainted.

He was thrust into an enclosure along the north side of which was an open shed in which were some fifty men. A high fence or stockade formed the remaining three sides of the quadrangle, the outside of which was patrolled by warriors; and Wood realized now that he was definitely a prisoner and far from being either an important or favored one, as the other inmates of the stockade were for the most part filthy, unkempt fellows, both white and black.

As Wood approached the enclosure every eye was upon him; and he knew that they were commenting upon him; and, from the tone of an occasional laugh, judged that he

was the butt of many a rough quip. He sensed antagonism
and felt more alone than he would have in solitary con-
finement; and then he heard his name called by some one
in the midst of the assemblage in the shed.

Immediately two men separated themselves from the
others and came to meet him. They were Spike and Troll.
A wave of anger swept through the American as the implica-
tion of their presence here pointed them out as the abductors
of Gonfala.

His face must have betrayed his emotions as he advanced
toward them; for Spike raised his hand in a gesture of warning.

"Hold on, now," he cried. "Gettin' hostile ain't goin' to get
us no place. We're in a Hell of a fix here, an' gettin' hostile
ain't goin' to help matters none. It'll be better for all of us
if we work together."

"Where's Gonfala?" demanded Wood. "What have you
done with her?"

"They took her away from us the day they captured us,"
said Troll. "We ain't seen her since."

"We understand she's in the palace," said Spike. "They
say the big guy here has fell for her. He's got her an' the
Gonfal, the dirty bounder."

"What did you steal her for?" Wood demanded. "If either
one of you harmed her——"

"Harm her!" exclaimed Troll. "You don't think I'd never
let nobody harm my sister, do you?"

Spike winked behind Troll's back and tapped his forehead.
"They ain't nobody harmed her," he assured Wood, "unless it was done after they took her away from us. And for
why did we bring 'er along with us? We had to 'ave 'er. We
couldn't work the Gonfal without 'er."

"That damned stone!" muttered Wood.

"I think they's a curse on it myself," agreed Spike. "It
ain't never brought nobody nothin' but bad luck. Look at me
and Troll. Wot we got for our pains? We lost the emerald;
now we lost the Gonfal, an' all we do is shovel dirt out o'
the elephant barns all day an' wait to see w'ich way they's
goin' to croak us."

As they talked they were surrounded by other prisoners
prompted by curiosity to inspect the latest recruit. They
questioned Wood; but, as he could not understand them nor
they he, they directed their questions upon Spike who replied in a strange jargon of African dialects, signs, and the

few words of the Athnean language he had picked up. It
was a wholly remarkable means of conveying thoughts, but
it apparently served its purpose admirably.

As Wood stood there, the object of their interest, he was
rapidly considering the attitude he should assume toward
Spike and Troll. The men were scoundrels of the first water,
and could command only his bitterest enmity. For the
wrong that they had done Gonfala it seemed to Wood that
they deserved death; yet they were the only men here with
whom he could talk, the only ones with whom he had any
interests in common. His judgment told him that Spike had
been right when he said that they should work together. For
the time being, then, he would put aside his just anger
against them and throw his lot in with them in the hope that
in some way they might be of service to Gonfala.

"They wants to know who you are an' where you comes
from," said Spike; "an' I told 'em you come from a country
a thousand times bigger than Athne an' that you was a juke
or somethin', like their officers. They's one of 'em in here
with us. See that big bloke over there standin' with his
arms folded?" He pointed to a tall, fine looking fellow who
had not come forward with the others. "He's a toff, or I
never seen one. He don't never have no truck with these
scrubs; but he took a shine to Troll and me, an' is learn-
in' us his language."

"I'd like to meet him," said Wood, for his first interest
now was to learn the language of these people into whose
hands fate had thrown him.

"Awright, come on over. He ain't a bad bloke. He's wot
they calls an elephant man. That's somethin' like bein' a juke
at home. They had some sort of a revolution here a few
months ago, an' killed off a lot of these here elephant men,
wot didn't escape or join the revolutionists. But this bloke
wasn't killed. They say it was because he was a good guy an'
everybody liked him, even the revolutionists. He wouldn't
join 'em; so they stuck him in here to do chamber work for
the elephants. These here revolutionists is like the gangsters in
your country. Anyway, they's a bad lot, always makin' trouble for decent people an' stealin' wot they ain't got brains
enough to make for themselves. Well, here we are. Valthor,
shake hands with my old friend Stanley Wood."

Valthor looked puzzled, but he took Wood's outstretched
hand.

"Cripes!" exclaimed Spike. "I'm always forgettin' you don't

know no English." Then he couched the introduction in the bastard language he had picked up.

Valthor smiled and acknowledged the introduction.

"He says he's glad to meetcha," translated Spike.

"Tell him it's fifty-fifty," said the American, "and ask him if he'll help me learn his language."

When Spike had translated this speech Valthor smiled and nodded, and there immediately began an association that not only developed into a genuine friendship during the ensuing weeks but gave Wood a sufficient knowledge of the Athnean language to permit free intercourse with all with whom he came in contact.

During this time he worked with the other slaves in the great elephant stables of Phoros, the dictator who had usurped the crown of Athne after the revolution. The food was poor and insufficient, the work arduous, and the treatment he received harsh; for the officers who were put in charge of the slaves had been men of the lowest class prior to the revolution and found a vent for many an inhibition when they were given a little authority.

During all this time he heard nothing of the fate of Gonfala, for naturally little news of the palace reached the slaves in the stables. Whether she lived or not, he could not know; and this state of constant uncertainty and anxiety told even more heavily upon him than did the hardships he was forced to undergo.

"If she is beautiful," Valthor had told him, "I think you need have no fear for her life. We do not take the lives of beautiful women—even the Erythra would not do that."

"Who are the Erythra?" asked Wood.

"The men who overthrew the government and placed Phoros on the throne of Zygo, king of Athne."

"She is very beautiful," said Wood. "I wish to God she were not so beautiful."

"Perhaps it will do her no harm. If I know Menofra, and I think I do, your friend will be safe from the attentions of Phoros at least; and if I know Phoros, he will not let any one else have her if she is very beautiful. He will always wait and hope—hope that something will happen to Menofra."

"And who might Menofra be?"

"Above all else she is a she-devil for jealousy, and she is the wife of Phoros."

This was slight comfort, but it was the best that was vouchsafed Wood. He could only wait and hope. There was little upon which to base a plan of action. Valthor had told him that there might be a counterrevolution to unseat Phoros and return Zygo to the throne; but in the slaves' compound there was little information upon which to base even a conjecture as to when, if ever, this might take place; as there was no means of communication between those confined there and Zygo's sympathizers in the city, while Zygo and most of his loyal nobles and retainers were hiding in the mountains to which they had escaped when revolution overwhelmed the city.

Among other duties that had fallen to the lot of Wood was the exercising of the elephant that was his particular charge. He had been chosen for this work, along with Valthor, Spike, and Troll, because of his greater intelligence than the ordinary run of slaves in the compound. He had learned quickly, and rode almost daily on the plain south of the city under a heavy escort of warriors.

They had returned to the stables one day from the field after the exercise period, which was always early in the morning, and were brushing and washing their huge mounts, when they were ordered to remount and ride out.

On the way to the plain they learned from the accompanying warriors that they were being sent out to capture a wild elephant that had been damaging the fields.

"They say he's a big brute and ugly," offered one of the warriors, "and if he's as bad as all that we won't all of us come back."

"Under Zygo, the nobles rode out to capture wild elephants, not slaves," said Valthor.

The warrior rode his mount closer to the Athnean noble. "They are all too drunk to ride," he said, lowering his voice. "If they were just a little drunk they might ride. If they were not drunk at all they would not have the nerve. We warriors are sick of them. Most of us would like to ride again under real elephant men like your nobleness."

"Perhaps you will," said Valthor, "—if you have the nerve."

"Hi-yah!" shouted a warrior ahead of them.

"They've sighted him," Valthor explained to Wood, who was riding at his side.

Presently they too saw the quarry emerging from a bamboo forest at the edge of the plain.

Valthor whistled. "He's a big brute, and if he's as ugly as they say we should have some real sport. But it's murder to send inexperienced slaves against him. Watch out for yourself, Wood. Just keep out of his way, no matter what the guards tell you to do. Make believe you can't control your elephant. Look at him! He's coming right for us. He's a bad one all right—not a bit afraid of us either, by Dyaus."

"I never saw a larger one," said Wood.

"Nor I," admitted Valthor, "though I've seen many an elephant in my time. He's got a blemish though—look at that tusk. It's much darker than the other. If it weren't for that he'd make a king's elephant all right."

"What are we supposed to do?" asked Wood. "I don't see how we could ever capture that fellow if he didn't want us to."

"They'll have some females ridden close to him, and try to work him gently toward the city and into the big corral just inside the gate. Look at that, now!"

Up went the big elephant's trunk, and he trumpeted angrily. It was evident that he was about to charge. The officer in command shouted orders to the slaves to ride the females toward him, but the officer did not advance. Like the other three with him, he was an Erythros and not of the noble class. Not having their pride or their code of honor, he could order others into danger while he remained in comparative safety.

Some of the slaves moved forward, but with no great show of enthusiasm; then the great beast charged. He barged right through the line of advancing females, scattering them to right and left, and charged for the bull ridden by the officer in command.

Screaming commands, the officer sought to turn his mount and escape; but the bull he rode was a trained fighting elephant which knew little about running away; besides, his harem of cows was there; and he was not going to relinquish that to any strange bull without a battle; so, torn between his natural inclinations and his habit of obedience to the commands of his rider, he neither faced the oncoming bull nor turned tail toward him; but swung half way around, broadside, in his indecision. And in this position the great stranger struck him with almost the momentum of a loco-motive run amok.

Down he went, pitching the officer heavily to the ground; but the fellow was up instantly and running—by far the stupidest thing he could have done; for almost any animal will pursue a thing that flees.

Hoarse screams for help mingled with the trumpeting of

the wild bull as the latter bore down upon his fleeing
victim. Valthor urged the female he rode into a trot in an
effort to head off the charge and distract the bull's attention, and Wood followed behind him; just why, he could
not have explained.

Valthor was too late. The bull overtook the terrified man,
tossed him three times, and then trampled him into the
dust of the plain until he was only a darker spot on the
barren ground.

It was then that Valthor and Wood arrived. Wood expected
nothing less than a repetition of the scene he had just
witnessed with either himself or Valthor as the victim, but
nothing of the kind happened.

The Athnean rode his cow quietly close to the great bull,
which stood complacently switching its tail, all the madness
having apparently passed out of him with the killing of
his victim; and Wood, following the example of Valthor,
closed in gently on the other side.

All this time Valthor was chanting in a low, sing-song
monotone a wordless song used by the elephant men of
Athne to soothe the great beasts in moods of nervousness
or irritation; and now to the cadence of his chant he added
words of instruction to Wood so that the two might work in
harmony to bring the wild bull to the city and into the
corral.

Between the two cows, which knew their parts well, the
bull was guided to captivity; while the officers, the warriors,
and the slaves trailed behind, happy and relieved that they
had not been called upon to risk their lives.

Valthor already held the respect of his fellow prisoners as
well as of the warriors who guarded them, and now Wood
took his place as a person of importance among them.

That word of the manner of the capture of the wild
elephant had reached the palace Wood had proof the following day when an officer and a detail of warriors came to
take him into the presence of Phoros.

"He wishes to see the fellow who helped Valthor capture
the rogue," said the officer.

Valthor leaned close and whispered, "He has some other
reason. He would not send for you just for that."

NIGHT WAS CREEPING stealthily out of its lair in the east, bringing its following of mystery and dark deeds and strange beasts that are not seen by day. Though the sun still colored the western sky with a fading tinge of red it was already dark and gloomy in The Pass of the Warriors that leads from the valley of Onthar to the valley of Thenar.

In Onthar is Cathne, the City of Gold; in Thenar is Athne, the City of Ivory; in The Pass of the Warriors was Tarzan of the Apes. Alone, he was going to Athne seeking a clew to the whereabouts of Gonfala.

Gemnon had tried to dissuade him from going without an escort; and so had Thudos, whom he had helped to seat upon the throne of Cathne.

"If you are not back within a reasonable time," Thudos told him, "I shall send an army to Athne to bring you back."

"If I am not back in a reasonable time," suggested the ape-man, "it may be because I shall be dead."

"Perhaps," agreed Thudos, "but they will not kill you unless they have to. They are always hard pressed to find enough slaves to carry on the work of the city, and they'd never destroy such a fine specimen as you. Like us, they also need men to fight in the arena."

"You would like that better than scrubbing elephants," said Gemnon, smiling.

Tarzan shook his head. "I do not like to fight or to kill, and there are worse things than scrubbing elephants."

And so he had gone, choosing to travel so that he would not have to cross the valley of Thenar by day, as he wished to approach and reconnoiter Athne unseen. That both valleys, especially Onthar, harbored many wild lions was a hazard he had to accept; but, except for the actual crossing of Thenar, he could take advantage of the protection of forests practically all of the way.

The hazard was great, for the lions of Thenar were not

all ordinary lions. Many of them were escaped hunting lions
of Cathne which had been often fed with human flesh and
trained to hunt men. For generations they had been bred
for speed and endurance; so that in all the world there were
no such formidable beasts of prey as these.

As night fell, Tarzan heard the roars of the great cats in
the valley he had quitted. With every sense alert he passed
through The Pass of the Warriors and entered the valley of
Thenar. As yet he had heard no lion roar coming from
that direction. The wind was in his face. It brought no
scent spoor of Numa, but he knew that it was carrying his
scent back in the direction of the hunting lions of Cathne.

He increased his speed, for though he had killed many a
lion he knew that no living creature could hope to survive
an attack by these beasts that often hunted in packs.

He was out now upon the open plain of Thenar. He could
still hear the roaring of the lions in Onthar. Suddenly they
took on a new note. He knew it well. It told him that they
had picked up the trail of some creature and marked it as
their quarry. Was it his trail?

A full moon rose above the mountains ahead of him,
lighting the floor of the valley, revealing the dark strip of
forest far ahead. The savage voices of the lions grew louder,
reverberating in the canyon called The Pass of the Warriors,
through which he had just come; then Tarzan knew that
the hunting lions of Cathne were on his trail.

You or I could not have counted the lions by their
voices; but to Tarzan the distinctive quality or character
of each voice was discernible, and thus he knew that five
lions were loping relentlessly to the kill. Once more he
quickened his pace.

He judged that the lions were about a mile in the rear of
him, the forest about three miles ahead. If no obstacle intervened he could reach the forest ahead of the lions; but
he was crossing an unfamiliar terrain known to him only
by the descriptions given him by Gemnon and Thudos, and
he knew that there might easily be some peculiarity of the
topography of the floor of the valley that would delay him
—a deep dry wash with overhanging banks of soft dirt
would do it.

On he trotted, his great chest rising and falling regularly,
his heartbeats scarcely accelerated by the exertion; but the
lions came even more swiftly. He knew from the sound of
their voices that they were gaining on him. Knowing them,

even as he did, he marvelled at their endurance, so unusual in lions; and was amazed at the results that could be attained by careful breeding. Now, for the first time, he broke into a run; for he knew that the moment they sighted him they would come on much faster than he could run for any great distance. It then would be just a question as to which could maintain the greatest speed for the longest distance.

No washes intervened nor other obstacle, and he came at last to within half a mile of the forest with sufficient distance and time to spare to assure him a reasonable margin of safety; then the unforeseen occurred. From the shadows of the forest a great lion stepped into view before him.

Those who would live long in the jungle must think quickly. Tarzan weighed the entire situation without losing a stride. The forest was his goal; one lion was less of a menace than five, and the one lion was all that stood between him and the forest. With a savage growl he charged the lion.

The beast had started to trot toward him; but now he stopped, hesitant. Would he hold his ground or would he break? Much depended upon whether he was an ordinary wild lion or a trained hunting lion. From the fact that he hesitated instead of carrying through his charge Tarzan guessed that he was the former.

The five lions from Onthar were gaining rapidly now. In the bright moonlight they must have caught sight of their quarry. Their voices proclaimed that. Now they were charging. Had they been wild lions they would have hunted in silence once their prey was marked, but the earth fairly trembled to their roars. Tarzan thought that they wasted too much energy thus, but he knew that they were trained to it so that the huntsmen could follow them even when they were out of sight.

Tarzan saw that the lion facing him was wavering. He was probably surprised at the tactics of the man-thing, at a quarry that charged him; and the roars of the five lions doubtless added to his nervousness. Only fifty yards separated them, and the lion had not made up his mind, when from the chest of the ape-man burst the savage challenge of the bull ape. It was the last straw—the lion wheeled and bounded back into the forest. A moment later Tarzan swarmed up a friendly tree as five angry lions leaped to seize him.

Finding a comfortable resting place, the ape-man broke off dead branches and threw them at the lions, calling them

Dango, Ungo, Horta, and other insulting names, ascribing vile tastes and habits to themselves and their ancestors. A quiet, almost taciturn, man, he was as adept in the use of the jungle billingsgate he had acquired from the great apes among which he had been raised. Perhaps the lions understood him; perhaps they did not. Who knows? Anyhow, they were very angry; and leaped high in air in vain efforts to reach him, which only made them angrier. But Tarzan had no time to waste upon them; and, keeping to the trees, he swung away toward the north and Athne.

He had timed himself to reach the city while it slept, and knew how to approach it from information given him by Gemnon and Thudos who had often visited Athne during the yearly truces when the two cities traded with one another. He passed half way around the city to the north side, which was less well guarded than the south.

Here he faced the greatest danger of discovery, for he must scale the wall in the light of a full moon. He chose a place far from the north gate, and crept toward the city on his belly through the garden stuff growing in the cultivated fields. He stopped often to look and listen, but he saw no sign of life on the city wall.

When he had come to within about a hundred feet of the wall, he arose and ran toward it at top speed, scaling it like a cat until his fingers closed upon the coping; then he drew himself up; and, lying flat, looked down upon the other side. A shedlike building abutted against the wall, and beyond this was a narrow street. Tarzan slipped to the roof of the shed, and a moment later dropped into the street.

Instantly a head was thrust from an open window and a man's voice demanded, "What are you doing there? Who are you?"

"I am Daimon," replied Tarzan in a husky whisper. Instantly the head was withdrawn and the window slammed shut. Tarzan, quick witted, had profited by something that Gemnon had told him—that the Athneans believed in a bad spirit that was abroad at night seeking whom it might kill. To Daimon they attributed all unexplained deaths, especially those that occurred at night.

Following the directions he had received, Tarzan moved through the narrow, shadowed streets toward the center of the city, coming at last to the walled enclosure where the palace stood. He had been told that here he would find guards only at the north and south gates. Other gates, if there were any, were securely fastened and seldom used.

As Tarzan approached the enclosure from the west, he encountered no gate and no guards. The wall was low compared with that which surrounded the city, and so proved no obstacle to the ape-man. Once over the wall he found himself in a garden of trees, shrubs, and flowers, a lovely place of soft, sweet fragrances; but for these he had no senses at the moment—he was searching for other scents than those of flowers.

Winding among small buildings and other gardens he came to a large building that he knew must be the palace; and here, to his surprise, he saw several rooms brilliantly lighted. He had thought that all would be asleep with the exception of the guards.

A number of old trees grew in the garden court that flanked this side of the palace, and in the security of their shadows Tarzan crossed to the building and looked in at one of the windows. Here he saw a large banquet hall down the length of which ran a long table at which a hundred or more men were seated, most of them in various stages of drunkenness.

There was much loud talk and laughter, and a couple of fights were in progress in which no one took any interest except the contestants. The men were, for the most part, coarse, common appearing fellows, not at all like the nobles of Cathne. The man at the head of the table was quite bestial in appearance. He pounded on the table with a great ham of a fist, and bellowed more like a bull than a man.

Slaves were coming and going, bringing more drink and removing empty goblets and dishes. Some of the guests were still eating, but most of them concentrated their energies and their talents upon the principal business of the evening —drinking.

"Didn't I tell you to fetch her?" shouted the large man at the head of the table, addressing the assemblage in general.

"Told who to bring what?" inquired another seated farther toward the foot of the table.

"The girl," shouted the large man.

"What girl, Phoros?"

"THE girl," replied Phoros drunkenly.

"Oh, THE girl," said some one.

"Well, why don't you bring her?"

"Bring who?"

"Bring THE girl," repeated Phoros.

"Who bring her?" asked another.

"You bring her," ordered Phoros.

The fellow addressed shook his head. "Not me," he said. "Menofra 'd have the hide off me."

"She won't know. She's gone to bed," Phoros assured him.

"I ain't takin' any chances. Send a slave."

"You'd better not send anyone," counselled a man sitting next to Phoros, one who did not seem as drunk as the others. "Menofra would cut her heart out and yours too."

"Who's king?" demanded Phoros.

"Ask Menofra," suggested the other.

"I'm king," asserted Phoros. He turned to a slave. The fellow happened to be looking in another direction. Phoros threw a heavy goblet at him, which barely missed his head. "Here, you! Go fetch the girl."

"What girl, master?" asked the trembling slave.

"There's only one girl in Athne, you son of a wart hog! Go get her!"

The slave hurried from the room. Then there ensued a discussion as to what Menofra would do if she found out. Phoros announced that he was tired of Menofra, and that if she didn't mind her own business he'd take her apart and forget to put her together again. He thought this such a good joke that he laughed immoderately and fell off his bench, but some of the others seemed nervous and looked apprehensively toward the doorway.

Tarzan watched and listened. He felt disgust and shame —shame, because he belonged to the same species as these creatures. Since infancy he had been fellow of the beasts of the forest and the plain, the lower orders; yet he had never seen them sink to the level of man. Most of them had courage and dignity of a sort; seldom did they stoop to buffoonery, with the possible exception of the lesser monkeys, who were most closely allied to man. Had he been impelled to theorize he would doubtless have reversed Darwin's theory of evolution. But his mind was occupied with another thought —who was "THE girl"? He wondered if she might not be Gonfala, but further speculation was discouraged by the coming of a large, masculine looking woman who strode into the room followed by the slave who had just been dispatched to bring the girl. So this was the girl! Tarzan looked at her in mild astonishment. She had large, red hands, a whiskered mole on her chin, and quite a noticeable mustache. In other respects she was quite as unlovely.

"What's the meaning of this?" she demanded, glaring at Phoros. "Why did you send for me at this time in the morning, you drunken lout?"

Phoros' jaw dropped; he looked wildly about at his companions as though seeking help; but he got none. Each of those who had not passed out completely was engaged in trying to appear dignified and sober.

"My dear," explained Phoros ingratiatingly, "we wanted you to join us and help celebrate."

" 'My dear' nothing!" snapped the woman; then her eyes narrowed. "Celebrate what?" she demanded.

Phoros looked about him helplessly. Bleary eyed and belching, he looked foolishly at the man sitting next him. "What were we celebrating, Kandos?"

Kandos fidgeted, and moistened his dry lips with his tongue.

"Don't lie to me!" screamed the woman. "The truth is that you never intended to send for me."

"Now, Menofra!" exclaimed Phoros in what was intended to be a soothing tone.

The woman wheeled on the frightened slave behind her. "Were you told to fetch me?" she demanded.

"Oh, great queen! I thought he meant you," whimpered the slave, dropping to his knees.

"What did he say to you?" Menofra's voice was raised almost to a shriek.

"He said, 'Go fetch the girl!' and when I asked him what girl, he said, 'There's only one girl in Athne, you son of a wart hog!' "

Menofra's eyes narrowed menacingly. "The only girl in Athne, eh? I know who you sent for—it's that yellow haired hussy that was brought in with the two men. You think you been fooling me, don't you? Well, you haven't. You just been waiting for your chance, and tonight you got drunk enough to muster up a little courage. Well, I'll attend to you; and when I get through with you, I'll fix the only girl in Athne. I'll send her to you, if there's anything left of you—I'll send her to you in pieces." She wheeled on the subdued and frightened company. "Get out of here, you swine—all of you!" Then she strode to the head of the table and seized Phoros by an ear. "And you come with me—*king!*" The title bristled with contumely.

ARZAN LEFT THE window and walked along the side of the building, looking up at the second floor. There, he surmised, would be the sleeping chambers. In some room above, doubtless, Gonfala was confined. Several vines clambered up the wall. He tested them, trying to find one that might bear his weight; and at last he came to some old ivy that had a stem that was as large around as his arm, a gnarled old plant that clung to the rough wall with a million aerial roots. He tried it with his weight; then, satisfied that it would bear him, he started to ascend toward a window directly above.

Close beside the open window he paused and listened, his sensitive nostrils classifying the odors that came from the chamber. A man slept within. Heavy breathing told him the man was asleep. Its stertorousness and odor told him that the fellow was drunk. Tarzan threw a leg across the sill and stepped into the room. He moved noiselessly, feeling his way through the darkness. He took his time, and gradually his eyes became accustomed to the blackness of the interior. He had the gift, that some men have in common with nocturnal animals, of being able to see in the dark better than other men. Perhaps it had been developed to a higher state of efficiency by necessity. One who can see by night in the jungle has a better chance of survival.

Soon he identified a darker mass on the floor near a side wall as the sleeper. That, however, was not difficult; the man's snores screamed his location. Tarzan crossed to the opposite end of the room and found a door. His fingers searched for lock or bolt and found the latter. It squeaked a little as he drew it back; but he had no fear that it would arouse the man, nor did it. The door opened into a dimly lighted corridor—an arched corridor along which were other doors and the arched openings into other corridors.

Tarzan heard voices. They were raised in angry altercation, and there were sounds of scuffling. The voices were those of Menofra and Phoros. Presently there was a loud scream followed by a thud as of a body falling; then silence. Tarzan waited, listening. He heard a door open farther up the corridor in the direction from which the voices had come; then he stepped back into the room behind him, leaving the door slightly ajar so that he could look out into the corridor. He saw a man step from a doorway and approach along the corridor. It was Phoros. He was staggering a little, and in his right hand he carried a bloody short-sword. His expression was bleary-eyed and vacuous. He passed the door from which Tarzan watched and turned into another corridor; then the ape-man stepped into the passageway and followed him.

When he reached the head of the corridor into which Phoros had turned, Tarzan saw the Athnean fumbling with a key at the lock of a door only a short distance ahead; and he waited until Phoros had unlocked the door and entered the room beyond; then the ape-man followed at a run. He wished to reach the door before Phoros could lock it from within, if such were his intention; but it was not. In fact, in his drunken carelessness, he did not even close the door tightly; and he had little more than entered the room when Tarzan pushed the door open and followed him.

The ape-man had moved with utter silence; so that though he stood just behind Phoros the latter was unaware of his presence. The room was lighted by a single cresset—a wick burning in a shallow vessel half filled with fat. Lying in one corner of the room, bound hand and foot, was Gonfala; in another corner, similarly trussed, was Stanley Wood. They both saw and recognized Tarzan simultaneously, but he raised a finger to his lips to caution them to silence. Phoros stood leering at his two prisoners, his gross body swaying unsteadily.

"So the lovers are still here," he taunted. "But why do they stay so far apart? Here, you stupid fool, watch me; I'll show you how to make love to the girl. She's mine now. Menofra, the old Hellcat, is dead. Look at this sword! See the blood? That's Menofra's blood. I just killed her." He pointed the sword at Wood. "And just as soon as I've shown you how a lover should behave I'm going to kill you."

He took a step toward Gonfala, and as he did so steel thewed fingers gripped his sword wrist, the weapon was torn from his hand, and he was thrown heavily to the floor.

"Quiet, or I kill," a low voice whispered.

Phoros looked into the cold grey eyes of an almost naked giant who stood above him with his own sword pointed at his breast. "Who are you?" he quavered. "Don't kill me. Tell me what you want. You can have anything if you'll not kill me."

"I'll take what I want. Don't move." Tarzan crossed to Wood and cut the bonds that held him. "Release Gonfala," he said, "and when you have done that bind this man and gag him."

Wood worked quickly. "How did you get here?" Tarzan asked him.

"I was searching for Gonfala. I followed her trail to this city; then they took me prisoner. Today Phoros sent for me. In some way, probably through some of his people overhearing Spike and Troll, he got the idea that I knew how to work the Gonfal. Spike had been bragging about its powers, but neither he nor Troll had been able to do anything with it. They had also told some one that Gonfala was the goddess of the big stone, and so he brought us together and told us to show him some magic. Our meeting was so sudden and unexpected that we gave ourselves away—it must have been apparent to any one that we were in love. Anyway, Phoros got it; maybe because he was jealous. He has been trying to make love to Gonfala ever since she was captured, but he was too scared of his wife to go very far with it."

When Gonfala was liberated Wood trussed up Phoros, and as he was completing the work they heard the sound of shuffling footsteps in the corridor. They all stood, tense and silent, waiting. Would the footsteps pass the door, or was some one coming to this room? Nearer and nearer they came; then they paused outside, as though he who walked was listening. The door was pushed open, revealing a horrible apparition. Gonfala muffled a scream; Wood recoiled; only Tarzan showed no emotion. It was Menofra. A horrible wound gashed her head and one shoulder. She was covered with blood; and reeled with weakness from the loss of it, but she still retained her wits.

Stepping quickly back into the corridor, she closed the door and turned the key that the drunken Phoros had left in the lock; then they heard her crying loudly for the guard.

"We seem to be nicely trapped," commented Wood.

"But we have a hostage," Tarzan reminded him.

"What a horrible sight," said Gonfala, shuddering and nodding in the direction of the corridor. "How do you suppose it happened?"

The ape-man jerked a thumb in the direction of Phoros. "He could tell you. I imagine that he's rather glad that we were here with him."

"What a sweet couple," said Wood, "but I imagine there are a lot of married couples who would like to do that to one another if they thought they could get away with it."

"What a terrible thing to say, Stanlee," cried Gonfala. "Do you think that we would be like that?"

"Oh, we're different," Wood assured her; "these people are beasts."

"Not beasts," Tarzan corrected. "They are human beings, and they act like human beings."

"Here comes the guard," said Wood.

They could hear men approaching at a run along the corridor; they heard their exclamations when they saw Menofra and their excited questioning.

"There is a wild man in there," Menofra told them. "He has set the two prisoners free, and they have bound and gagged the king. They may kill him. I don't want them to; I want him for myself. Go in and capture the strangers and bring the king to me."

Tarzan stood close to the door. "If you come in without my permission," he shouted, "I will kill the king."

"It looks like you were on a spot, Phoros," said Wood, "no matter what happens. If Menofra gets you she'll hand you plenty." Phoros could make no reply because of the gag.

The warriors and the queen were arguing in the corridor. They could come to no decision as to what to do. The three prisoners in the room were no better off. Tarzan was puzzled. He told Wood as much.

"I knew an Athnean noble well," he said, "and through him I was led to believe that these people were rather noble and chivalrous, not at all like those I have seen here. There was a rumor in Cathne that there had been some change in government here, but the natural assumption was that another faction of the nobility had come into power. If these people are of the nobility, our friend Spike must be at least an archbishop."

"They are not of the nobility," said Wood. "They are from the lowest dregs of society. They overthrew the king and the nobility a few months ago. I guess they are pretty well ruining the country."

"That accounts for it," said Tarzan. "Well, I guess my friend, Valthor, can't help me much."

"Valthor?" exclaimed Wood. "Do you know him? Why say, he's the only friend I have here."

"Where is he? He'll help us," said Tarzan.

"Not where he is, he won't. He and I were fellow slaves at the elephant stables."

"Valthor a slave!"

"Yes, and lucky to be that," Wood assured him. "They killed off all the other members of the nobility they caught —except a few that joined 'em. The rest escaped into the mountains. Every one liked Valthor so much that they didn't kill him."

"It is a good thing that I didn't take any chances when I came here," remarked the ape-man. "They'd heard these rumours in Cathne; so I came in after dark to investigate before I tried to find Valthor or made myself known."

There was a rap on the door. "What do you want?" asked Tarzan.

"Turn the king over to the queen and we won't harm you," said a voice.

Phoros commenced to wriggle and squirm on the floor, shaking his head vigorously. Tarzan grinned.

"Wait until we talk it over," he said; then, to Wood, "Take the gag out of his mouth."

As soon as the gag was removed Phoros choked and spluttered before he could articulate an understandable word, so frightened and excited was he. "Don't let her have me," he finally managed to say. "She'll kill me."

"I think you have it coming to you," said Wood.

"Maybe we can reach a bargain," suggested Tarzan.

"Anything, anything you want," cried Phoros.

"Our freedom and a safe escort to The Pass of the Warriors," demanded the ape-man.

"It is yours," promised Phoros.

"And the big diamond," added Wood.

"And the big diamond," agreed Phoros.

"How do we know you'll do as you agree?" asked Tarzan.

"You have my word for it," Phoros assured him.

"I don't think it's worth much. I'd have to have something more."

"Well, what?"

"We'd want to take you with us and keep you close to me where I could kill you if the bargain were not kept."

"That too. I agree to everything, only don't let her get her hands on me."

"There is one more thing," added Tarzan. "Valthor's freedom."

"Granted."

"And now that you've got all that arranged," said Wood, "how in Hell are we going to get out of here with that old virago holding the fort with the guard out there? Have you ever been to a coronation, Tarzan?"

The ape-man shook his head.

"Well, take Phorsie out there, my friend, and you'll see a king crowned."

"I don't know what you're talking about, but I don't intend taking him out of here until I have some assurance that his promises will be carried out." He turned to Phoros. "What can you suggest? Will the guard obey you?"

"I don't know. They're afraid of her. Everybody's afraid of her, and Dyaus knows they have reason."

"We seem to be getting no where with great facility," commented Wood.

Tarzan crossed to Phoros and removed his bonds. "Come to the door," he directed, "and explain my proposition to your wife."

Phoros approached the door. "Listen, dear," he said ingratiatingly.

"Listen nothing, you beast, you murderer," she screamed back at him. "Just let me get my hands on you—that's all I ask."

"But darling, I was drunk. I didn't mean to do it. Listen to reason. Let me take these people out of the country with an escort of warriors and they won't kill me."

"Don't 'darling' me, you, you—"

"But, my own little Menofra, listen to reason. Send for Kandos, and let us all talk it over."

"Go in there, you cowards, and drag them out," Menofra shouted to the guardsmen.

"Stay out there!" screamed Phoros. "I am king. Those are the king's commands."

"I'm queen," yelled Menofra. "I tell you to go in and rescue the king."

"I'm all right," shouted Phoros. "I don't want to be rescued."

"I think," said the officer of the guard, "that the best thing to do is summon Kandos. This is no matter for a simple officer of the guard to decide."

"That's right," encouraged the king; "send for Kandos."

They heard the officer dispatch a warrior to summon Kandos, and they heard the queen grumbling and scolding and threatening.

Wood stepped to the door. "Menofra!" he called. "I have an idea that perhaps you hadn't thought of. Let Phoros accompany us to the border; then when he comes back you'll have him. That will save a lot of trouble for all concerned."

Phoros looked troubled. He hadn't thought of that either. Menofra did not answer immediately; then she said, "He might trick me in some way."

"How can he trick you?" demanded Wood.

"I don't know, but he'd find a way. He has been tricking people all his life."

"He couldn't. You'd have the army. What could he do?"

"Well, perhaps it's worth thinking about," admitted the queen; "but I don't know that I could wait. I'd like to get my hands on him right now. Did you see what he did to me?"

"Yes. It was terrible," sympathized Wood.

It was not long before the warrior returned with Kandos. Menofra greeted him with a volley of vituperation as soon as he came in sight, and it was some time before he could quiet her and get the story. Then he led her away where none could overhear, and they whispered together for sometime. When they had finished, Kandos approached the door.

"It is all arranged," he announced. "The queen has given her permission. The party will start shortly after sunrise. It is still dark, and the trail is not safe by night. Just as soon as you and the escort have had your breakfasts you may go in peace. Have we your promise that you will not harm the king."

"You have," said Tarzan.

"Very well," said Kandos. "I am going now to arrange for the escort."

"And don't forget our breakfasts!" called Wood.

"I most certainly will not," promised Kandos.

23

S TANLEY WOOD WAS in high spirits. "It commences to look as though our troubles were about over," he said. He laid a hand on Gonfala's tenderly. "You've been through a lot, but I can promise you that when we get to civilization you'll be able to understand for the first time in your life what perfect peace and security mean."

"Yes," said Tarzan, "the perfect peace and security of automobile accidents, railroad wrecks, aeroplane crashes, robbers, kidnapers, war, and pestilence."

Wood laughed. "But no lions, leopards, buffaloes, wild elephants, snakes, nor tsetse flies, not to mention shiftas and cannibals."

"I think," said Gonfala, "that neither one of you paints a very pretty picture. You make one almost afraid of life. But after all it is not so much peace and security that I want as freedom. You know, all my life I have been a prisoner except for the few short weeks after you took me away from the Kaji and before Spike and Troll got me. Perhaps you can imagine then how much I want freedom, no matter how many dangers I have to take along with it. It seems the most wonderful thing in the world."

"It is," said Tarzan.

"Well, love has its points, too," suggested Wood.

"Yes," agreed Gonfala, "but not without freedom."

"You're going to have them both," Wood promised.

"With limitations, you'll find, Gonfala," warned Tarzan with a smile.

"Just now I'm interested in food," said Gonfala.

"And I think it's coming." Wood nodded toward the door. Some one was fumbling with the key. Presently the door opened far enough to permit two pots to be shoved inside the room; then it was closed with a bang.

"They are taking no chances," commented Wood as he crossed the room and carried the two vessels back to his companions. One contained a thick stew; the other, water.

"What, no hardware?" inquired Wood.

"Hardware? What is that?" asked Gonfala; "something to eat?"

"Something to eat with—forks, spoons. No forks, no spoons, no Emily Post—how embarrassing!"

"Here," said Tarzan, and handed his hunting knife to Gonfala. They took turns spearing morsels of meat with it and drinking the juice and the water directly from the pots, sharing the food with Phoros.

"Not half bad," commented Wood. "What is it, Phoros?"

"Young wether. There is nothing tastier. I am surprised that Menofra did not send us old elephant hide to chew on. Perhaps she is relenting." Then he shook his head. "No, Menofra never relents—at least not where I am concerned. That woman is so ornery she thinks indigestion is an indulgence."

"My!" said Gonfala, drowsily. "I am so sleepy I can't keep my eyes open."

"Same here," said Wood.

Phoros looked at the others and yawned. Tarzan stood up and shook himself.

"You, too?" asked Phoros.

The ape-man nodded. Phoros' lids drooped. "The old she-devil," he muttered. "We've all been drugged—maybe poisoned."

Tarzan watched his companions fall into a stupor one by one. He tried to fight off the effects of the drug. He wondered if any of them would awaken again; then he sagged to one knee and rolled over on the floor, unconscious.

*   *   *

The room was decorated with barbaric splendor. Mounted heads of animals and men adorned the walls. There were crude murals done in colors that had faded into softness, refined by age. Skins of animals and rugs of wool covered the floor, the benches, and a couch on which Menofra lay, her body raised on one elbow, her bandaged head supported by one huge palm. Four warriors stood by the only door; at Menofra's feet lay Gonfala and Wood, still unconscious; at her side stood Kandos; at the foot of the couch, bound and unconscious, lay Phoros.

"You sent the wild-man to the slave pen as I directed?" asked Menofra.

Kandos nodded. "Yes, queen; and because he seemed so strong I had him chained to a stanchion."

"That is well," said Menofra. "Even a fool does the right thing occasionally."

"Thank you, queen," said Kandos.

"Don't thank me; you make me sick. You are a liar and a cheat and a traitor. Phoros befriended you, yet you turned against him. How much more quickly would you turn against me who has never befriended you and whom you hate! But you won't, because you are a coward; and don't even think of it. If I ever get the idea for a moment that you might be thinking of turning against me I'll have your head hanging on this wall in no time. The man is coming to."

They looked down at Wood whose eyes were opening slowly and whose arms and legs were moving a little as though experimenting with the possibilities of self-control. He was the first to regain consciousness. He opened his eyes and looked about him. He saw Gonfala lying beside him. Her rising and falling bosom assured him that she lived. He looked up at Kandos and the queen.

"So this is the way you keep your word?" he accused; then he looked about for Tarzan. "Where is the other?"

"He is quite safe," said Kandos. "The queen in her mercy has not killed any of you."

"What are you going to do with us?" demanded Wood.

"The wild-man goes to the arena," replied Menofra. "You and the girl will not be killed immediately—not until you have served my purpose."

"And what is that?"

"You shall know presently. Kandos, send for a priest; Phoros will soon awaken."

Gonfala opened her eyes and sat up. "What has happened?" she asked. "Where are we?"

"We are still prisoners," Wood told her. "These people have double-crossed us."

"Civilization seems very far away," she said and tears came to her eyes.

He took her hand. "You must be brave, dear."

"I am tired of being brave; I have been brave for so long. I should like so much to cry, Stanlee."

Now Phoros regained consciousness, and looked first at

one and then at another. When his eyes fell on Menofra
he winced.

"Ah, the rat has awakened," said the queen.

"You have rescued me, my dear!" said Phoros.

"You may call it that, if you wish," said Menofra coldly;
"but I should call it by another name, as you will later."

"Now, my darling, let us forget the past—let bygones
be bygones. Kandos, remove my bonds. How does it look
to see the king trussed up like this?"

"It looks all right to me," Menofra assured him, "but
how would you like to be trussed up? It could be done
with red hot chains, you know. In fact, it has been done.
It's not a bad idea; I am glad you suggested it."

"But, Menofra, my dear wife, you wouldn't do that to
me?"

"Oh, you think not? But you would try to kill me with
your sword so that you could take this wench here to wife.
Well, I'm not going to have you trussed up with red hot
chains—not yet. First I am going to remove temptation
from your path without removing the object of your temptation. I am going to let you see what you might have en-
joyed."

There was a rap on the door, and one of the warriors
said, "The priest is here."

"Let him in," ordered Menofra.

Wood had helped Gonfala to her feet, and the two were
seated on a bench, mystified listeners to Menofra's cryptic
speech. When the priest had entered the room and bowed
before the queen she pointed to them.

"Marry these two," she commanded.

Wood and Gonfala looked at one another in astonishment. "There's a catch in this somewhere," said the former.
"The old termagant's not doing this because she loves us,
but I'm not looking any gift horse in the mouth."

"It's what we've been waiting and hoping for," said
Gonfala, "but I wish it could have happened under different conditions. There is something sinister in this. I don't
believe that any good thought could come out of that
woman's mind."

The marriage ceremony was extremely simple, but very
impressive. It laid upon the couple the strictest obligations
of fidelity and condemned to death and damned through
eternity whomever might cause either to be unfaithful to
the other.

During the ceremony Menofra wore a sardonic smile, while Phoros had difficulty in hiding his chagrin and anger. When it was concluded, the queen turned to her mate. "You know the laws of our people," she said. "King or commoner, whoever comes between these two must die. You know that don't you, Phoros? You know you've lost her, don't you—forever? You would try to kill me, would you? Well, I'm going to let you live—I'm going to let you live with this wench; but watch your step, Phoros; for I'll be watching you." She turned to the guard. "Now take them away. Take this man to the slave pen, and see that nothing happens to him, and take Phoros and the wench to the room next to mine; and lock them in."

*   *   *

When Tarzan regained consciousness he found himself chained to a stanchion in a stockaded compound, an iron collar around his neck. He was quite alone; but pallets of musty grass, odd bits of dirty clothing, cooking utensils, and the remains of cooking fires, still smouldering, disclosed the fact that the shed and the yard was the abode of others; and he conjectured correctly that he had been imprisoned in a slave pen.

The position of the sun told him that he had been under the influence of the drug for about an hour. The effects were passing off rapidly leaving only a dull headache and a feeling of chagrin that he had been so easily duped. He was concerned about the fate of Wood and Gonfala, and was at a loss to understand why he had been separated from them. His active mind was occupied with this problem and that of escape when the gate of the compound opened and Wood was brought in by an escort of warriors who merely shoved the American through the gateway and departed after relocking the gate.

Wood crossed the compound to Tarzan. "I wondered what they had done with you," he said. "I was afraid they might have killed you." Then he told the ape-man what Menofra had decreed for Gonfala. "It is monstrous, Tarzan; the woman is a beast. What are we to do?"

Tarzan tapped the iron collar that encircled his neck. "There is not much that I can do," he said ruefully.

"Why do you suppose they've chained you up and not me?" asked Wood.

"They must have some special form of entertainment in view for me," suggested the ape-man with a faint smile.

The remainder of the day passed in desultory conversation, principally a monologue; as Tarzan was not given to garrulity. Wood talked to keep from thinking about Gonfala's situation, but he was not very successful. Late in the afternoon the slaves were returned to the compound, and immediately crowded around Tarzan. One of them pushed his way to the front when he caught a glimpse of the prisoner.

"Tarzan!" he exclaimed. "It is really you?"

"I am afraid it is, Valthor," replied the ape-man.

"And you are back, I see," said Valthor to Wood. "I did not expect to see you again. What happened?"

Wood told him the whole story of their misadventure, and Valthor looked grave. "Your friend, Gonfala, may be safe as long as Menofra lives; but she may not live long. Kandos will see to that if he is not too big a coward; then, with Menofra out of the way, Phoros will again come to power. When he does, he will destroy you. After that there would not be much hope for Gonfala. The situation is serious, and I can see no way out unless the king and his party were to return and recapture the city. I believe they could do it now, for practically all of the citizens and most of the warriors are sick of Phoros and the rest of the Erythra."

A tall black came close to Tarzan. "You do not remember me, master?" he asked.

"Why, yes; of course I do," replied the ape-man. "You're Gemba. You were a slave in the house of Thudos at Cathne. How long have you been here?"

"Many moons, master. I was taken in a raid. The work is hard, and often these new masters are cruel. I wish that I were back in Cathne."

"You would fare well there now, Gemba. Your old master is king of Cathne. I think that if he knew Tarzan was a prisoner here, he would come and make war on Athne."

"And I think that if he did," said Valthor, "an army from Cathne would be welcome here for the first time in history; but there is no chance that he will come, for there is no way in which he may learn that Tarzan is here."

"If I could get this collar off my neck," said the ape-man, "I could soon get out of this slave pen and the city and bring Thudos with his army. He would come for me to save my friends."

"But you can't get it off," said Wood.

"You are right," agreed Tarzan; "it is idle talk."

For several days nothing occurred to break the monotony of existence in the slave pen of the king of Athne. No word reached them from the palace of what was transpiring there; no inkling came of the fate that was in store for them. Valthor had told Tarzan that the latter was probably being saved for the arena on account of his appearance of great strength, but when there would be games again he did not know. The new masters of Athne had changed everything, deriding all that had been sacred to custom and the old regime. There was even talk of changing the name of Athne to The City of Phoros. All that prevented was the insistence of the queen that it be renamed The City of Menofra.

Every morning the slaves were taken to work, and all day long Tarzan remained alone, chained like a wild animal. Imprisonment of any nature galled The Lord of the Jungle; to be chained was torture. Yet he gave no sign of the mental suffering he was enduring. To watch him, one might have thought that he was content. Seething beneath that calm exterior was a raging sea of anger.

One afternoon the slaves were returned to the pen earlier than usual. The guards that herded them in were unusually rough with them, and there were several officers not ordinarily present. They followed the slaves into the pen and counted them, checking off their names on a scroll carried by one of the officers; then they questioned them; and from the questions Tarzan gathered that there had been a concerted attempt on the part of a number of slaves to escape, during which a guard had been killed. During the excitement of the melee several slaves had escaped into the bamboo forest that grew close upon the eastern boundary of the cultivated fields of Athne. The check revealed that three were missing. Were they ever recaptured, they would be tortured and killed.

The officers and warriors were extremely brutal in their handling of the slaves as they questioned them, trying to force confessions from them that they might ascertain just how far-reaching the plot had been and which slaves were the ring-leaders. After they left the pen the slaves were in a turmoil of restlessness and discontent. The air was surcharged with the static electricity of repressed rebellion that the slightest spark would have ignited, but Valthor counselled them to patience.

"You will only subject yourselves to torture and death," he told them. "We are only a handful of unarmed slaves. What can we do against the armed warriors of the Erythra? Wait. As sure as Dyaus is in heaven some change must come. There is as much discontent outside the slave pen as within it; and one day Zygo, our king, will come out of the mountains where he is hiding and set us free."

"But some of us are slaves no matter who is king," said one. "I am. It would make no difference whether Zygo or Phoros were king—I should still be a slave."

"No," said Valthor. "I can promise you all that when Zygo comes into power again you will all be set free. I give you my word that it will be done."

"Well," said one, "I might not believe another, but all know that what the noble Valthor says he will do, he will do."

It was almost dark now, and the cooking fires were alight, and the slaves were cooking their poor meals in little pots. Jerked elephant meat constituted the larger part of their diet; to this was added a very coarse variety of turnip. From the two the men made a stew. Sometimes those who worked in the fields varied this diet with other vegetables they had been able to steal from the fields and smuggle into the pen.

"This stew," remarked Wood, "should be full of vitamins; it has everything else including elephant hair and pebbles. The elephant hair and the pebbles might be forgiven, but turnips! In the economy of mundane happiness there is no place for the turnip."

"I take it that you don't like turnips," said Valthor.

Since Tarzan had been brought to the slave pen, Troll and Spike had kept to themselves. Spike was very much afraid of the ape-man; and he had managed to impart this fear to Troll, although the latter had forgotten that there was any reason to fear him. Spike was worried for fear that, in the event they were liberated, Tarzan would find some way to keep the great diamond from him. This did not trouble Troll who had forgotten all about the diamond. The only thing that Troll remembered clearly was that Gonfala was his sister and that he had lost her. This worried him a great deal, and he talked about it continually. Spike encouraged him in the delusion and never referred to the diamond, although it was constantly the subject of his thoughts and plannings. His principal hope of retrieving it lay in the possibility that the rightful king of Athne would regain his throne, treat him as a guest instead of a prisoner, and return the Gonfal to him; and he knew from conversations he had had with other prisoners that the return of Zygo was just between a possibility and a probability.

As the slaves were eating their evening meal and discussing the escape of their three fellows an officer entered the compound with a detail of warriors, one of whom carried an iron collar and chain. Approaching the shed, the officer called Valthor.

"I am here," said the noble, rising.

"I have a present for you, aristocrat," announced the officer, who until the revolution had been a groom in the elephant stables of Zygo.

"So I see," replied Valthor, glancing at the collar and chain, "and one which it must give a stable-boy much pleasure to bring me."

The officer flushed angrily. "Be careful, or I'll teach you some manners," he growled. "You are the stable-boy now, and I am the aristocrat."

Valthor shook his head. "No, stable-boy, you are wrong. You will always be a stable-boy at heart, and way down deep inside you you know it. That is what makes you angry. That is what makes you hate me, or think that you hate me; you really hate yourself, because you know that you will always be a stable-boy no matter what Phoros tells you you are. He has done many strange things since he drove out the king, but he cannot make a lion out of a jackal's tail."

"Enough of this," snapped the officer. "Here you, snap the collar about his neck and chain him to the stanchion beside the wild-man."

"Why has Phoros thus honored me?" inquired Valthor.

"It was not Phoros; it was Menofra. She is ruling now."

"Ah, I see," said the noble. "Her psychology of hate for my class is more deeply rooted than yours, for it springs from filthy soil. Your vocation was at least honorable. Menofra was a woman of the street before Phoros married her."

"Well, have your say while you can, aristocrat," said the officer, tauntingly, "for tomorrow you and the wild-man die in the arena, trampled and gored by a rogue elephant."

24

Death

THE OTHER SLAVES were furious because of the sentence imposed upon Valthor, who was to die, the officer had told him before he left, in punishment for the outbreak that had resulted in the death of an Erythros warrior and the escape of three slaves and as a warning to the others. Valthor had been chosen ostensibly not because he had been charged with fomenting rebellion among the slaves, but really because he was popular among them and an aristocrat.

Wood was horrified by the knowledge that Tarzan was to die, Tarzan and Valthor, both of whom were his friends. It seemed to him absolutely inconceivable that the mighty heart of the Lord of the Jungle should be stilled forever, that that perfect body should be broken and trampled in the dust of an arena to satisfy the blood lust of ignorant barbarians.

"There must be something that we can do," he said; "there's got to be. Couldn't we break those chains?"

Tarzan shook his head. "I have examined mine carefully," he said, "and tested it. If it were cast iron, we might break a link; but it is malleable and would only bend. If we had a chisel—but we haven't. No, there is nothing to do but wait."

"But they are going to kill you, Tarzan! Don't you understand? They are going to kill you."

The ape-man permitted himself the shadow of a smile. "There is nothing unique in that," he said. "Many people have died; many people are dying; many people will die—even you, my friend."

"Tarzan is right," said Valthor. "We must all die; what matters is how we die. If we meet death courageously, as befits warriors, there will be no regrets. For myself, I am glad that an elephant is going to kill me; for I am an elephant-man. You know what that means, Tarzan; for you have

been to Cathne where the lion-men are the nobles; and you
know with what pride they bear the title. It is the same here,
except that the nobles are the elephant-men. As they breed
lions, we breed elephants; their god, Thoos, is a lion; our
Dyaus is an elephant. The nobles who escaped the Erythros
revolution took him into the mountains with them, for the
Erythra, who have no god, would have killed him."

"If I were to have my choice of the manner in which I
were to die," said Tarzan, "I should prefer the lion to the
elephant. For one thing, the lion kills quickly; but my real
reason is that the elephant has always been my friend; my
very best friend, perhaps; and I do not like to think that a
friend must kill me."

"This one will not be your friend, Tarzan," Valthor reminded him.

"No, I know it; but I was not thinking of him as an in-
dividual," explained Tarzan. "And now, as, with all our
talk, we have arrived nowhere, I am going to sleep."

The morning of their death dawned like any other morning. Neither spoke of what was impending. With Wood they
cooked their breakfasts, and they talked, and Valthor
laughed, and occasionally Tarzan smiled one of his rare
smiles. Wood was the most nervous. When the time came
for the slaves to be taken to their work he came to say good-
bye to the ape-man.

Tarzan laid a hand upon his shoulder. "I do not like to
say good-bye, my friend," he said.

If Wood had known how rare was the use by Tarzan of
that term "my friend" he would have been honored. He
thought of many animals as friends, but few men. He liked
Wood, his intelligence, his courage, his cleanness.

"Have you no message you would like to send to—to—"
Wood hesitated.

Tarzan shook his head. "Thank you, no," he said. "She
will know, as she always has."

Wood turned and walked away, following the other slaves
out of the stockade. He stumbled over the threshold, and
swore under his breath as he drew a palm across his eyes.

It was afternoon before they came for Tarzan and Valthor, half a hundred warriors and several officers, all in their
best trappings, their freshly burnished arms shining in the
sun.

In front of the palace a procession was forming. There
were many elephants richly caparisoned and bearing howdahs
in which rode the new-made nobility of Athne. All the

howdahs were open except one elaborate pavilion. In this sat Menofra alone. When Valthor saw her he laughed aloud. Tarzan turned and looked at him questioningly.

"Look at her!" exclaimed the noble. "She could not be more self-conscious if she were naked. In fact that would not bother her so much. The poor thing is trying to look the queen. Note the haughty mien, and the crown! Dyaus! she is wearing the crown to the arena—and wearing it backwards. It is worth dying to see."

Valthor had not attempted to lower his voice. In fact it seemed that he raised it a little. His laughter had attracted attention to him, so that many listened and heard his words. They even reached the ears of Menofra. That was apparent to all who could see her, for her face turned fiery red; and she took the crown off and placed it on the seat beside her. She was so furious that she trembled; and when she gave the command to march, as she immediately did, her voice shook with rage.

With the hundred elephants in single file, the many warriors on foot, the banners and pennons, the procession was colorful; but it lacked that something that would have made its magnificence impressive. There was nothing real about its assumed majesty, and the entire pageant was colored by the spuriosity of its principal actors. This was the impression that it made upon the Lord of the Jungle walking in chains behind the elephant of Menofra.

The procession followed the main avenue to the south gate through lines of silent citizens. There was no cheering, no applause. There were whispered comments as Valthor and Tarzan passed; and it was plain to see that the sympathies of the people were with Valthor, though they dared not express them openly. Tarzan was a stranger to them; their only interest in him lay in the fact that he might serve to give them a few minutes of thrills and entertainment in the arena.

Passing through the gate, the column turned toward the east, coming at last to the arena, which lay directly east of the city. Just outside the main gate, through which the procession entered the arena, Tarzan and Valthor were led from the line of march and taken to a smaller gate which led through a high palisade of small logs into a paddock between two sections of a grandstand. The inner end of the paddock was formed by a palisade of small logs; and was similar to the outer end, having a small gate opening onto the arena. The ape-man could not but notice the flimsy con-

struction of the two palisades, and idly wondered if the entire arena were as poorly built.

In the compound there were a number of armed guards;
and presently other prisoners were brought, men whom Tarzan had not before seen. They had been brought from the
city behind the elephants of lesser dignitaries who had ridden in the rear of Menofra. Several of these prisoners, who
spoke to Valthor, were evidently men of distinction.

"We are about the last of the aristocracy who did not escape or go over to the Erythra," Valthor explained to Tarzan. "Phoros and Menofra think that by killing off all their
enemies they will have no opposition and nothing more to
fear; but as a matter of fact they are only making more
enemies, for the middle classes were naturally more in sym-
pathy with the aristocracy than with the scum which con-
stitutes the Erythra."

About four feet from the top of the inner palisade was
a horizontal beam supporting the ends of braces that held
the palisade upright, and upon this beam the prisoners were
allowed to stand and witness what took place in the arena
until it was their turn to enter. When Tarzan and Valthor
took their places on the beam the royal pageant had just
completed a circuit of the arena, and Menofra was clumsily
descending from the howdah of her elephant to enter the
royal loge. The grandstands were about half filled, and
crowds were still pouring through the tunnels. There was little noise other than the shuffling of sandaled feet and the
occasional trumpeting of an elephant. It did not seem to
Tarzan a happy, carefree throng out to enjoy a holiday; but
rather a sullen mob suppressed by fear. A laugh would have
been as startling as a scream.

The first encounter was between two men; one a huge
Erythros warrior armed with sword and spear; the other a
former noble whose only weapon was a dagger. It was an
execution, not a duel—an execution preceded by torture. The
audience watched it, for the most part, in silence. There
were a few shouts of encouragement from the loges of the
officials and the new nobility.

Valthor and Tarzan watched with disgust. "I think he
could have killed that big fellow," said the ape-man. "I saw
how he might be easily handled. It is too bad that the other
did not think of it."

"You think you could kill Hyark?" demanded a guard
standing next to Tarzan.

"Why not?" asked the ape-man. "He is clumsy and stupid; most of all he is a coward."

"Hyark a coward? That is a good one. There are few braver among the Erythra."

"I can believe that," said Tarzan, and Valthor laughed.

Hyark was strutting to and fro before the royal box receiving the applause of Menofra and her entourage, slaves were dragging out the mutilated corpse of his victim, and an officer was approaching the paddock to summon forth the next combatants.

The guard called to him, "Here is one who thinks he can kill Hyark."

The officer looked up. "Which one thinks that?" he demanded.

The guard jerked a thumb toward Tarzan. "This wild-man here. Perhaps Menofra would like to see such an encounter. It should prove amusing."

"Yes," said the officer, "I should like to see it myself. Maybe after the next combat. I'll ask her."

The next prisoner to be taken into the arena was an old man. He was given a dagger to defend himself; then a lion was loosed upon him.

"That is a very old lion," said Tarzan to Valthor. "Most of his teeth are gone. He is weak from mange and hunger."

"But he will kill the man," said Valthor.

"Yes, he will kill the man; he is still a powerful brute."

"I suppose you think you could kill him, too," jeered the guard.

"Probably," assented the ape-man.

The guard thought this very funny, and laughed uproariously.

The lion made short work of the old man, giving him, at least, a merciful death; then the officer came, after they had driven the lion back into his cage with many spears, and said that Menofra had given assent to the fight between Hyark and the wild-man.

"She has promised to make Hyark a captain for killing two men in one afternoon," said the officer.

"This one says he can kill the lion, too," screamed the guard, rocking with laughter.

"But Hyark is going to kill your wild-man now; so we will never know if he could kill the lion," said the officer, pretending to be deeply grieved.

"I will fight them both at once," said Tarzan; "that is if Hyark is not afraid to go into the arena with a lion."

"That would be something to see," said the officer. "I will go at once and speak to Menofra."

"Why did you say that, Tarzan?" asked Valthor.

"Didn't I tell you that I'd rather be killed by a lion than an elephant?"

Valthor shook his head. "Perhaps you are right. At least it will be over sooner. This waiting is getting on my nerves."

Very soon the officer returned. "It is arranged," he said.

"What did Hyark think of it?" asked Valthor.

"I think he did not like the idea at all. He said he just recalled that his wife was very ill, and asked Menofra to give some one else the honor of killing the wild-man."

"And what did Menofra say?"

"She said that if Hyark didn't get into the arena and kill the wild-man she would kill Hyark."

"Menofra has a grand sense of humor," remarked Valthor.

Tarzan dropped to the ground and was taken into the arena, where the iron collar was removed from about his neck and he was handed a dagger. He walked toward the royal box below which Hyark was standing. Hyark came running to meet him, hoping to dispatch him quickly and get out of the arena before the lion could be loosed. The men at the lion's cage were having some difficulty in raising the door. The lion, nervous and excited from his last encounter, was roaring and growling as he struck at the bars trying to reach the men working about him.

Hyark held his spear in front of him. He hoped to thrust it through Tarzan the moment that he came within reach of him. There would be no playing with his victim in this encounter, his sole idea being to get it over and get out of the arena.

Tarzan advanced slightly crouched. He had stuck the dagger into the cord that supported his loin cloth. The fact that he came on with bare hands puzzled the crowd and confused Hyark, who had long since regretted that he had accepted the challenge so boastfully. He was not afraid of the man, of course; but the two of them! What if the man avoided being killed until the lion was upon them? The lion might as readily leap upon Hyark as upon the other. It was this that added to Hyark's confusion.

They were close now. With an oath, Hyark lunged his spear point at the naked breast of his antagonist; then Tarzan did just what he had planned to do, knowing as he did his own agility and strength. He seized the haft of the spear and wrenched the weapon from Hyark's grasp, hurling it to the ground behind him; then Hyark reached for his sword; but he was too slow. The ape-man was upon him; steel thewed fingers seized him and swung him around.

A great shout went up from the crowd—the lion was loosed!

Grasping Hyark by the collar of his jerkin and his sword belt, the ape-man held him helpless despite his struggles. For the first time the crowd became really vocal. They laughed, jeering at Hyark; they screamed warnings at the wild-man, shouting that the lion was coming; but Tarzan knew that already. From the corner of an eye he was watching the carnivore as it came down the length of the arena at a trot. He could get a better estimate of the beast now as it came closer. It was a small lion, old and pitifully emaciated. Evidently it had been starved a long time to make it ravenous. Tarzan's anger rose against those who had been responsible for this cruelty, and because of it there was born in his mind a plan to avenge the lion.

As the lion approached, Tarzan went to meet it, pushing the frantic Hyark ahead of him; and just before the beast launched its lethal charge, the ape-man gave Hyark a tremendous shove directly toward the great cat; and then Hyark did precisely what Tarzan had anticipated he would do—he turned quickly to one side and broke into a run. Tarzan stood still—not a muscle moved. He was directly in the path of the lion, but the latter did not hesitate even an instant; it turned and pursued the fleeing Hyark, the screaming, terrified Hyark.

"The brave Hyark will have to run much faster if he hopes to get his captaincy," said Valthor to the guard. "He would have been better off had he stood still; the lion was sure to pursue him if he ran. Had he stepped to one side and stood still, the lion might have continued his charge straight for Tarzan. At least he would have had a chance then, but he certainly cannot outrun a lion."

Just in front of the loge of Menofra the lion overtook Hyark, and the screaming man went down beneath the mangy body to a mercifully quick end. Before his final struggles had ended the starving beast commenced to devour him.

Tarzan came up the arena toward the royal loge and the feeding lion. On the way he picked up Hyark's discarded spear and crept silently onto the lion from the rear; nor did the lion, occupied with his greedy feeding, see the approaching man. The crowd sat tense and silent, marvelling, perhaps,

at the courage of this naked wild-man. Closer and closer to
the lion crept Tarzan; and still the lion fed upon the carcass
of Hyark, unconscious of the ape-man's presence. Directly
behind the carnivore Tarzan laid the spear upon the ground.
He had brought it only as a measure of safety in the event
his plan miscarried. Then, with the swiftness and agility of
Sheeta the panther, he leaped astride the feeding cat and
grasped it by the mane and the loose hide upon its back, lifting it bodily from its kill and at the same time swinging
around and whirling the beast with him, roaring and striking,
but futilely. It was the lightning quickness of his act that
made it possible—that and his great strength—as, with one
superhuman effort, he flung the beast into the royal loge;
then, without a single backward glance, he turned and walked
back toward the prisoners' paddock.

The lion's body struck Menofra and knocked her from her
chair; but the lion, frightened now and bewildered, thought
for the moment only of escape; and leaped to an adjoining
loge. Here he lashed out with his taloned paws to right and
left among the screaming nobility. From one loge to another
he leaped, leaving a trail of screaming victims, until he
chanced upon a tunnel, into which he darted and galloped
to freedom beyond the amphitheater.

The stands were in an uproar as the populace cheered
Tarzan as he entered the paddock and took his place again
beside Valthor on the cross-beam. The guard who had ridi-
culed him looked at him now in awe, while the other prisoners
praised and congratulated him.

"Menofra should give you a wreath and a title," said Valthor, "for you have given her and the people such entertainment as they have never seen before in this arena."

Tarzan looked across at the royal loge and saw Menofra
standing in it apparently unhurt. "The lion missed a golden
opportunity," he said; "and as for the wreath and the title, I
do not deserve them; for it was the lion, not Menofra or the
people, that I was trying to entertain."

When the stands had quieted down and the wounded been
removed, the officer in charge returned to the paddock. "You
were a fool," he said to Tarzan, "to throw the lion into
Menofra's loge. If you hadn't done that, I believe she would
have given you your liberty; but now she has ordered that
you be destroyed at once. You and Valthor go in next. You
will take your places in the center of the arena immediately."

"I wish," said Valthor, "that you might have had a better

reception in The City of Ivory. I wish that you might have known my own people and they you. That you should have come here to die is tragic, but the fates were against you."

"Well, my friend," said Tarzan, "at least we have seen one another again; and—we are not dead yet."

"We shall be presently."

"I think that perhaps you are right," agreed the ape-man.

"Well, here we are. Have you any plan?"

"None," replied Tarzan. "I know that I cannot throw an elephant into Menofra's loge."

"Not this one," said Valthor. "I know him. I helped capture him. He is a devil and huge. He hates men. They have been saving him for this, and they will probably kill him afterward—he is too dangerous."

"They are opening the elephant paddock," said Tarzan. "Here he comes!"

A great elephant charged, trumpeting, through the opened gates. At first he did not appear to notice the two men in the center of the arena, and trotted around close to the stands as though searching for an avenue of escape; then quite suddenly he wheeled toward the center and trotted toward the two men.

Tarzan had noted his great size and the one tusk darker than the other, and on the screen of memory was pictured another scene and another day—hyenas at the edge of a pit, snapping at a huge elephant with one dark tusk, while above circled Ska the vulture.

The elephant's trunk was raised, he was trumpeting as he came toward them; and then Tarzan stepped quickly forward and raised a hand with the palm toward the beast.

"Dan-do, Tantor!" he commanded. "Tarzan yo."

The great beast hesitated; then he stopped. Tarzan walked toward him, motioning Valthor to follow directly behind him, and stopped with one hand upon the trunk that was now lowered and feeling exploratively over the ape-man's body.

"Nala Tarzan!" commanded the ape-man. "Nala tarmangani!" and he pulled Valthor to his side.

The elephant raised his trunk and trumpeted loudly; then he gathered first one and then the other in its folds and lifted them to his head. For a moment he stood swaying to and fro as Tarzan spoke to him in low tones; then, trumpeting again, he started off at a trot around the arena while the spectators sat in stunned amazement. The great beast had completed half the oval and was opposite the prisoners' paddock when Tarzan gave a quick command. The elephant wheeled sharply to the left and crossed the arena while Tarzan urged him on with words of encouragement in that strange mother of languages that the great apes use and the lesser apes and the little monkeys and that is understood in proportion to their intelligence by many another beast of the forest and the plain.

With lowered head the mighty bull crashed into the flimsy palisade at the inner end of the paddock, flattening it to the ground; then the outer palisade fell before him; and he carried Tarzan and Valthor out onto the plain toward freedom.

As they passed the main gate of the amphitheater and headed south they saw the first contingent of their pursuers issuing from the arena and clambering to the howdahs of the waiting elephants, and before they had covered half a mile the pursuit was in full cry behind them.

While their own mount was making good time some of the pursuing elephants were gaining on him.

"Racing elephants," commented Valthor.

"They are carrying heavy loads," observed the ape-man: "five and six warriors beside a heavy howdah."

Valthor nodded. "If we can keep ahead of them for half an hour we've a good chance to get away." Then he turned from the pursuers and looked ahead. "Mother of Dyaus!" he exclaimed. "We're caught between a wild bull and a hungry lion—the Cathneans are coming, and they're coming for war. This is no ordinary raid. Look at them!"

Tarzan turned and saw a body of men that approximated an army coming across the plain toward them, and in the van were the fierce war lions of Cathne. He looked back. Closing in rapidly upon them were the war elephants of Athne.

25

Battle

THINK WE YET have a chance to escape them both," said Valthor. "Turn him toward the east. Zygo and his loyal followers are there in the mountains."

"We do not have to run away from our friends," replied Tarzan.

"I hope they recognize you as a friend before they loose their war lions. They are trained to leap to the backs of elephants and kill the men riding there."

"Then we'll approach them on foot," said the ape-man.

"And be caught by the Erythra," added Valthor.

"We shall have to take a chance; but wait! Let's try something." He spoke to the bull, and the animal came to a stop and wheeled about; then Tarzan leaped to the ground, motioning Valthor to follow him. He spoke a few words into the ear of the elephant, and stepped aside. Up went the great trunk, forward the huge ears; as the mighty beast started back to meet the oncoming elephants.

"I think he'll hold them up long enough for us to reach the Cathnean line before they can overtake us," said Tarzan.

The two men turned then and started toward the advancing horde of warriors—toward ranks of gleaming spears and golden helmets and the lions of war on golden chains. Suddenly a warrior left the ranks and ran forward to meet them; and when he was closer, Tarzan saw that he was an officer. It was Gemnon.

"I recognized you at once," he cried to the ape-man. "We were coming to rescue you."

"How did you know that I was in trouble?" demanded Tarzan.

"Gemba told us. He was a prisoner with you in the slave pen; but he escaped, and came straight to Thudos with word that you were to be killed."

"Two of my friends are still prisoners in Athne," said Tarzan, "and now that you have caught many of the warriors of Phoros out here on the plain in a disorganized condition——"

"Yes," said Gemnon; "Thudos realized his advantage, and we shall attack at once as soon as we get back to the lines."

Valthor and Gemnon had met before, when Valthor was a prisoner in Cathne. Thudos the king welcomed them both, for Gemba had told him of the Erythra; and naturally his sympathies were with the aristocracy of Athne.

"If Thoos is with us today," he said, "we shall put Zygo back upon his throne." Then, to an aide, "Loose the lions of war!"

The great bull with the dark tusk had met the first of the war elephants of Athne head on with such a terrific impact that all the warriors were hurled from the howdah and the war elephant thrown to the ground; then he charged the next and overthrew it, whereat the others scattered to avoid him; and a moment later the war lions of Cathne were among them. They did not attack the elephants, but leaped to the howdahs and mauled the warriors. Two or three lions would attack a single elephant at a time, and at least two of them succeeded ordinarily in reaching the howdah.

The commander of the Erythros forces sought to rally his men and form a line to repel the advance of the Cathneans; and while he was seeking to accomplish this, the Cathnean foot warriors were upon them, adding to the rout that the great bull had started and the lions almost completed.

The Erythros warriors hurled spears at their foes and sought to trample them beneath the feet of their mounts. The Cathneans' first aim was to kill the mahouts and stampede the elephants, and while some warriors were attempting this, others pressed close to the elephants in an endeavor to cut the girths with their sharp daggers, precipitating the howdahs and their occupants to the ground.

The shouts of the warriors, the trumpeting of the elephants, the roars of the lions, and the screams of the wounded produced an indescribable bedlam that added to the confusion of the scene and seemed to raise the blood lust of the participants to demonic proportions.

While a portion of his forces was engaging the Erythra on the plain before the city, Thudos maneuvered the remainder to a position between the battle and the city, cutting off the Erythra retreat; and with this and the killing of their commander the Athneans lost heart and scattered in all directions, leaving the city to the mercy of the enemy.

Thudos led his victorious troops into Athne, and with him marched Tarzan and Valthor. They liberated Wood and the other prisoners in the slave pen, including Spike and Troll; and then, at Wood's urgent pleading, marched to the palace in search of Gonfala. They met with slight resistance, the palace guard soon fleeing from the superior numbers that confronted them.

Tarzan and Wood, led by a palace slave, hurried to the apartment where Gonfala was confined. The door, fastened by a bolt on the outside, was quickly opened; and the two men entered to see Gonfala standing above the body of Phoros, a dagger in her hand.

At sight of Wood, she rushed forward and threw herself into his arms. "Word just reached him that Menofra is dead," she said, "and I had to kill him."

Wood pressed her to him. "Poor child," he whispered, "what you must have suffered! But your troubles are over now. The Erythra have fallen, and we are among friends."

After the fall of Athne, events moved rapidly. Zygo was summoned from the mountains and restored to his throne by his hereditary enemies, the Cathneans.

"Now you can live in peace," said Tarzan.

"Peace!" shouted Thudos and Zygo almost simultaneously. "Who would care to live always in peace?"

"I replace Zygo on the throne," explained Thudos; "so that we Cathneans may continue to have foes worthy of our arms. No peace for us, eh, Zygo?"

"Never, my friend!" replied the king of Athne.

For a week Tarzan and the other Europeans remained in Athne; then they set off toward the south, taking Spike and Troll and the great diamond with them. A short march from Athne they met Muviro with a hundred warriors coming to search for their beloved Bwana, and thus escorted they returned to the ape-man's own country.

Here Tarzan let Spike and Troll leave for the coast on the promise that neither would return to Africa.

As they were leaving, Spike cast sorrowful glances at the great diamond. "We'd orter get somethin' out o' that," he said. "After all, we went through a lot o' hell on account of it."

"Very well," said Tarzan, "take it with you."

Wood and Gonfala looked at the ape-man in astonishment, but said nothing until after Troll and Spike had departed; then they asked why he had given the great diamond to two such villains.

A slow smile touched the ape-man's lips. "It was not the Gonfal," he said. "I have that at home. It was the imitation that Mafka kept to show and to protect the real Gonfal. And something else that may interest you. I found the great emerald of the Zuli and buried it in the Bantango country. Some day we'll go and get that, too. You and Gonfala should be well equipped with wealth when you return to civilization —you should have enough to get you into a great deal of trouble and keep you there all the rest of your lives."